the Stubborn Suitor

the Stubborn Suitor

ALEXA WILDER

The Stubborn Suitor, Complete Series

Find out more about the author and upcoming books online at **www.alexawilder.com**

Also by Alexa Wilder

Don't Miss Out on New Releases, Free Stories and More!!

Join Alexa's Readers Group!

AlexaWilder.com/readers-group/

Visit Alexa on Facebook:

Facebook.com/AuthorAlexaWilder

The Wedding Rescue

The Courtship Maneuver

The Stubborn Suitor

The Reckless Secret

The Temptation Trap

The Surprising Catch

Drew Sloane can't get Cami Hendricks out of his mind. After he let her down one too many times, will Cami let Drew into her heart?

Cami Hendricks has a lot on her plate. She's a single mom, works full-time, and her ex is a nightmare. Plus, every time she sees her mother, Cami has to tolerate her jabs about her weight. As if all that wasn't enough, the first guy Cami thinks she might really like seems to be playing games with her. His hot and cold attitude is not what she needs, especially with her ex playing hardball for full custody of her daughter.

Drew Sloane is torn - he can't get Cami out of his mind. Ever since he met her at a party, all he can think of is her beautiful face and her luscious body. But the timing couldn't be worse. Before he can dedicate himself to winning Cami, Drew has a delicate personal situation he has to clear up. Now that Cami has lost all trust in him, can he convince her that she's all he wants?

CONTENTS

the Stubborn Suitor

BOOK ONE

CHAPTER ONE
Cami

"Hey, Cami," Ashley said, leaning over the counter of the nurses' station. "It's slow right now. Why don't you go ahead and take your lunch break?"

Cami glanced at her watch and was surprised to find that it was already after noon. She was over half-way through her ten-hour shift and well past due for a break. The Emergency Room of Sacred Heart Hospital, where Cami Hendricks worked as a nurse, had been unusually busy for a Tuesday morning, and the time had gotten away from her.

"Sure," Cami said with a smile, knowing that Ashley wouldn't be able to take her own break until after Cami had returned from hers. "I won't need the full half-hour. I'm just going to grab a snack and a protein bar."

"No need to rush!" Ashley called from behind her as Cami made her way towards the staff locker rooms. "And you'll need more than a protein bar to make it 'til five. Take your time."

Cami nodded absentmindedly before turning the corner. In the locker room, she grabbed her purse and immediately checked her phone. As a single mother of a three-year-old, Cami was always worried about her daughter. If it wasn't against hospital policy, she'd keep her cell with her at all times in case of an emergency.

But for now, her mother knew the direct number for the ER nurses' station, where Cami spent most of her time. If something went wrong at home, or there was any issue with her daughter Madison, Cami had no doubt that her mother would be able to easily contact her. Still, like any mother, she worried.

She smiled as she looked at the picture on her phone's lock screen, a beautiful photo of Madison greeting her. The girl's strawberry blonde hair was quite a bit lighter than Cami's own fiery red, but the vibrant green eyes of her daughter matched her own, as did the mischievous smile of the three-year-old staring back at her. Every time Cami picked up her phone and looked at the picture, her heart lurched a little, swelling with pride and love. Before Madison, Cami hadn't known that it was possible to love someone this much.

After smiling down at the picture for a moment, Cami swiped to unlock her phone. She couldn't help but groan a little in frustration. Instead of any calls or texts from her mother—who often sent her picture messages of Madison throughout the day, even if

Cami could only see them on her breaks—there were two missed calls and a text from her ex-husband, Ken.

Call me! was all the text read. Cami rolled her eyes, really not wanting to deal with whatever the irresponsible bastard had to say during her short break. It was Ken's turn to take Madison this Friday, and he was probably trying to get out of it. He only had her every other weekend, but he still ended up canceling half the time. As much as she didn't want to talk to him now, Cami knew that if she waited until after her shift, she'd definitely be too tired to deal with his crap.

Instead of calling him back immediately, Cami made her way towards the cafeteria. Once she was armed with strong coffee and a protein bar, she found a secluded area outside to make the call. Steeling herself, and aided by a much-needed caffeine and sugar boost, she dialed the number of her ex.

"Hey, Cam," Ken said instead of hello.

His voice was a little too chipper, and Cami immediately knew something was up. She also hated the intimate way he still referred to her, despite the hostile divorce. It was like the last two years had never happened.

"What's so important, Ken?" Cami asked, not bothering to keep the exasperation out of her voice. "You need to make this quick. I'm on my break."

"Do you have a moment to talk? If not, I can call

back later. There are a few things I need to talk to you about."

"I won't have time after my shift," Cami replied flatly. "I'll be tired and I'll have Madison. Just tell me whatever it is that you need to talk to me about so badly."

"Okay, yeah," Ken replied, but then said nothing else.

"Just spit it out, Ken," Cami demanded, growing even more frustrated. Her break was dwindling, and she didn't have time to waste on yet another bout of her ex's shit.

"I just wanted to let you know—before you saw it on Facebook or something—that I asked Natalie to marry me last weekend. And she said yes."

"Oh," was all Cami could think of to say.

Ken had begun dating Natalie almost immediately after their split. In fact, Cami had a sneaking suspicion that he'd begun seeing the blonde even before Cami had finally left him.

Natalie was everything Cami was not. She was tall and thin, where Cami was short and voluptuous. While Cami had always been proud of her curves, Ken had often made comments about her needing to lose weight—especially after the birth of Madison. That was only one of many reasons why she'd eventually decided to divorce him. There had also been the drinking, the partying, and—if her suspicions were true—the cheating.

Still, Cami couldn't help the small pang of jealousy creeping up her spine. It's not like she wanted Ken back or anything. She was definitely happy to be rid of him. But he had so easily found someone new to warm his bed, while Cami hadn't even been on a date in over a year. She loved Madison, and being a mother was her number-one priority. Yet she still yearned for someone to share her life with.

"So yeah," Ken began after an awkward moment of silence. "I just thought you should know, since she'll be a part of the family officially now. She'll be Madison's stepmom."

That statement made Cami cringe. She didn't want to imagine that woman having anything to do with Madison, much less being considered a parental figure.

"Well," Cami replied curtly. "Congratulations. I wish you every happiness. Now, if you don't mind, I need to get back to my break."

"Actually," Ken replied. "There's something else I want to talk to you about."

"What?" Cami couldn't keep the added level of annoyance out of her voice, but she really didn't care.

"Natalie has put in a notice at her job," Ken replied. "She wants to be a housewife."

She just wants to live off your money, Cami thought, but she didn't say this aloud. If he wanted to marry a gold-digger, so be it. He was smart enough to make sure she wouldn't get anything in the divorce—same as he had done to Cami. Four years of marriage, and Cami had walked away with a menial monthly child support payment and no spousal support. That's what happens when your husband comes from a family full of lawyers and has unlimited funds, all while you can barely afford the cheapest lawyer in the phone book.

"Good for her," is all Cami said in reply.

"So we were thinking," Ken continued, "since you work so much, and Natalie is going to be a homemaker, Madison could spend more time with us. In fact, I was thinking that it would make more sense if we took over primary custody."

It took a moment for his words to sink in. Ken had never really seemed to be all that interested in more custody than he already had. In fact, it was often difficult to get him to keep Madison on the weekends he was already scheduled to have her. And now, he was expecting to take over primary custody.

Cami couldn't help but laugh: it had to be a joke.

"It's not funny," Ken replied. "I'm serious."

"Ken, there is no way you could handle any more custody than you already have. And there is absolutely no way I am giving up primary custody of Madison."

"You don't get to decide that on your own," Ken replied. His friendly tone was gone, and he was beginning to sound angry.

"No, Ken, the lawyers decided that during the divorce. And you agreed upon it."

"Yeah, well that was then. This is now. Natalie will be a stay-at-home mom. That's what Madison needs. It's more than you can provide for her."

"You have no idea what Madison needs!" Cami was nearly shouting now and she saw a few heads turn towards her in the courtyard. She swallowed and continued in a calmer, quieter tone. "Ken, where is this even coming from? I can't even get you to keep your scheduled time with Madison. Why are you asking for more now?"

"Things are different now. Natalie and I are getting married. We're going to be a family."

"That's awesome," Cami replied sarcastically. "Start your own family."

"We can't," he said quietly. "Natalie can't have kids."

Cami knew that she probably should have felt bad at hearing such a revelation, but instead she was incensed.

"So what?" she asked, voice rising again. "You think you can just take *my* daughter away from me to play house with? That's not going to happen."

"Yes, it will," Ken voice was forceful and confident. It made Cami cringe. "I was hoping we could work this out like adults, but obviously you're being too immature."

"*I'm* being immature?" Cami gasped. "You're the one that thinks he can just decide to take my daughter away from me."

"Think about this rationally," Ken said. "Natalie and I can give her things you can't. You work ten-hour shifts at the hospital. You barely ever see her as it is."

"That's not true," Cami snapped. "I only work those long shifts so I have three days off a week to spend with Madison. You have no idea what you're talking about. You don't have the slightest clue what Madison needs."

"I know she needs security. I can provide that for her. Natalie and I can. We can provide for her."

"I'm providing for her just fine, no thanks to you!"

"Like I said, Cam, I was hoping to do this like civilized adults, but it is obvious that it's not going to happen, so I'll have my lawyer contact your lawyer. We'll have a sit-down sometime next week. If it has to go before a judge, so be it. I *will* be getting custody of my daughter."

Cami felt nauseated. Angry tears were sliding down her face, and she extended her hand to hold the phone away from her, so that Ken wouldn't be able to hear her distress. She knew that if Ken insisted on taking this to court, he would most likely win. He had money. He had fancy lawyers. Cami didn't even have a lawyer of her own. She could look up the lawyer she'd used during the divorce, but that idiot hadn't been much help then and she couldn't risk losing now.

Absentmindedly, Cami realized that Ken was still talking. She gently pushed the phone back against her ear.

"...that would be easiest. Just give me the name of your lawyer. I can have Gil get in touch with him directly, since you obviously can't handle this yourself." Cami cringed, both at the thought as well as the mention of Gil Dubois, Ken's lawyer and an old friend of the family. He had been the one to make sure that Cami walked away from the divorce with absolutely nothing.

"I don't have that information on me," Cami replied, making sure her voice sounded even and calm, though she felt anything but. "I'll have to get back to you with that."

"That's fine. I'll get it from you when I pick up Madison this weekend."

With that, Ken hung up. Cami appreciated that he hadn't tried to say goodbye or feign any sort of niceties. He'd made his intentions clear. He wasn't going to give up without a fight.

Cami stared down at her phone until the lock screen reappeared, along with the green-eyed, freckled face of Madison. No matter what, she couldn't lose her daughter. She didn't know how yet, but she would find a way to fight.

CHAPTER TWO
Cami

For a long time after she hung up the phone, Cami sat in the courtyard staring off into space. The conversation with her ex-husband had caught her completely by surprise. She'd never once considered that Ken would one day decide that he wanted more custody of their daughter.

And, as infuriating as this truth was, if Ken really meant to fight her on this, he would probably win. He had the money and the connections to manipulate the legal system in his favor. Cami wasn't even sure that she could afford a lawyer.

The most frustrating part of the situation was that Cami knew Ken didn't really care about Madison—not the way that she did. He didn't really care about anyone but himself. He was immature, irresponsible, and self-involved. He only ever saw Cami—and then Madison, once she was born—as possessions, trophies he could show off.

Ken had always been after Cami to lose weight, not because he didn't like her body—she knew from experience that he loved her curves—but because he didn't want people to see him with a "fat wife." When he'd actually said those very words to Cami—during one of his many drunken stupors—she'd known it was time to leave.

Now he had Natalie, who really was the perfect trophy wife. She was beautiful and poised. She put up with his drinking and his partying, and had no desire for a career of her own. But that wasn't enough for him. Nope. Now he wanted a perfect little family—and for that, he needed Madison.

Well, he couldn't have Madison. Cami didn't know how yet, but she would make sure of that. Cami was a great mother. She wasn't confident about a lot of things, but this was one fact she knew about herself. She was great at taking care of Madison.

Yes, Cami worked full-time, but she left her daughter with her mother, so it wasn't like the child was with a stranger for forty or fifty hours a week. She was with Grandma, who spoiled her rotten.

Cami couldn't afford to give up her job. But more than that, she didn't want to. She'd worked hard to get where she was and she was proud of her accomplishments. It was also a way for her to make sure that Madison would have everything she needed in life. Ken had, so far, not proven himself to be much of a provider.

And yet, he thought he could walk in now and demand more custody, just because he had the means to provide for Madison financially?

Cami could feel tears of frustration—and fear—sliding down her cheeks. She knew that she'd spent too much time out in the hospital courtyard, and her break was probably long over, but it was a while before she could pull herself off the bench and head inside. Only the thought of poor Ashley, probably starving and waiting for her turn to take a break, was what motivated her to finally rise from her position.

In the bathroom, she splashed water onto her pale face. She had a fair complexion at the best of times, but at the moment she looked as white and pasty as a ghost. Her green eyes were red-rimmed and swollen, and there were red blotches all over her skin.

Cami knew that she couldn't go back to work like this. The ER was stressful enough, with patients often scared and in pain. It was the job of the nurses to be calm and confident—not looking like a zombie that just rose from the grave.

Retrieving her makeup bag from her locker, Cami reapplied her foundation and a little blush to make her look a little more alive. She practiced her smile for a minute before heading back out into the emergency room.

"Took you long enough," Ashley replied as Cami leaned over the computer to clock back in.

"Sorry," Cami said, offering an apologetic smile.

Ashley squinted and studied Cami's face, her large amber eyes growing worried.

"Are you okay?" she asked after a moment.

"Yeah," Cami replied, as confidently as she was able. It obviously didn't convince Ashley, who just raised an eyebrow, so Cami continued. "Just dealing with the ex. You know how it is."

"Don't I ever," Ashley replied, shaking her head. Cami knew that Ashley had gone through a painful divorce herself, just last year. "But if you really are okay, I'm gonna head out on my break. The burn victim in room five will need more morphine soon. They can't take him up to surgery for another hour, so we're just easing his pain for now. Other than that, everything is pretty quiet."

"Thanks, Ashley," Cami muttered, examining the charts. "No, you go take your break. I'll be fine here. God knows, you deserve it!"

Ashley nodded and headed off as Cami grabbed the burn victim's chart and headed into his room.

Cami tried hard to push the conversation with Ken—and all that it entailed—out of her mind as she began to check the patient's vital signs. But she couldn't stop thinking about the "what ifs."

What if Ken *did* get primary custody of Madison? What if he and Natalie raised her to be part of their perfect little cookie cutter family? What if she wasn't able to tuck Madison in every night and tell her she loved her? What if Natalie was doing that instead?

Cami blinked tears out of her eyes yet again and tried to focus on administering the shot of morphine to the patient via the IV, but her hands were shaking so badly that she had to step back for a moment and take a deep breath. Once she'd calmed down a little, Cami realized that she'd almost forgotten to scan the patient's wristband, so she moved towards the bed to do so before administering the drug. She scanned the band, then the morphine she was about to administer, only to receive a shrill beep from the machine. Something wasn't right.

Looking down, Cami began to study the patient's wristband, then his chart. Suddenly, her blood ran cold, heavy with a realization. This was not the patient she was supposed to administer the morphine to. She'd almost administered an extremely strong narcotic to the wrong person. This patient's chart stated that he was already on a similar medication. A second dose could have been extremely dangerous.

Cami felt sick—even sicker than she had been after her conversation with Ken. This was a rookie mistake—one she'd never made before. In fact, not even rookies made this mistake. The entire point of scanning all patient wristbands and all meds was to make sure something like this never happened. And yet, she had been so preoccupied that she'd almost done so. Had her hands not been shaking so badly that she'd had to take a moment, she could have potentially killed a patient.

That thought sent her dashing to the employee restroom, where she began retching up the protein bar she'd eaten for lunch. After a few minutes, she finally took a few deep breaths. She reminded herself that it was the stress and anxiety that had almost caused her to make such a mistake, and that if she didn't calm down now, there was a chance she might actually make such a mistake again.

Cami couldn't help but wish that her best friend, Maggie Emerson, was working.

When Maggie had first started as an emergency room nurse last year, Cami hadn't thought they'd get along. In fact, when she'd learned that Maggie's father was on the hospital's board of trustees, she'd assumed Maggie had only been given a position because of that fact. Maggie was from a wealthy family similar to Ken's, and Cami had expected the woman to be just as irresponsible and self-involved as her ex-husband.

In the beginning, Cami had had trouble understanding why Maggie was even working as a nurse—with the money her family had, she probably didn't have to work at all.

How wrong had she been. Cami quickly realized that her assumptions were completely unfounded. Maggie was the most warm, caring person she'd ever met. Despite not having to work for a living—or even simply being able to take up a position in her family's company—Maggie had chosen to become a nurse because she wanted to help people.

She also had a wicked sense of humor—a trait that quickly endeared her to Cami. They took to spending their breaks together, then hanging out outside of work. Between marriage, work, and motherhood, Cami hadn't had time to develop any close friendships in the last few years. Maggie quickly became her best friend. On weekends when Madison was with Ken, the two would go out on the town or simply chill at home with a bottle of wine, bitching about men, or the inability to find clothing that properly fit their voluptuous bodies.

Maggie had a way of understanding Cami like no one else ever had. She could always calm Cami down and make her laugh. But, unfortunately, she was off today—when Cami needed her the most.

Once she was no longer dry heaving, Cami headed into the locker room and texted Maggie to see if they could hang out later that evening. She really needed to see her best friend, but it wasn't just that. With the Emerson family's wealth and connections, perhaps she would be able to recommend a good (affordable) lawyer, or at least offer tips on how to work the system.

After Cami put her phone away, she spent a few minutes alone in the locker room, breathing deeply and trying to calm down. It wasn't until she was completely focused and sure that she wouldn't make any more mistakes that she headed back out to the ER—ready to administer morphine to the *correct* patient.

CHAPTER THREE
Cami

Cami was disappointed when, after her shift, she was finally able to read the reply text from Maggie.

Sorry CamiBear, can't tonight. Have some boring family dinner that I'm required to sit through. Call you after!

Cami cringed at the awful nickname. At least she'd convinced Maggie not to use it at work—the last thing she needed was the entire emergency room calling her CamiBear. Maggie started calling her that after she decided that Cami looked like a huggable teddy-bear. Cute? Yes. Professional? Not so much. Swallowing her disappointment, Cami carefully typed out a response.

No worries. Need to spend some time with the little monster anyway. Call me later. I have something I really need to talk to you about.

Cami wasn't lying; she really did need to spend some quality time with Madison. After all of the fears that had been stampeding through her head all afternoon, she wanted nothing more than to hold her daughter, to kiss her and tell her how much she loved her.

Being Madison's mother was what gave her life meaning. Yes, Cami enjoyed her job at the hospital and she loved helping people. She loved her time relaxing with Maggie and she really did hope to someday meet a man she could spend the rest of her life with. But all of those things paled in comparison to the joy and meaning Cami found in being a mother. With the threat of having that taken away from her, she wanted nothing more than to crawl into bed with her "little monster" and read bedtime stories until they both fell asleep.

Unfortunately, one thing Cami was not in the mood for was dealing with her mother. She loved her mom dearly; the woman had raised Cami alone after her father had left when Cami was ten. And she was eternally grateful now that her mother provided free childcare four days a week while Cami worked. She knew her mother loved her and only wanted the best for her, but sometimes that desire for the "best" could come off as judgmental or condescending.

Yet there wasn't much Cami could do to avoid her mom this evening. She had to pick up her daughter, after all.

Cami parked and slowly climbed the stairs to her mother's second-story apartment. She used her own key to let herself in and was surprised to find the place uncharacteristically quiet. Usually, Madison would greet Cami at the door with shrieks of "Mommy!!!" before throwing herself into her arms.

The only sound to greet her now was the gentle hum of the air conditioning as Cami made her way into the apartment. The old, worn leather sofa was empty, as was the rocking chair. The room was dark and abandoned. It reminded Cami of the countless nights she'd spent alone in the apartment as a child while her mother worked. Very little had changed in this place over the last two decades, besides some added portraits of Madison on the walls, and a new-ish flat-screen TV.

She wandered into the kitchen, where she found her mother at the table, a cup of tea in her hand as she flipped through a gossip magazine. She looked tired, with her gray hair pulled back in a messy bun, loose tendrils falling in front of her drooping eyelids. She looked up as Cami entered the room, offering her daughter a loving but weak smile.

"Cami, I didn't hear you come in," she said.

"Where's Madison?" Cami asked, coming to stand next to the older woman.

"She's passed out in the bedroom. We went to the park, and she spent the afternoon running around with a neighbor's dog. She was exhausted."

"Sorry I missed that," Cami said with a sad smile.

She could picture the little monster, running

through the grass after the mutt, shrieking with joy. She smiled at her mother, who was now looking at her with an inquisitive expression. She must have seen the stress on Cami's face. Cami really wasn't ready to have that conversation with her mother, so she turned to go.

"I better get her home."

"No rush," the older woman said. She patted the chair next to her. "Come, have a seat."

Cami thought about arguing, but knew that she'd never win that fight against her mother. Besides, her mom didn't spend much time around other adults. She owed her a few minutes of visiting. So Cami pulled out the chair and sat down beside her.

"You look tired," the older woman said as Cami relaxed into the chair. "You work too much!"

"I really don't want to get into this with you again, Mom." Cami was emotionally and physically exhausted, and she really didn't want to rehash this argument once again.

"You're missing out on so much of her childhood," her mother replied, changing approaches to continue her point when Cami clearly didn't want to talk about it.

Cami sighed deeply, wishing she hadn't taken a seat. The truth was, she *did* feel like she was missing parts of Madison's childhood. But that was the point of working long hours four days a week. She then had three full days to spend with Madison—at least when her daughter wasn't spending the weekend at her father's house. But she was doing her best—or what she thought was best for Madison.

"I don't have a choice, Mom," she replied indignantly.

"Of course, you do! You could work part-time. Move in here with me. That way you wouldn't miss so much of your baby's childhood."

"I can't do that, mom. You know I can't." Cami was growing angry. "This apartment only has two rooms."

"I can sell this place and move into a town home or something."

"Not going to happen, Mother," Cami said.

The thought of living with her mom sent another wave of nausea through her stomach. Cami loved her and was eternally grateful for the support she offered in taking care of Madison, but she would pull her hair out if she had to live with the woman.

"Something has to happen, honey," her mom replied. "You work too damn much."

"Why is everyone saying that today?"

"Who else has been saying that?" the older woman questioned.

Cami sighed. She definitely did not want to get into Ken's phone call with her mother. She'd only worry and make things all the more stressful.

"No one, Mom. I just…I don't have a choice. Ken has made it clear he isn't going to help, so if I want

Madison to have everything she deserves in life, I have to work. You worked more than I do when I was growing up. I turned out fine."

Cami's mother eyed her speculatively for a moment, as if she disagreed with Cami having turned out fine, but she thankfully didn't respond. She simply sipped her tea and looked back down at her magazine.

"Besides," Cami continued, too indignant to let the topic fall just yet, "I love my career. I've worked hard to get where I am. I love helping people. I feel like I'm making a difference in the world."

Her mother just hummed, but didn't look up from the magazine. They sat in silence for a few minutes, her mother reading while Cami collected her thoughts. She was just about to get Madison and head home when her mother spoke again.

"I worked two jobs while you were growing up because I had to. I had no other options," she said after a moment.

"And I do?" Cami really didn't know where her mother was going with this, and she didn't want to know.

"I was older than you are. I had less going for me. You're still young. You have a beautiful face."

Cami cringed at the word *face*. Now she definitely knew where the conversation was heading and she didn't want to have it. She moved to stand but her mom put a forceful hand on her shoulder.

For a woman her age, she had a surprising level of strength.

"Just sit here for a second and hear me out," she said. "You owe me that much."

Cami hated when her mother brought up all the free childcare she was giving. But it was true—Cami did owe her mother a lot. So she gritted her teeth and sank back into the chair. She allowed her mother to push the open magazine over until it was sitting in front of Cami. It was open to an article about celebrity diets.

"You have such a beautiful face," her mother repeated. "If you just lost a little weight, you'd have no trouble catching yourself a man."

"I'm not fat, Mother," Cami said through gritted teeth.

"No one said you were," her mom said softly. She leaned forward to brush a loose lock of Cami's hair behind her ear. "But you could stand to lose a few pounds. I'm not saying that to be mean, sweetheart. I'm only trying to help. Right now, you have so much going for you. You're young and smart and vivacious. That head of hair of yours is just to-die-for. You know how many women wish they were natural redheads? Millions of dollars are spent in salons each year trying to recreate what God gave you naturally. And those eyes… you have your father's eyes—so big and green. Not to mention your skin—so clear. Most redheads are covered with freckles."

"There is nothing wrong with freckles," Cami said defensively. "Madison has freckles."

"All I'm saying, dear, is that, with a little weight loss, you could be absolutely stunning."

Cami bit her tongue. She knew that her mother meant well. In her warped mind, she thought she was offering her daughter a piece of helpful advice, not trampling on her self-esteem. Cami tried not to let the words get to her, but she couldn't help but feel hurt.

"You would have men falling all over you," her mother continued. "If you lost a little weight, you would easily be able to catch yourself a guy. You could marry someone who would support you, so you didn't have to work. Support you and Madison."

"I already married a man who was wealthy enough to support me," Cami spat bitterly. "And we both know how that turned out. I'm never going to rely on another man to take care of me! Especially not some hypothetical one that will only appear after I starve myself!"

With that, Cami pushed her chair away from the table and stood up. She stomped from the room before her mother had a chance to respond. Cami really wasn't interested in anything she had to say at the moment.

Her mood was quickly lifted, however, as she found herself in the guest bedroom, leaning over her sleeping child. Madison was in the middle of potty training, and was wearing a pull-up and nothing else. She was stretched out on her stomach, with her strawberry curls twisting against her freckled back. She had one thumb in her mouth, while the other hand clutched the corner of her purple blankie.

Cami considered waking her daughter in order to help her dress, but she really didn't have the heart to do so—not when Madison looked so peaceful and precious in sleep. Instead, she wrapped the little girl in the comforter and carried her out against her shoulder.

Her mother was standing in the hall as Cami walked by, but Cami didn't raise her eyes to look at the older woman.

"Good night, sweetheart," her mom said exasperatedly, seemingly unaware of the hurtful words she'd uttered only a few minutes earlier.

"'Night, Mom," Cami replied quietly, so as not to wake her daughter, before exiting the apartment.

She tucked Madison into her car seat—a difficult task while still wrapped in the comforter—and kissed her forehead before starting the car and heading home.

Cami barely made it out of the parking lot before the weight of the day caught up with her. Sadness, anxiety, and frustration washed over her, twisting her body into knots. Tears, refusing to be contained, began to pour down her face. Within moments, she was crying so hard that she could barely drive. Unwilling to put her daughter in danger, she pulled over to the side of the road and put the car in park. Shoving her fist into her mouth so as not to wake Madison with her heaving sobs, she silently wept against the steering wheel.

CHAPTER FOUR
Cami

Cami sat at the side of the road until she had no more tears left to cry. She felt oddly numb as she made the ten-minute drive home.

Madison woke while Cami was trying to remove her from her car seat, which was just fine with Cami. As exhausted as she was, she was more than happy to spend some quality time with her pride and joy. She gave Madison a bath, watching as the happy three-year-old splashed in the water. Cami allowed the shock and numbness of the day to wash away, replaced by the love and joy she found in her daughter. She then curled up next to her baby in her own bed, reading her stories that Madison was too young to understand, until the little girl drifted off to sleep.

Cami considered allowing herself to drift off as well, but it was barely eight o'clock. She'd only eaten a protein bar for lunch, which she hadn't even been able to keep down, so she begrudgingly pulled herself out of bed. After carefully lifting Madison and carrying her to the crib in her nursery, Cami spent a few minutes simply gazing at her darling baby girl.

I cannot lose her, she thought. *I will not allow Ken to take her away from me!*

Yes, Cami worked full-time. But even on the days she worked, she was always home in time to bathe her daughter and tuck her into bed. The only times that Madison went to bed without a goodnight story and a kiss from her mother were the nights she spent with her father. Ken was wrong. Her own mother was wrong.

"I'm a great mom," Cami said out loud. "I am what's best for Madison!"

Eventually, Cami's stomach began to rumble, so she made her way to the kitchen to microwave something easy for dinner. After a quick meal of frozen burritos, Cami settled on the sofa to relax with a generous glass of red wine and all of the TV shows she'd been meaning to catch up on.

Cami was just getting into the latest episode of *The Voice* when her phone rang. She'd completely forgotten that Maggie had promised to call her after the family dinner. Cami was exhausted and considered not answering the phone, but decided that a conversation with Maggie may be exactly what she needed.

"Hey," she said, picking up the call. "How was dinner?"

"Meh. I'll tell you all about it in a minute. What's up with you? You said you had something you really needed to talk to me about."

Cami exhaled. For a moment, she'd hoped that Maggie had forgotten all about that, and that they could just spend some time chatting about superfluous stuff. But it didn't seem like that was the case. Maggie was quiet, waiting for Cami to speak.

"I talked to Ken today," Cami divulged.

"Yeah? He isn't trying to cancel with Madison this weekend, is he? Because I have plans for us, girl."

"No, actually," Cami began. "He…he um…he wants more custody of Madison. In fact, he wants primary custody."

"What?" Maggie asked. "He can't even handle the custody he has now."

"I know," Cami replied with a bitter laugh. "But he and Natalie are getting married. I guess he thinks that Madison will be the icing on the cake of his perfect little life. Natalie wants to be a stay-at-home mom."

"Well, then she needs to pop out some kids of her own."

"Apparently, she can't have kids."

"That doesn't mean she can have yours!" Maggie said angrily.

It warmed Cami's heart to hear Maggie jump to her defense. "I know. But he has lots of money and amazing lawyers and, now, apparently a stay-at-home wife. I work full-time and can't even afford the crappy attorney that represented me during my divorce."

"You're a great mom," Maggie said.

"I know that. You know that. I don't know if I'll be able to convince a judge of that."

"He's not going to take Madison away," Maggie said confidently.

"How can you be so sure?" Cami asked, feeling the stifling fear from earlier that day sinking back into her chest. "He wants to meet with me and my lawyer next week. I don't even have a lawyer."

"Relax. We'll get you one. I'll talk to my dad. He knows lots of lawyers."

"There's no way I can afford any of the attorneys your family knows."

"I'm sure they'd be willing to pro-rate their fees. I'll explain the circumstances. We'll figure something out together. We will not allow that rat bastard to steal Madison!"

Cami wanted to trust Maggie, but she knew that her best friend was overly idealistic. She meant well, but Maggie didn't have a lot of experience with the way the world worked outside of her privileged upbringing. Still though, Cami couldn't help but smile. It was good to have someone in her corner. Someone other than her well-meaning but condescending mother.

"How was your dinner?" Cami asked, trying to change the subject.

"Ugh… if I had taken a shot every time my mother mentioned that I need to lose weight, I'd be shitfaced right now."

For the first time that day, Cami found herself giggling.

"I know exactly what you mean," she said. "My mother gave me a talking-to today, too. I'm pretty sure that her exact words were, 'if you lost weight, you'd be able to catch yourself a man.' *Catch a man…* as if they are fish. As if I need a man to rescue me—to take care of me."

"Shoot, girlfriend, you don't need no man," Maggie agreed.

"Damn straight. And the thing is… I have no trouble attracting men. Neither of us does."

That was the truth. Whenever the two friends went out, they always had guys falling all over themselves to buy them drinks. Lots of men actually wanted a woman with curves on her body.

"I know, right?" Maggie responded. "Our problem isn't catching men… it's catching men who aren't complete dicks."

"Exactly! I'm beginning to think that they're extinct."

"Speaking of, though," Maggie said, "I have an opportunity for us—an opportunity to catch even more of these rare, elusive men your mother speaks of…though I cannot guarantee they won't be dicks."

"Do tell," Cami said, becoming intrigued.

"So, the family dinner tonight was actually about a party my dad and brother are throwing this weekend at the beach house. It's gonna be part business, part pleasure. There will be a bunch of rich, snooty people there talking business, but there will also be boating and cocktails and sun tanning."

"Sounds like fun!" Cami stated.

"Good," Maggie responded. "Because you're coming."

"I am?"

"Yeah. You said Ken has Madison this weekend, right?"

"Yeah, he's supposed to. And I doubt he'll cancel, since he's obsessed with custody right now."

Bitterness and fear began to seep back into Cami's chest, but Maggie must have noticed because she quickly moved the conversation away from Cami's ex.

"Good. Then you're coming. I'm required to be there all weekend and I cannot bear to do it without you. Grant is bringing some of his friends as well. And I know there will be some other eligible bachelors our age. It's going to be fun, I promise!"

"First you say that you're required to go—and can't possibly handle it without me. Then you promise me it will be fun. You're sending me mixed messages."

"It will be fun," Maggie assured her, a little more confidently. "Especially, if you're there. And if it isn't, we'll just keep drinking until it is."

"Sounds like a plan," Cami said, smiling as she thought about sipping cocktails on the beach—or on a boat.

She couldn't remember the last time she'd been on a boat. At some point, she'd gone sailing with Ken and his family, but it had been miserable because, well, it had always been that way with Ken and his family.

After finalizing their plans, Maggie hung up the phone. Cami sipped her wine as she thought about the weekend that lay ahead of her. She could still feel the stress and fear sitting heavy at the pit of her stomach, but she also felt happy and hopeful for the first time all day. She still had to deal with the lawyer situation and gear up for a meeting with Ken next week, but at least she had something to keep her mind off those things over the weekend.

CHAPTER FIVE
Cami

The rest of the week passed uneventfully. Cami continued to feel anxious and scared about the future custody battle, but she did her best to push it to the back of her mind so there would be no more almost-mistakes at work.

She dropped Madison off at Ken's a little earlier than usual on Friday, so she could get ready for her weekend away. Her ex-husband was still at work when she arrived, but Natalie was there to greet them at the door, cooing over Madison in a way that made Cami's stomach turn. Cami offered her fakest smile before quickly kissing her daughter goodbye. She had the urge to turn around, pluck Madison out of Natalie's arms, and take her right back home. But she couldn't be the one to break the custody agreement—not when she was about to fight for it to remain as it was. So she kissed

Madison once more and headed home, struggling to hold back tears as she left her daughter with the blonde bimbo.

Thankfully, she didn't have much time to stew in her own self-pity. Maggie showed up at her house soon after Cami returned home.

"What are you doing here so early?" Cami asked, surprised to see her best friend in her doorway. "I thought I was supposed to meet you at your house in a couple of hours."

"I told the driver to meet us here," Maggie said with a smirk, pushing her jet-black hair out of her face as she moved past Cami and into the house. "I knew you'd need help picking out appropriate weekend wear. You never dress sexy enough."

"I'm the working mother of a three-year-old. I don't have time for sexy," Cami said as she followed Maggie through the house towards her room.

"You do this weekend," Maggie replied with a mischievous grin. "There will be a lot of single, attractive men at this party. We're going to make the most of it."

Without waiting for an invitation, Maggie began sifting through Cami's walk-in-closet, pulling out a few skimpy dresses Cami had purchased but never really wore.

"Why would I need cocktail dresses at the beach?" Cami asked skeptically.

"For all the cocktail parties," Maggie replied, as if the answer was obvious. "There will be one tonight and another one tomorrow night on the deck."

"Exactly how many people are coming to this weekend getaway?" Cami asked, realizing that she may have had the wrong idea about what this weekend would entail.

"A few," Maggie replied noncommittally as she moved to Cami's dresser and began to root around in the swim wear drawer. "Thank God I forced you to buy a nice swimsuit!"

Cami smiled, looking at the 50s-style one-piece Maggie was holding up. Maggie tossed it onto the bed along with all of the other clothes she'd picked out—way too many for a two-day trip to the beach. She grabbed the little green dress and pushed it into Cami's hands, along with a strapless bra and matching panties.

"Shower, then put this on while I pack. The car will be here in an hour!"

After the shower, Maggie fussed over Cami's hair and makeup, blowing the gorgeous red locks out before curling them into perfect ringlets. Cami's hair was her favorite feature, though she had very little time to do much with it in recent years, so it spent most of its time up in a ponytail or a bun. Now, it fell around her shoulders, framing her voluptuous chest—which was nearly falling out of the little green dress Maggie had picked out. Thankfully, Maggie agreed to let her go easy on the make-up, allowing her natural peaches-and-cream complexion and large green eyes to speak for themselves.

Maggie got ready with her, before both women took a minute to appreciate themselves in the mirror. Maggie was wearing a little purple dress, her cute black hair adorned with matching amethyst clips. Cami had to admit that they both looked amazing. She wasn't sure what the weekend was going to hold, but they looked good enough to conquer anything at the moment.

Their transportation arrived right on time—a big black town car, ready with a bottle of champagne for the girls to enjoy during the hour-long drive to the beach.

Cami had never been to the Emerson family beach house before. As soon as the car pulled through the gates, she realized that it wasn't as much a beach house as it was a beach mansion—a three-story building sprawling along the shore, complete with an enormous lounging patio and a dock where a few boats were anchored. It looked more like a small hotel than a family beach house.

"Of course this is your beach house," Cami said to Maggie, rolling her eyes.

Maggie just giggled as the car pulled to a stop in front of the mansion. Cami reached for the door, but there was already someone there, opening it from the outside. An older gentleman dressed in a suit smiled as he held the car door for her.

"Welcome, ladies," he said, nodding his head to Cami and Maggie.

Once they were out of hearing distance, Cami turned to Maggie and whispered, "What was that? You have a door man?"

"Not normally," Maggie replied. "We have an entire staff for the weekend, since there will be so many guests. But normally there's just the cleaning lady—and sometimes a cook."

Cami couldn't help but feel out of place. It was all fun and games when she was getting ready. Alone with Maggie, she never felt like she didn't belong. Maggie wasn't snooty, and Cami never really felt the class difference between them. Here, however, gazing up at the enormous mansion her family owned, Cami began to feel like she maybe shouldn't have come.

Maggie pulled Cami's hand, showing her into the house, where a large foyer led to a spiraling staircase.

"Come on," Maggie said, grabbing Cami's arm and leading her towards the stairs. "Let's put our stuff away, then I'll show you around."

The girls were sharing a room on the third floor, with large bay windows that overlooked the ocean.

"How many bedrooms does this place have?" Cami asked as she watched the waves crashing against the shore.

"Ten," Maggie said, coming to stand behind her. "Not including the rooms on the first floor, which are used as offices."

"And yet, we're sharing a room?" Not that Cami was complaining. Having Maggie close was a source of comfort in such an overwhelming place.

"Yeah, all the rooms are full this weekend. We even have a few friends staying at a hotel down the road."

"So, when you said that there would just be 'a few' people here this weekend, that was a bit of an understatement."

Maggie turned back to her, swallowing visibly.

"I didn't mean to deceive you, I just really wanted you to come and I was scared you wouldn't, if you knew the truth. It will be fun, I promise. My brother is here, along with his friends Declan and Preston. You've met them before, a couple of times. And there are others, too; I know you'll like them. We'll just avoid the snootier people who are only here for business."

Cami nodded, though she was still unsure. But she was here, after all. There was no going back, so she might as well make the most of it. Plus, she had to admit to herself that she really did look fabulous.

* * *

By the time the girls made it downstairs for cocktail hour, the deck was already full of people. Cami felt a little self-conscious and out of her league, but she reminded herself that no one knew she was a single working mother.

Maggie pulled her towards the bar for another glass of champagne before directing her through the crowd to a group of people around their own age. Cami recognized Maggie's brother, Grant, immediately. He gave her a warm smile and a big hug.

"Great to see you, Cami," he said as he released her. "You remember Declan and Preston, right?"

Cami turned towards his two best friends, whom she'd met on a number of occasions. She nodded and smiled.

"And," Grant continued, ushering her towards a man she'd never met before. "This is Drew Sloane. He's another close friend of mine. Drew, this is Maggie's best friend, Cami."

Cami looked up into the face of the most breathtakingly attractive man she'd probably ever seen. He had big amber eyes and dark, messy hair. When he smiled at her, dimples appeared in either cheek, and his eyes crinkled in the most adorable way.

"Nice to meet you, Cami," he said in a deep, buttery voice, putting his hand out to shake hers. His grip was warm and firm around her own, leaving her fingers tingling even after he'd pulled away. It was as if he sent tiny electric shocks up her hand and arm, and then down her spine.

"Nice to meet you, too," she said after a minute,

trying to will herself to stay calm and not become flustered.

"Cami works with me at the hospital," Maggie said, coming up behind her. Her best friend had obviously noticed that she was nervous, and Cami appreciated the support. "Drew went to business school with Grant. He started his own company that's now worth two-and-a-half billion dollars."

Cami felt her eyes grow wide. It was overwhelming enough to be talking to such an attractive man—finding out that he was a billionaire just made it all the more difficult. She was so out of her league.

Drew seemed to notice her discomfort, as he stepped close to her and placed a hand on the bare spot on her back. Her skin was on fire beneath his touch, but she tried not to show any emotion.

"Don't listen to her," he whispered into her ear. "She exaggerates."

Cami couldn't help but smile. "So you're not a ridiculously wealthy businessman?" She arched her eyebrow.

"I've had *some* success, but nothing too out of the ordinary. What about you? You're a nurse?"

"Yeah, I work with Maggie in the emergency room at Sacred Heart General."

"That's so much more exciting than business," he replied, his face still close enough to her ear for his voice to be heard over the crowd, though he wasn't speaking loudly.

"Not as lucrative though, I'm guessing," Cami responded.

"You save lives. That's so much more meaningful. You can't put a price tag on that."

Cami couldn't help but smile at that. She looked into his deep, whiskey-colored eyes. She could get lost in those eyes. It was as if the air around them had somehow thickened, even though they were outside. The word she was looking for in her head was *chemistry*. They talked about it in romance novels all the time, Cami thought, and here it was, completely palpable between her and this gorgeous stranger.

He smiled back and held her gaze for a moment until Cami noticed that they were alone. When had they left the group and moved to the side of the deck, facing the ocean? Cami hadn't even noticed that familiar faces no longer surrounded her. And, at the moment, she really didn't care.

The moment was shattered, however, when an older couple approached them.

"Drew," the man said, putting out a hand.

Drew turned towards them in greeting. The woman, dressed impeccably in a tailored Chanel pantsuit, matching pearls included, looked judgmentally upon Cami.

"I'm gonna go refresh my drink," Cami told Drew. "Do you need anything?"

"I'm fine, thanks," Drew replied, offering her a warm smile before she turned to go.

Cami made her way through the crowd towards the bar, where she ordered another glass of champagne. She took a few sips before heading back in Drew's direction, wanting to give him a moment to ditch the snotty older couple. She could feel a burst of excitement wash through her as she watched the gorgeous man. She hadn't met anyone this promising since her divorce. Drew was excruciatingly hot, but also sweet and attentive. Cami could barely believe her luck as she reclaimed her spot by his side.

"Now all we need to do is deal with the tax problem," the older man was saying to Drew.

"I'm just so sick of the poor always trying to make a claim on our hard-earned money," his wife complained.

Cami felt a surge of anger at the woman's statement. She just wanted him to tell these people off so that Drew and her could get back to their conversation. She looked at him imploringly, but he was just smiling sweetly at the horrible couple, seemingly agreeing with them.

"If they want more money, they just need to get out there and earn it," the older man said. "Just like you did, right, son?"

"Yep," Drew said, nodding his head in agreement.

Cami couldn't believe it. The excitement she'd been feeling only minutes before was suddenly turning to nausea. How had she thought this guy was anything special? He was just another wealthy, entitled ass.

Turning away from Drew without another glance, she scanned the room, looking around for her friends. She saw Maggie's bright purple dress across the deck, still standing with her brother and his friends. Cami quickly made her way over to them.

"There you are," Maggie said as she approached. She then looked over Cami's shoulder. "Where's Drew?"

"I have no idea," Cami lied.

Something in her voice must have betrayed her frustration, because Maggie raised her eyebrow questioningly. Thankfully, before she could interrogate Cami on the subject, Grant's friend Declan stepped right up beside her and Maggie.

He slipped a hand around Maggie's waist and smiled at her wickedly. Cami knew that her friend had always found Declan attractive, in a roguish sort of way. His sandy blond hair was perpetually in disarray, and his blue eyes were teasing and warm.

"So, ladies," he began, "how are things at the hospital?"

"Things at the hospital are good," Cami replied, seeing that her friend was getting just a little too intoxicated to answer the question. Maggie was grinning wide into Declan's eyes.

"That's good," Declan responded, still smiling seductively at Maggie.

Cami couldn't remember why Maggie had never developed a serious crush on the guy. He was warm and fun and very attractive. "How are things with… umm…what do you do again?" She was embarrassed she couldn't recall what Declan did for living.

"Most of the time, he lives off his trust fund," Preston offered with a smirk.

"That's not true," Declan responded. "I'm also an attorney at Creighton and Callahan. Perhaps you've heard of the firm? We represent Sacred Heart Hospital."

"Yeah, I think I have," Cami replied. She noticed that Maggie was eyeing Declan up and down, probably imagining him shirtless, given that the guys pecs were straining against his thin summer shirt.

Really, she thought, *why* hasn't *Maggie ever thought of Declan in any serious way?*

Before she could think too much about it, however, a waitress came by with a tray full of champagne. Everyone grabbed a glass, and, as the woman turned to go, Cami watched Declan's eyes follow her rear end while she made her way back towards the house.

That's *why she's never developed a crush on Declan*, she reminded herself. Maggie knows him well, she's just too drunk right now to think straight. The guy flirted with practically anything with breasts. Every time Cami had been out with a group he was a part of, she'd watched him flirt with all the attractive girls. He was nothing but a playboy. As unobtrusively as possible, she moved away from Declan to stand closer to Maggie, hoping to maybe rescue her soon.

"Speaking of the hospital," Preston said, turning to talk to the two girls. "I have a question."

"What?" Maggie asked, eyeing him with suspicion.

"You know my car accident a few months ago?"

Cami didn't know that Preston had been in an accident, but Maggie nodded.

"How are you?" she asked, finally looking away from Declan.

"Oh, I'm fine now," he brushed the question off. "I was sent to Sacred Heart but neither of you fine ladies were there to take care of me. Instead, the most beautiful woman I'd ever seen stitched me up. Not that you two aren't beautiful, but this woman was a goddess. She had the most beautiful skin and dark hair. Big, full lips. Man, she was gorgeous."

Cami immediately recognized that he was describing Ashley. But Ashley had recently come out of a disastrous marriage to a husband who constantly cheated on her. If Preston was anything like Declan—and Cami was pretty sure that he was—then Ashley would be much better off if Preston never knew her name.

Maggie seemed to be on the same page, as she looked at Cami with a knowing smirk and winked.

"I don't know who you're talking about," Maggie said to Preston, completely straight-faced.

"Liar," Preston accused. He then turned towards Cami, a sad, pleading look on his handsome face.

"Come on, Cami. You have to help me out. Just give me a name."

"Don't you work for the hospital?" Cami asked, remembering that Grant had mentioned it the first time she and Preston had been introduced.

"I'm on the board. That's not at all the same. I don't have access to the employee files."

"I'm not suggesting that you look up her file," Cami responded, shocked at his assumption. "I just meant… can't you go in to the ER and ask for her again?"

"Not without a name. Just give me a name," he begged. "Just a name. That's all I ask."

"Nope," both girls said in unison, then giggled at their identical responses.

Cami almost felt a little sorry. Preston didn't seem like a bad guy. But all of the men at this party looked like they were too wealthy for their own good and were most likely playboys. Ashley deserved something serious if she were ever to get in another relationship. If Preston wasn't serious enough to try finding her himself, he didn't deserve a chance with her.

Finally, Preston gave up and the conversation switched to something about ski resorts—a topic Cami had absolutely no opinion on. She was staring off into the sea when Declan stepped up behind her.

"How about the two of us go for a walk?" he asked.

"How about not?" Cami responded, surprised. Mere moments ago the man had his arm wrapped around Maggie's waist.

"I only wanted to ask you why your BFF won't talk to me or ever take my calls, but I guess I'll leave you to your negative thoughts." Declan looked like a kicked puppy for a moment, and Cami immediately felt bad. He was probably a little drunk and just felt lonely. And Maggie did just brush him off unceremoniously just a few seconds ago. But then Cami remembered his roving eyes.

"Why don't you go ask that waitress to take a walk with you?"

At least Declan had the sense to look sheepish. He nodded and eventually left her alone. Cami felt a little sorry for him, but she didn't need a man like that. She turned back towards the ocean, watching the sunset over the waves.

"I'm perfectly happy alone," she said under her breath. "Perfectly happy!"

CHAPTER SIX
Cami

It was late, and most of the party had long since cleared out by the time Cami decided to call it a night. Maggie had disappeared a while ago, stating that she needed to catch up on her beauty sleep. Cami knew that her friend had simply drunk too much and needed to crash.

Cami had wandered out onto the dock alone, watching the seagulls dive into the ocean. She was more than a little tipsy herself as she made her way back towards the house.

"Hey," came a voice from behind her, making her jump and spin around. Drew was leaning against the deck railing, smiling at her. "Sorry. I didn't mean to startle you."

"It's fine," Cami replied, a little more sternly than she intended.

"You disappeared earlier," he pointed out.

"You seemed occupied. I didn't want to intrude."

"I'm not occupied now," he said with a smirk.

Cami was reminded of all the other cocky, playboy men at this party.

"I am," she replied. "I'm going to bed."

"Come on," he said, pushing himself off the rail and slinking towards her. "It's still early." He held up the bottle of champagne, as if to signify that the party wasn't over.

"Are you drinking alone out here on the deck?"

"I am celebrating…alone…out here on the deck. When you say it like that, it sounds pathetic. But it wouldn't be pathetic if you were celebrating with me."

Drew smiled, and Cami was yet again reminded of how absolutely handsome he was. She wanted to turn and walk away. But she was already more than a little tipsy, and Drew had the charm and the good looks to spare. Cami was having a hard time coming up with a reason to say no.

Drew must have seen her hesitation, because he smirked and moved even closer to her, sneaking a hand around her shoulder to rest against her back. Once again, her flesh tingled at the warmth of his touch. She couldn't help but wonder what it would feel like to have those large, strong hands on other parts of her body.

"Come on," he said with a smirk. "Let's take a walk."

Drew led Cami down the steps onto the beach, where they both kicked off their shoes and left them beneath the deck. They passed the bottle of champagne back and forth as they strolled along the sand, the tide gently lapping at their bare feet.

Cami couldn't help but think that this was the kind of thing that happened to *other* people—late night walks on the beach with the sexiest man alive, sharing a bottle of champagne. This was the life an heiress was meant to lead, not a single working mother.

"Who am I right now?" she asked herself under her breath.

"What?" Drew asked, leaning in.

"What are we celebrating?" Cami asked, not wanting him to know what she'd actually muttered.

"Um..." Drew looked out into the ocean for a moment, pensive. "Opportunities," he replied finally, lifting the bottle of champagne to his lips and taking a deep drink before handing it over to her.

She watched his tongue dart out and swipe at the wetness on his lips, causing a different type of wetness to pool between Cami's legs. In an attempt to ignore her body's reaction, she chugged the remaining champagne, then frowned down at the empty bottle.

"You drank it all," Drew cried in mock anger. "How dare you!"

"Sorry-not-sorry," Cami replied with a smile, feeling like a teenager for the first time in years.

She couldn't help but laugh when Drew nudged her gently with his shoulder, pushing her further into the ocean. The waves began breaking around her knees, and she shrieked at the cold water, running back towards the shore.

Cami hadn't felt this young or alive in years. She adored Madison and loved being a mother. But, she realized, sometimes she missed feeling playful and carefree. She laughed and splashed in the water with Drew like a child, pushing him into the waves until his pants were wet up to the knees.

"Now, you've done it!" he growled, turning towards her with mock anger in his eyes.

Cami laughed and lunged away from him, frolicking further down the beach.

"Uh-oh," she said a few minutes later, stopping to stare at her empty hands.

"What?" Drew asked, coming up to stand beside her.

"The champagne bottle. I don't know what I did with it. I littered!"

"Don't worry about it," Drew replied. He was close to her now, his warm hand on her back once again. "I'm sure some of the staff are charged with picking up any trash left on the beach."

Cami winced at how snobbish Drew sounded. She hated the idea of relying on *staff* to clean up after her. She was once again reminded of how this was definitely not her life.

"I can't just leave it out here for someone else to pick up!" she implored.

"Well, you aren't going to find it tonight," Drew replied, gently rubbing circles on her back. "I'll tell you what...we'll let it go tonight, and tomorrow morning I'll come out here and find it myself."

Cami relaxed once again, leaning into Drew's caress. She couldn't help but wonder how she'd gotten him so wrong earlier in the evening. Right now, he didn't seem so snobbish at all. He seemed sweet and genuine and truly interested in her.

She allowed him to lead her towards the beach, where they both sat down in the sand and stared out at the ocean. Or rather, it was Cami who was staring out at the ocean. After a moment, she realized that Drew was staring at her. She turned her eyes towards him, and her breath caught at his hungry look.

One moment they were staring at each other, the next, they were kissing. Cami didn't know how it started, but what she did know was that Drew's lips were suddenly on her own, hard and hungry, his tongue seeking entrance into her mouth.

For a split second, Cami froze. She had not been with a man since her divorce and hadn't planned on being with one now. But Drew had been so sweet, and he was so sexy, and his lips felt delicious against her own. So Cami finally allowed herself to relax, leaning into the kiss and opening her mouth to let him in.

Drew moaned as he explored her lips with his tongue, and the next thing she knew, Cami was being pressed back against the sand. Drew never moved his lips from her own as he stretched out half on top of her.

Eventually, he *did* have to pull back for air, but he continued to kiss and lick his way down her neck, his hands exploring her body through the thin fabric of her dress. When his firm fingers squeezed and caressed her breasts, Cami couldn't help but arch into him.

At her reaction, Drew pulled away from her and sat up. Cami tried to sit up as well, but a hand on her shoulder kept her pinned down as Drew moved to straddle her.

His eyes met hers for a second questioningly as his fingers gently traced the low-cut neckline of her dress. Cami wasn't exactly sure what he was asking of her, but she nodded anyway, her body too on fire to say no.

Drew's fingers grasped the top of her strapless dress, pulling it, along with her bra, down and over her chest. Her large breasts bounced free and Drew released another moan of pleasure, grinding his hips down against Cami's. She could feel the press of his substantial erection rubbing against her thigh.

When he moved down to lick at one hard nipple, then the other, it was Cami's turn to cry out. Her nipples had always been extremely sensitive and it had been years since anyone had shown them any attention.

Drew attached his lips to her swollen tip, sucking and nibbling it gently. He brought a hand up to the other breast, pulling and tweaking the nipple until Cami was overwhelmed with pleasure.

When they'd first started dating, Ken had seemed to love her body. But as he grew to resent her weight in the later years of their marriage, he'd spent less and less time with foreplay. And he never worshiped her breasts the way that Drew was doing it right now. Drew was licking and sucking and biting one nipple, than the other. Whichever breast wasn't in his mouth was being manipulated by his large, warm hands.

The tingling his touches had caused earlier was nothing compared to the fire in her skin at this moment. She thrashed beneath him, bucking her hips in an attempt to gain even the slightest amount of friction between her legs.

Drew shifted to the side, pulling Cami close as he wound his hand into her hair. He continued to kiss and lick her neck and chest, sucking and biting bruises onto the swell of her breasts before soothing the sensitive flesh with his tongue. His other hand gave her nipple one last pull before slowly sliding down her body. He caressed her thighs for a moment before pushing up under her dress. He stroked her through her wet panties, causing Cami to twist and moan even more, opening her legs in encouragement.

After a few moments of teasing, Drew slipped a hand inside her underwear, exploring her wet, slippery folds. He slid two fingers deep inside her aching body, and Cami pressed down on them. Soon, she was riding on his thick fingers. He brought his thumb up to circle her clit in the same rhythm, and Cami was overwhelmed with pleasure. She could feel Drew grinding his hard cock against her thigh as he fingered her.

"You are so sexy," he whispered huskily and continued to press his fingers deep into her. "Watching you writhe beneath me is almost enough to make me come in my pants."

That was all it took to send Cami over the edge. She shook as pleasure overwhelmed her body for what felt like hours.

When she finally came back to herself, Cami was suddenly extremely self-conscious. She was half-naked on a beach where anyone could see her, allowing a man she hardly knew—a man who had acted like a complete ass earlier in the evening, nonetheless—to put his hands all over her body.

Cami quickly sat up and pushed Drew off her. He looked at her questioningly, and she suddenly felt a little guilty. He had given her an amazing orgasm, after all, and she was about to leave him high and dry. But that wasn't enough of a reason to have sex with this near-stranger.

"I'm sorry," she said as she pulled her bra and dress back up over her chest. "This was a bad idea. We're in public, and I'm really drunk. I've never done anything like this. I would never do anything like this sober."

Drew nodded, looking guilty himself.

"I understand," he said. "I'm sorry, too."

Cami was more than a little surprised by his response, expecting him to be angry that she'd denied him. Instead, he stood and offered her his hand. She allowed him to pull her up, and together, they walked back to the house in silence. It was more than a little awkward, but less so than she was expecting it to be.

They grabbed their shoes from beneath the deck and headed inside.

Drew, who was staying on the third floor, offered her a meek "goodnight" on the landing before continuing up towards his room.

Cami crawled into bed, a weird mix of satisfaction and embarrassment coursing through her veins as she slowly drifted off to sleep.

CHAPTER SEVEN
Cami

Cami awoke to what felt like someone drilling into her head. She opened her eyes, only to have the sensation intensify with the addition of the bright morning sun. Shutting her eyes immediately, she groaned and rolled over, burying her head beneath a pillow.

Unfortunately, Cami had completely forgotten that she was sharing a room—and the big, king-sized bed—with her best friend. The pillow she was now burrowed beneath must have belonged to Maggie, as it was quickly yanked away from her with an angry growl.

"I hate you. And I'm never drinking again," Maggie whined from next to Cami on the bed.

"Champagne hangovers are the worst," Cami agreed.

She tried her best to go back to sleep, but the events of the previous evening came crashing through her memory suddenly, and all thoughts of relaxation disappeared. After a few more frustrating moments, she slowly sat up and opened her eyes once again. Her head was still throbbing, but she knew it wouldn't get any better without a lot of water and a few aspirin. Coffee and food probably wouldn't hurt either.

At the thought of food, Cami's stomach growled. As sick as she felt, she was also starving.

"I don't think I ate anything yesterday," Cami said aloud as she thought over the events of the previous day.

She'd been too stressed out in the morning by the prospect of having to leave Madison with Ken to have any sort of appetite. Then Maggie had shown up, and they'd started drinking in the town car. There had been food served later in the evening, but Cami had been too full of champagne to pay it much mind. She was sure paying for that now.

Cami slowly crawled out of bed and limped towards the bathroom to take a hot shower. She decided to forego washing her hair, as the curls from yesterday had settled into a soft, windswept look that was actually quite becoming. After drying off, she slipped into a pink sundress that complemented her complexion and headed back into the bedroom.

Maggie was still in bed, head now covered by blankets.

"Are you getting up?" Cami asked, somewhat hesitant to head downstairs without her best friend there.

"No!" Maggie replied, her voice muffled by the blankets. "I'm staying in bed at least until noon! Go on without me. I'm sure there's a huge breakfast spread already prepared."

Cami stood in the room, deliberating for a moment. She really didn't want to go down there alone, especially not with the chance that she'd run into Drew. But her throbbing head and growling stomach made the final decision for her. She left the room and made her way hesitantly downstairs to the large dining area.

Maggie hadn't been lying. There was an enormous breakfast spread laid out in the dining hall, where heated dishes kept eggs, pancakes, and waffles warm. There was also a wide array of what appeared to be fresh-baked pastries as well as fresh fruit.

Cami let out a pleased sound when she saw the coffee carafe. After helping herself to a large mug and a bottle of water, she grabbed a plate of eggs and croissants and headed towards the empty deck. She sucked down the water immediately and was sipping her coffee when she was startled by an empty champagne bottle, covered in sand, now placed beside her plate.

Drew was standing next to her, a self-satisfied smile on his face. The dimpled grin made her shudder a little, and she looked away from his gorgeous face. Instead, Cami stared at the bottle for a moment, finding it hard to believe that Drew had gotten up and gone in search of the bottle as promised this morning, even after she'd stopped things while they were practically in the middle of almost going all the way.

But there was the bottle, sitting right next to her coffee mug—and there was Drew, looking completely proud of himself.

"Thank you," Cami said after a moment, offering him a warm smile. She didn't really know what else to say.

"You're welcome," he said in reply, sitting next to her. "How are you feeling today?"

"Like someone drilled a hole in my head," Cami answered, massaging her temple.

"Yeah—that's how I felt too when I woke up this morning. You need more water," he told her, looking at the empty bottle. He stood once again. "I'm going to get some food. I'll grab you another."

While Drew was gone, Cami stared out into the ocean contemplatively. She really *had* been wrong about Drew. He was sweet and understanding. He kept his word—even when he'd been denied an orgasm.

Drew quickly returned, not only sliding a water bottle towards her when he arrived, but also a few aspirin.

"Thank you!" Cami replied genuinely, grateful for so much more than just the water and pills. He really was a conscientious man.

"You're welcome," he said again as he sat down across from her and started on a large plate of eggs.

They were silent for a few moments, both caught up in their own thoughts as they ate. But it was a comfortable silence, companionable.

"Mind if I join you?" came a soft voice from behind her, and Cami turned to see a woman she'd never met before. The woman was absolutely gorgeous—tall and thin with dark hair and high cheekbones.

"Sure," came Drew's reply.

Cami turned to see a big smile on Drew's face as the beautiful stranger sat down next to him on the bench—a little too close to be polite, in Cami's opinion. Drew didn't seem bothered by it, though. He just stared at her for a moment with a wide grin on his face, almost as if he were in a daze, before turning to Cami.

"Cami, this is Analise. Analise, this is Cami—she works with Grant's sister Maggie at Sacred Heart General."

"You're a nurse, too?" Analise asked in a condescending tone.

"Yep," Cami replied, pursing her lips.

"Analise is a model," Drew offered, seemingly oblivious to the tension between the two women.

"Yeah," Analise replied smugly. "I just returned from Milan. That's why I didn't arrive until late last night." She turned back towards Drew with a pouty look on her face that made Cami want to vomit. "I looked for you last night but I couldn't find you anywhere."

"Yeah…I…took a little walk."

Drew didn't even look over at Cami as he said this. It was almost like she didn't exist. Cami was suddenly feeling like the third wheel. She sat for a few more minutes, trying to force herself to finish her breakfast. But the conversation between Drew and Analise remained insular. Their voices were hushed and they were turned in towards each other as he asked about Milan.

Eventually, Cami couldn't stomach it anymore. She rose and took her dishes to the kitchen before heading out towards the beach. She just didn't understand Drew.

When they were alone, he seemed like the sweetest, most genuine guy in the world. He'd gone back to retrieve their bottle from the beach as promised, even after she'd refused to have sex with him. And, speaking of sex, when she'd asked him to stop, he did—right away, with no questions asked.

But when he was around other people, he seemed like such an ass, bitching about the poor and drooling all over models. She really didn't need that kind of hot-and-cold attention, she decided.

Cami was pulled from her thoughts by the ringing of her phone. She reached into her little bag and pulled out her cell, surprised to see that Ken was calling.

"Ken," she acknowledged.

"Cami," he said, his voice curt. "Sorry to bother you on your little vacation."

He said the words with such a condescending tone that she considered hanging up on him. She'd already gotten enough condescension this weekend to last a lifetime. Cami was grateful that she didn't hang up a second later, however, when Ken continued.

"Madison is sick and she wants to talk to you."

Cami stopped in her tracks, heart racing.

"Sick? How sick?" she demanded. "What are her symptoms? I can be there in less than two hours."

"There's no need. It's just a little fever. She'll be fine. I wouldn't have called at all except she is demanding to talk to you."

Cami wasn't convinced by Ken's words and was already walking back towards the house, making plans to call a cab, when her daughter came on the line.

"Mommy!" the sweet little voice sang.

At three years old, Madison's speech was not fully developed, but she was able to communicate well enough. Cami never had any trouble understanding her, at least.

"Hey, sweetheart. How are you feeling?"

"Daddy says fever."

"How's your tummy? Does your tummy hurt?"

"Hurts." There were a few sniffles through the line, then, softly, "Miss you!"

"I miss you too, sweetie. Do you want me to come get you?"

"Yes," Madison replied. "Come get me. Wanna go home."

There was a sound as the phone was snatched from Madison's hand, and she could hear her daughter whining as Ken spoke.

"You will not come and get her. She's fine. We called the pediatrician and followed his directions. He said it's just a stomach bug. The fever is already going down. This is my weekend, and you have no right to even offer."

Cami bit her lip, almost ready to argue. But she didn't want to press her luck right now—not with the custody battle about to begin. Ken must have been able to read her thoughts.

"Speaking of custody," he began, "my lawyer still hasn't heard from yours. You need to have your attorney call Gil by Monday, or we'll begin the process without your representation present."

"It's the weekend, Ken," Cami said angrily. "I'll be sure to have someone contact you by Monday. Now put my daughter back on the phone. I want to say goodbye."

"You better not offer to come pick her up again," he warned before passing the phone to Madison.

"Mommy!" Madison shrieked happily once she was back on the phone. She really did sound better already, Cami had to admit. "You coming?"

"Nope, baby. I'm sorry. It's your time with your daddy right now. And you're feeling better."

"No!" Madison shrieked angrily into the phone. "I wanna go home."

There was another rustle, and once again Ken was on the phone.

"See what you started?" he demanded angrily. "Thanks for that."

He then promptly hung up. Cami gritted her teeth, willing herself not to cry. Her head still hurting, she was confused over the hot-and-cold treatment by Drew, and now the custody battle was once again front and center in her mind. She took a few deep breaths, willing herself to calm down. She then flipped through her phone, praying that the number for her former lawyer's office was still in her contacts.

She did still have the number, and, even though the lawyer himself wasn't in the office on Saturdays, there was a polite secretary who took down her information and promised that he'd call her first thing on Monday morning.

Feeling slightly better, Cami made her way back towards the beach house, mentally preparing herself for the forthcoming custody battle.

"Cami…there you are." She turned towards Drew, who was wandering along the deck. "I was just looking for you. You disappeared a little while ago."

Cami was taken aback. He'd practically ignored her once *Analise* had shown up, but now he was acting like nothing had happened. His back-and-forth personality was making her head hurt. She didn't have time for this.

"Yeah, well, you seemed a little indisposed," Cami snapped before strolling back towards the house.

She didn't turned around as she left Drew standing on the porch. She heard him call her name, but she was already on the stairs, heading back up to her room.

CHAPTER EIGHT
Cami

When Cami made it back to their room, Maggie had finally joined the land of the living—though only just barely. She was sitting up in bed, her black hair in complete disarray, a far-away look in her eyes.

"I think I might be dead," she said as Cami entered the room and shut the door behind her.

"No dear, you're just hung over," Cami replied. "I doubt you'd be in this much pain if you were actually dead."

"True," Maggie agreed as she pulled herself up and out of bed. She passed by Cami on her way towards the bathroom and stopped. "Are you okay?" she asked.

Cami thought about telling Maggie everything—about admitting what had happened last night between her and Drew and detailing all of his confusing behavior. Maggie knew Drew, after all. Perhaps she could shed some light on the situation.

In the end, however, Cami decided to keep the information to herself. Maggie was a little too eager to see Cami dating again, and Cami wasn't completely sure that Maggie wouldn't push her towards Drew simply to get her some action. Unfortunately, Cami had absolutely no interest in action—not if it didn't come along with commitment.

"I talked to Ken this morning," she said instead, deciding on a partial truth. "Madison is sick."

"Oh no," Maggie gasped. "Do you need to leave? I can get you a car."

"No," Cami replied, distraught. "I want to be with her. But, when I mentioned it to Ken, he freaked out. He started talking about our custody agreement. He was bugging me again about my lawyer, so I went ahead and called the guy who helped with my divorce."

"Doesn't he suck?" Maggie asked.

"Yes," Cami admitted. "But he's all I can afford at the moment. And I don't really have time right now to look for another lawyer anyway. Ken is set on meeting next week."

Maggie opened her mouth like she wanted to argue, but quickly closed it again. Instead, she nodded.

"I'm really sorry, Cami," she finally said after a moment, placing a comforting hand on her friend's arm. "I'm sure everything will turn out fine. And I'll still talk to my dad about it."

"Sounds good," Cami replied, though it was a

blatant lie. She was becoming more and more worried about the impending custody battle as each day passed.

"Let's spend the day lounging on the beach," Maggie suggested suddenly. "I think it will cheer us both up. I'm going to go shower really quick, then I'll be ready to go."

While Maggie was in the shower, Cami dressed in her new swimsuit, a black one-piece with white polka dots, specifically designed for girls with curves. It hugged her hips and chest just right, while minimizing her waist. She pulled on a sheer swimsuit cover and a big hat and glasses to complete the ensemble.

"You, darling, look like a fifties movie star!" Maggie exclaimed as she exited the bathroom.

She was in a yellow two-piece with a high waist that also flattered her figure—purchased from the same website. Though Cami and Maggie had similar body types, Cami had never found the self-assurance for a two-piece bathing suit. She was a little envious of Maggie's confidence.

"You too!" Cami replied.

"We can trade at some point," Maggie offered. "We're the same size."

"I don't know if I could pull that off," Cami said skeptically.

"Of course, you can!" Maggie replied. "Next time we go swimming, we're switching suits! Our housekeeper can wash them after today."

"Deal," Cami said, though she was still a little unsure. But she knew better than to argue with her best friend once Maggie had made her mind up about something.

Maggie grabbed a late breakfast, and the girls made their way to the beach. The temperature had risen quite a bit since Cami had been out on the beach earlier. The sand was hot against their feet as they carried beach chairs out near the ocean. They put their chairs in the surf, so that water lapped at their feet each time the tide came in.

Cami closed her eyes and angled her face up towards the sun. She let all of her problems from the last week melt away as she felt the warmth of the sun on her face and the cold tickle of the waves on her toes.

"This is perfect," Cami sighed after a while. "You're right. It's exactly what we needed."

"Do you know what would make this even more perfect?" Maggie asked.

"What?"

"Cocktails."

"I thought you were never drinking again," Cami replied. She couldn't help but laugh.

"That was champagne. But I could go for a margarita. And I'm pretty sure there are some already premixed in the fridge."

"Really?" Cami asked, though that didn't really surprise her. It was as if the Emerson family had thought of everything for this party.

"Yeah. I can go grab us some."

"No," Cami said, rising from her chair. "I need to reapply my sunblock anyway—I'm a fair-skinned redhead after all. My body wasn't made to tan, only burn."

"Awesome," Maggie responded, relaxing back down into her chair. "If you go into the kitchen, there will be someone there to help you get the cocktails in order."

"Be right back," Cami called as she headed towards the house.

The mansion was surprisingly empty. Maggie had mentioned that most of the men were on the golf course a few miles away, talking business. Cami couldn't help but wonder where the women were, then. Wherever they were, she was thankful for the quiet atmosphere.

The house wasn't as deserted as she thought it was going to be, however. As she stepped into the corridor, she heard a couple arguing in a small alcove near the dining room.

"You're drunk," a soft feminine voice declared. "And I saw you grab that woman's ass. You can't deny it. I saw it with my own eyes."

"You don't know what you're talking about," a man snapped back at her.

"You have a problem, Robert."

"Shut up, Elsie!" The man was shouting now. He was slurring his words, obviously drunk even though it was only early afternoon. "It's not like you're one to talk, with the way you've been stuffing your face all weekend."

"How dare you," the woman responded. "You know that's not true."

"You say that," the man sneered, "but you're gaining weight by the minute. I think you're the one with the problem here, not me."

"How can you say that?" sobbed the woman. "You're drunk at one in the afternoon. You're sexually harassing the staff—in front of your wife."

Cami moved slightly further into a small corridor, so that she could see into the alcove while remaining hidden. The woman in question wasn't fat at all, simply curvaceous like Cami and Maggie were. She had long dark hair and large doe eyes, which were filled with tears. She was beautiful, if one could ignore the look of hurt and humiliation on her face. The man in question, substantially larger and taller than her, was leaning over her menacingly.

Cami watched in horror as he reached out and grabbed hold of the woman's arm. She struggled to get away but he wouldn't let her go. Instead, he leaned forward even more, until his face was almost pressed against hers.

"You do not get to talk to me like that, woman," he growled.

Cami was just about to step out of the corridor and intervene, when another masculine voice rang through the hall.

"Let go of her right this moment, Robert!" Drew demanded as he stalked into the room from the kitchen. He didn't seem to notice Cami, standing just down the hall.

The drunken man—Robert—turned towards Drew, glowering, but didn't let go of the woman.

"Don't you dare tell me how to talk to my wife?"

"I can and will tell you how to treat my sister. You better let go of her right now and walk away, or you will find yourself extremely sorry."

Drew wasn't as tall as Robert, but he still seemed intimidating as he got right up in the drunken man's face. The two men glared at each other for a moment before Robert pushed the woman away and stomped off.

"You better pack your bags and call a car, Robert. I don't want to see you again this weekend," Drew called after him. "Or I cannot be held responsible for my actions."

"Calm down, D," the woman said, reaching out to grab Drew's arm.

"Are you okay, Els?" he asked, studying the woman with concern in his eyes.

"No," she admitted, looking down.

"What are you doing Elsie? Why are you still with him?" Drew asked quietly.

"It's not always like this," Elsie replied.

"It should *never* be like this," Drew said emphatically. "I thought you said he quit drinking."

"He did," she said, tears still streaming down her face. "But then he started again."

"How long?" Drew demanded.

"About a month, this time," Elsie admitted.

Drew growled angrily, but he pulled the woman into a tight hug.

"You have to leave him, Els," he said against her hair.

"But what about Robbie?" she asked, distraught.

"It's better for him to grow up without a father than with one who's an abusive alcoholic. Do you really want Robbie to learn how to treat women from him?"

The woman closed her eyes and buried her face in Drew's shoulder, but she shook her head.

"You're a great big brother," she said after a moment. "I don't know what I'd do without you."

"Yes, you do," Drew said with a smile. But his smile quickly turned into a frown. "And you deserve so much more than Robert." Elsie didn't respond, so Drew continued. "You're an amazing woman, Elsie. You're smart and funny and beautiful. You have so much going for you. You deserve someone who is going to love you the way you need to be loved—someone who is going to teach Robbie to be the kind of person you want him to be."

Elsie nodded against her brother's chest.

Cami suddenly felt like she was eavesdropping on a very personal moment—which most definitely she was. She quietly slunk back the way she came, exiting the house then walking much louder back down the hall in an attempt to alert Drew and Elsie to her presence.

But the siblings either didn't hear her or didn't care whether or not they were seen, because they remained where they were, hugging each other in the alcove. Drew was patting Elsie's hair as his sister sobbed.

Cami couldn't help but feel a slight pang of envy as she regarded the siblings. Yes, Elsie was in a bad situation. Her husband reminded Cami of Ken in so many ways that it kind of terrified her. In fact, Cami was pretty sure that she and Ken had arguments almost identical to the one she'd just overheard.

But at least Elsie had her brother. Cami would have given anything to have someone like that in her corner while she was going through her divorce—someone to love her and stick up for her as unconditionally as Drew seemed to.

Cami's mom had been there for her. And her mother really had meant well. But she had also been hypercritical and didn't truly understand why Cami had chosen to leave Ken, despite the drinking and the partying and the possible cheating. When her mother looked at Cami's ex-husband, all she saw were dollar signs. It was hard to convince someone who had worked herself to the bone for decades just to scrape by that money wasn't the answer to every problem.

Shaking her head in an attempt to change her train of thought, Cami slipped past the siblings and moved towards the stairs. After grabbing the sunblock from the room she and Maggie were sharing, Cami headed towards the kitchen. She couldn't help but notice that Elsie and Drew had disappeared.

"Can I help you?" asked a middle-aged woman in a black and white uniform.

Cami smiled at the woman. "Yeah, I think. Maggie told me that there was a ready-made stock of margaritas in here."

"Yes, of course." The woman gave her a kind smile. "How many do you need?"

"Oh, it's just Maggie and I," Cami replied as the woman reached into the fridge to pull out a large pitcher full of margarita mix.

"Are you out on the patio, dear?" the woman asked as she pulled out two delicate fishbowl glasses.

"No, actually. We're on the beach."

"Oh," the woman said, frowning at the glasses. "Then these probably won't do."

Instead, she pulled two large, insulated cups out of the cabinet, filling them up with the icy mixture before affixing them with lids and straws. Cami's eyes widened. The cups were huge, and Cami felt certain that she and Maggie were doomed to another batch of hangovers on the way home. She grabbed two large water bottles to make sure they stayed hydrated, then headed out the door.

In the main dining room, Cami came face-to-face with Drew. She remembered how she had left things between them that morning and opened her mouth to speak, but was quickly interrupted.

"Come on, Drew," Grant called as he turned and headed into his office. Drew offered her a small smile before following behind Grant.

Cami walked back to the beach while replaying every interaction she'd had with Drew in the last twenty-four hours—as well as the one she'd witnessed between him and his sister. The man was so confusing.

"Took you long enough," Maggie bitched as Cami handed her a cup and a bottle of water.

"Quit complaining!" Cami demanded with a smile.

Once again, Cami considered discussing Drew with Maggie. She really was mystified by his actions. At some moments, he seemed so sweet and genuine. At others, he came off as completely snobby and self-involved. Cami would chalk his constantly changing demeanor up to his trying to get into her pants—only he'd been so protective and supportive of his sister. He really did seem like a truly nice guy—except when he wasn't, that is.

Cami spent the remainder of her afternoon sipping her margarita in the sun while contemplating the enigma that was Drew Sloane. By the time the girls made their way back towards the house, Cami was pretty sure that she *did* like Drew. After all, she'd witnessed him being open and kind more times than she'd seen him be snobby and rude.

That evening, she would give him another chance, she decided. Perhaps they could take another walk, get to know each other a little bit better. She even wondered whether or not he had been assigned his own room, though Cami kept telling herself that it was too early to think about sex.

Only, Cami couldn't stop thinking about sex—sex with Drew. The memories of the previous night, though covered with the shiny haze of inebriation, were nothing short of amazing. It had been years since a man had touched her, and Drew seemed to know exactly how to push her buttons. She'd had a better orgasm on his fingers than Ken had given her…perhaps ever. Maybe, just maybe, Cami thought, if they really connected tonight, she'd be willing to finish what they started the night before.

* * *

Cami took extra time getting ready, sweeping her hair back to the side and giving herself a bit more dramatic eye makeup to match the little black cocktail dress she was wearing. Once again, she looked at herself in the mirror and conceded that she was smokin' hot.

When the girls headed down to dinner after freshening up, Cami was disappointed to find that the large crowd from the night before had returned.

Surveying the masses, she was finally able to spot Drew near the bar.

"I'll be right back," Cami said to Maggie before heading in Drew's direction.

As she approached, she realized that he was in a deep conversation with the snooty older couple from the night before. She hesitated for a second, but eventually decided that she was not about to let some rude old snobs stop her from a potentially awesome romance. Taking a deep breath, she made her way through the rest of the crowd.

She was less than ten feet away when the model from this morning—Analise, Cami remembered her name to be—sauntered up next to Drew. She handed him a drink before moving even closer and putting an arm around his waist. To Cami's horror, Drew returned her easy affection, wrapping an arm around her bony shoulders and rubbing circles against Analise's back the same way he'd done to Cami the night before.

Cami cringed as she watched the pair. They moved together naturally, as if they'd been with each other for a while. Cami couldn't help but wonder whether or not they actually were a couple.

Had Drew cheated on Analise with Cami? With that thought, Cami felt sick. She needed a drink. She continued walking again, this time past the group that Drew was a part of, to the bar, where she ordered a strong cocktail.

She took a long sip of her beverage before turning from the bar to scan the crowd for Maggie. Unfortunately, Drew happened to be staring right at her, and she accidentally met his eye. He offered her a small, almost sad smile. Cami didn't return it. She turned instead and walked towards the other side of the patio.

She was more than ready for this weekend to be over.

CHAPTER NINE
Drew

Drew was speaking to a group of investors when he noticed Cami at the bar. The little black dress she was wearing perfectly accentuated her pert, round ass. As she leaned over the bar, the skimpy fabric rode up a little, revealing her taunting milky thighs. He remembered what it had been like to run his hand up those legs the night before.

He tried not to let his investors realize he was no longer paying attention, still smiling and nodding along with their conversation...but his mind was on Cami's delectable body. It wasn't just her body, though. Cami also had the most stunning face he'd ever seen: beautiful alabaster skin; soft, pouty lips; large emerald eyes that shone with intelligence—all framed by fiery red hair that bounced around her head, thick and lustrous.

Drew realized that he was waxing poetic about a woman he barely knew, when his future—the future he'd worked so hard to build—was standing right in front of him. Drew shook his head to clear his mind, then smiled weakly at the group of investors—men he'd grown to hate over the course of the last few weeks. Unfortunately, they were also men that he knew he needed in order to get him where he was going. Self-involved men only out to make money, yes, but needed just the same.

He glanced around the group before him. They were all so different from Cami. He'd only known her for a short period of time, but she'd proven herself to be completely unpretentious, kind, and funny. She was also extremely caring. Hell, she'd wanted to go searching for an abandoned champagne bottle in the middle of the night simply because she didn't want to add to the workload of the staff. She was exactly the kind of woman he could see himself settling down with.

"Isn't that right, Drew?" James Cook, president of the investment firm, was asking.

"That's right," Drew agreed, though he had no idea what they were talking about.

He shook his head again, berating his own lack of focus. He didn't have time to date right now. He could think about settling down later. Tonight, he needed to woo his investors.

He offered one last longing look towards Cami's curvaceous back. As if on cue, she turned towards him, giving him a perfect view of her large breasts, which were nearly spilling out of the top of her dress. Her huntress eyes met his, and he felt the chemistry between them sizzle, like the night before. But it was the briefest of sparks, gone as soon as it started. He offered her a small smile, sad that he couldn't be over there with her. Perhaps they could catch up later.

Cami shot a pointed look at Analise Cook, James's daughter, who was still unfortunately hanging off Drew's arm. Cami then rolled her eyes and turned away, disappearing into the crowd. Drew felt something inside his gut coil into a bitter nausea.

Cami couldn't possibly think that he was interested in Analise, could she? Analise was attractive, sure, in a cold, calculating way. She had none of Cami's heat, nor her kindness. She was like an emaciated prune, compared to Cami, who was a delectable, fresh, mouth-watering plum. Of course Cami didn't know that, but she had to realize that he wouldn't have let things get so heated last night if he had feelings for another woman.

But how would she know that? She didn't really know him from Adam. And right now, he did have his arm wrapped around Analise Cook—though that was only because she initiated it, and he couldn't afford to push her away and offend her father and thus alienate the investors. But then again, Cami couldn't know that.

Quit obsessing over Cami, he commanded himself again. He would have plenty of time to date once this deal was done. He only needed to impress these people for another few weeks. He could hold out that much longer. He could wrap his arm around Analise's bony frame and pretend to care about her modeling career. He could laugh at James and Nancy Cook's awful, elitist jokes.

It's a means to an end, he reminded himself.

However, no matter how hard he tried, he couldn't seem to get his mind off Cami. He continued to nod and smile, half listening to the conversation so that he could add a comment here or there. But his mind was miles away—or right across the deck, where Cami was laughing with Grant, his sister, and a bunch of their friends.

His mind wandered to the night before, the way she'd writhed beneath him so wantonly, shaking with desire at the mere touch of his mouth and fingers. Her lavish breasts had undulated as she twisted in pleasure. She'd been so wet, so hot and tight around his fingers. He couldn't help but think about how hot and tight it would feel wrapped around his cock.

He'd gone up to his room last night and thought about just that as he'd stroked his rigid cock. He'd pumped into his fist, imagining it was Cami's wet heat. He'd come harder than he had in a long time—with a partner or without.

Despite all this, right now he was right where he needed to be—right where he'd always wanted to be—standing in the middle of a group of multi-million dollar investors. Yet Drew couldn't help but wish that everyone else would just disappear. He wanted nothing more than to be alone with Cami, to watch her smile and hear her laugh, then listen to her moans mingle with his own as he buried himself deep within her.

Just a few more weeks, he reminded himself, as he forced a laugh at another stupid joke. *I can make it a few more weeks.*

CHAPTER TEN
Cami

After walking away from Drew, Cami had spent the remainder of the night getting drunk with Maggie, Grant, and their friends. She tried to push every single thought of Drew Sloane out of her mind as she sipped cocktail after cocktail.

Maggie was almost as drunk as she was, hanging off Declan in a way that Cami was sure she'd regret in the morning. She made a mental note to make sure Maggie ended up back up in the room with her. She wasn't going to let her best friend make a drunken mistake like the one Cami had made the night before.

Just thinking about it sent another wave of frustration through Cami. She knew better than to fool around with strange men—especially when she'd been drinking. This was why she was single in the first place. That was exactly what she and Maggie had been discussing on the phone the other night—after their mothers had both tried to pick apart their weight. Cami had absolutely no lack of interested men. It was just that all of the men that were interested in her turned out to be jackasses. Or, perhaps *all* men were jackasses, she thought with a chuckle.

But Drew had been such a sexy, seemingly sweet jackass.

Cami shook her head, willing thoughts of Drew out of her mind. That didn't work, so she flagged down a server to order another drink.

By the time Cami and Maggie finally stumbled up to their room, it was after midnight and they were both completely wasted. Maggie crashed face-first onto the bed and immediately fell asleep on top of the comforter.

Cami took her time getting ready for sleep, brushing her teeth, washing her face, and slipping into a comfortable little pair of soft shorts and a silky camisole. But even after that entire routine, she lay in bed awake. She couldn't rid her mind of images of Drew.

It was one thing if he didn't like her at all—if he had just turned out to be a total ass. But he hadn't. The scene she'd encountered with his sister had been completely genuine. And the way he'd looked at her last night on the beach—like she was the answer to all of his problems—that had been genuine, too. Plus, their chemistry, when they were together, was undeniable.

With a growl of frustration, Cami rolled onto her back. She was extremely thirsty, she realized. Not wanting to wake up dehydrated and excruciatingly hung over for the second morning in a row, she decided to make a quick trip to the kitchen and get a bottle of water. Then she'd be able to sleep, she reasoned.

Cami debated whether or not to leave the room in her skimpy sleepwear. She didn't have a robe to throw over, or even some comfortable sweats. So, changing would require pulling on one of her sexy little dresses, which she really didn't have the energy to do. It was almost one in the morning, she reasoned to herself. The likelihood of running into anyone at this time of night was slim to none.

She wondered for a moment whether or not she would even consider walking around a strange mansion in the middle of the night barely dressed if she was completely sober. Probably not, she decided, but headed down the stairs anyway.

She chugged an entire bottle of water while standing in front of the fridge, than grabbed a second bottle to take back up to her room. If she didn't end up drinking it, Maggie probably would.

Cami was just turning to go, when she came face-to-face with Drew, who was just entering the kitchen. They stood silently for a moment, eyes hungrily roving over each other's body.

Drew looked completely rumpled and unkempt—it was the sexiest that Cami had ever seen him. He was still wearing his clothes from the previous evening, though his shirt was untucked and partially unbuttoned, with the sleeves rolled up past the elbow. And his tie seemed to have had disappeared. His dark hair was sticking out in every direction, as if he'd been running his hands through it.

Or someone else had been running her hands through it. The picture of Drew and Analise frolicking on the beach—just like Cami and Drew had the other night—flickered through her mind.

"Excuse me," Cami said angrily, trying to push past Drew. But he was a solid form against her, all toned hard muscle, refusing to let her through.

"Cami," he whispered, pushing further into her. "It's just…a really bad time." His breath hitched as his chest pressed against her breasts—which were only covered by a slim slip of silk. "It's a bad time for me to meet a girl I really like."

"I'm sorry to hear you and Analise are having problems," she snarled, trying her best to move around him towards the door.

"Fuck Analise," she heard him whisper under his breath.

And then he was all over her. His hot mouth claimed hers, kissing and licking at her lips until she opened for him. His hands wound down her body until they reached the perky flesh of her ass. After squeezing tightly, he used his grip to pull her up as if she weighed nothing, closer to his mouth. Instinctively, she wrapped her legs around his waist and allowed him to press her against the wall.

His tongue continued to dominate her mouth as he ground his hardening length against her crotch. Cami couldn't help but press back, while all of her common sense was washed away by the surge of adrenaline and want.

Once Cami was securely pressed against the wall, Drew released her ass and allowed his hands to explore her body, moving up until they were cupping and squeezing the ample flesh of her soft breasts. She moaned and pressed into his touch, relishing the way his thumbs made delicious circles over her swollen, aching nipples.

Drew's mouth moved from her lips, trailing kisses down her neck and cleavage. He licked at the bead of sweat clinging between her breasts before moving further down to mouth at her nipples through the thin silk of her camisole.

Cami was going crazy. She wanted nothing more than to reach down and release his cock, so that he could fuck her right there in the middle of the kitchen, pressed against the wall.

It was that crazy thought that finally snapped Cami out of her alcohol and hormone induced craze.

"What am I doing?" she asked herself, pushing against Drew's chest until he backed up and allowed her to slide down his body until her feet touched the floor. She quickly maneuvered past him and ran towards the stairs.

"Cami, wait," Drew called after her, but Cami didn't stop until she was back in her and Maggie's bedroom, the door safely locked behind her.

Once there, with Maggie still sleeping soundly on the bed next to her, Cami finally allowed herself to take a shaky breath. Her legs were suddenly wobbly, and she began to slide down until she was sitting on the floor, with her back against the wall. She drew her knees up and pressed her face against them.

"What am I doing?" she asked herself again.

The man was obviously crazy. He was hot and cold—he didn't know his own mind. He had another woman—possibly his girlfriend—hanging off him half the time. Then he would look at her in a way that made her body catch on fire, and the next thing she knew they'd be grinding together like horny teenagers.

She had more self-respect than that. She deserved a man who would value her. Cami's mind wandered back to the scene between Drew and his sister earlier that day. He'd told her almost that exact same thing. He'd seemed so sweet and caring at the time—a good older brother.

God, she wanted *that* Drew. Why couldn't she have *that* Drew?

"Because the man is crazy," she said aloud. "Maybe he has a multiple-personality disorder."

"What?" Maggie asked, suddenly sitting up in bed and glaring at Cami. Her hair was sticking up in every direction again and there was dried drool in the corner of her mouth.

"You're going to make some man very happy one day," Cami quipped playfully.

"What?" Maggie asked again, tilting her head to the side in confusion.

"Nothing. Sorry. Go back to sleep," Cami said soothingly.

"Why are you on the floor?" Maggie asked.

"No reason. Just go back to sleep."

Maggie continued to stare at her questioningly for a moment, then zoned out. Falling back against the comforter, she immediately fell back to sleep—apparent by the gentle snores reverberating through the room.

Cami remained seated on the floor for a long time, deep in thought. With everything she was going through with her ex and Madison, the last thing she needed was some stupid guy sending her mixed signals.

But, try as she might, she just couldn't get Drew out of her head.

CHAPTER ELEVEN
Cami

Cami was physically and emotionally exhausted the following morning as she and Maggie climbed into the back of a town car for the long ride home. Despite her best effort the night before, Cami was much more hung over than she was hoping to be.

Cami didn't actually drink much on a regular basis—just a glass of wine here or a cocktail there. She reckoned that she'd drank more this weekend than she had the entire year prior. And she was paying for it today.

On top of the physical repercussions, Cami was also feeling disgusted with herself, as well as Drew. She couldn't believe she'd let him make out with her again last night. She felt used, though she wasn't even sure why.

Not surprisingly, Maggie was even more hung over than Cami and was in absolutely no mood to talk on the ride home. The women sat in silence, faces pressed against opposite windows as the car slowly made its way back to the city.

Cami arrived home by early afternoon and wasn't scheduled to pick up Madison until later in the evening. She knew better than to show up early—not with the way Ken had been acting. Instead, she took a long, hot bath, followed by a nap.

She was still not back to her normal self by the time she arrived at Ken's door at seven sharp, but the beautiful face of her smiling baby girl made everything better.

The sight of Natalie carrying Madison out of the house was a little upsetting, but Cami quickly pushed that thought aside to take her daughter into her arms.

"Mom!" Madison squealed in delight.

Cami felt like she could squeal with joy as well, though she refrained from it in front of her ex and his fiancée.

Ken was acting uncharacteristically nice. He even smiled as he handed Cami Madison's diaper bag.

"See you this week," he said as she walked towards the car.

She only nodded coldly. Like she needed to be reminded that she would soon have to fight for custody of her daughter.

Madison had already eaten dinner at Ken's house, so Cami simply gave her a bath before tucking her into bed next to her. She read a few goodnight stories as her daughter clung to her more tightly than usual. She wondered if Ken had said something to her about spending more time with them, or if she was simply picking up on Cami's emotions.

Either way, Madison fell asleep with her face pressed against her mother's chest, Cami gently stroking her soft little curls. Cami didn't even consider getting up to put her daughter to bed in her own room, opting instead to drift off to sleep with the little angel in her arms.

By the following morning, the little angel had turned into a little monster.

"I don't want to go to Nana's house," Madison sobbed, kicking and fighting as Cami tried to buckle her into her car seat.

It broke Cami's heart knowing that her daughter was just as exhausted as she was and wanted nothing more than to spend the day at home with her mommy.

But Madison lacked the vocabulary to understand that while she'd been away from Mommy all weekend, Mommy hadn't actually been at work, and she was required to go in today. This was one of the reasons why she hated any rotation in which her days off fell on the weekend. Most nurses loved those rotations, but to Cami, they simply meant she didn't get to spend her days off with her daughter every other week.

Madison cried all the way to Cami's mother's house and was still sobbing when Cami brought her inside.

"What's wrong?" her mom asked as she took the little girl into her arms and rocked her soothingly.

"She didn't want to come today," Cami admitted, though she knew her mother would give her a hard time.

"Then don't go to work," she replied. "Take the day off to spend with your daughter."

"You know I can't, Mom."

"Yes, you can. Call in sick."

"I can't, Mom. I can't afford it. I only have four shifts a week. I can't give one up."

"Yes you can, Camilla," her mother chided, though she was still whispering soothingly against Madison's ear between chastisements to Cami.

One thing Cami really could commend her mother for was how great she was with Madison. It was the reason why she continued to use her mother as a babysitter, despite her criticisms—that and the fact that she watched Madison for free, of course.

"I really can't. Not right now," Cami replied.

Her mother must have heard the seriousness in her voice, because she looked up from where she was soothing Madison to sleep in order to meet Cami's eyes.

"Why? What's wrong?"

"Ken is suing for more custody. He's engaged and he thinks that his new stay-at-home wife would be a better option for Madison than me."

Cami held her breath, half expecting her mother to side with Ken. Her mom had just been on her case because she worked too much and she'd always valued Ken's money.

"That rat bastard," her mother growled, surprising Cami. Madison stirred a little, but her mom continued to rock her as she spoke to Cami. "He seriously thinks some bimbo is a better caregiver for Madison than her own mother and grandmother?"

"He's crazy, Mom," Madison replied, sinking down on the sofa beside her.

"Exactly. He's crazy. You have nothing to worry about."

"But I do. Ken has money and lawyers and connections. I can barely afford the lawyer I used during the divorce. He's going to screw me now just like he screwed me then."

Tears began to slide down Cami's face as she finally admitted that there was a chance she could lose the case—a chance that she could lose primary custody of her daughter.

"Oh, honey," her mom singsonged, leaning forward to wrap the arm around Cami. "Don't worry, kiddo. We'll figure something out. We'll make sure we don't lose Madison."

After the surprisingly cathartic conversation with her mother, Cami's day improved. The emergency room was slow, but not slow enough to make the day drag. There were no fatalities, and everything ran along smoothly.

On her first break, she found that she had a voice mail from her lawyer, letting her know that he had called Ken's attorney and scheduled a preliminary meeting for Friday. She called him back and they discussed what Cami should expect from the meeting. They were just going to go over the different custody options, the lawyer explained. No changes were actually going to be made during the meeting, he assured her. He seemed confident, so Cami felt better.

* * *

On Tuesday, Maggie was scheduled for the same shift as Cami, which always made the day go by faster. They even made plans to take their lunch break at the same time.

"So..." Maggie began over a bowl or beef stir-fry in the hospital cafeteria. "Have you heard from Drew?"

Cami's mouth fell open mid-bite and her broccoli fell from her fork onto the table. How had Maggie known about Drew? She'd never mentioned anything to her. And why would she think that Drew would call her?

"Why would you think I'd hear from Drew?" Cami asked, trying to sound casual. From the smirk on Maggie's face, she could tell that she'd failed.

"I don't know," Maggie said mischievously. "It seemed like the two of you really hit it off."

"What makes you think that?" Cami demanded, her voice actually getting a little loud.

She didn't mean to be so defensive, but she'd spent the last two days trying to forget about Drew Sloane and she didn't understand why Maggie was suddenly bringing him up.

Maggie looked away, an odd look on her face. She bit her lip as if she was contemplating saying something. Unless Cami was mistaken—which she never was when it came to her best friend—Maggie almost looked guilty.

"What?" Cami asked, though she wasn't sure if she even wanted to know the answer at this point.

"Don't be mad, okay?" Maggie said after a moment. "I'll tell you, but you have to promise not to be mad."

"I can't promise that," Cami replied, growing more worried by the minute. "There's a large chance that whatever you're about to say actually *will* make me mad, and then I'll be a liar."

"Fine," Maggie said, letting out a sigh. "Just promise you won't freak out… and that you'll give me a chance to explain myself."

"Sure. Now spill," Cami demanded, trying to mentally prepare herself for whatever Maggie had to say.

"So… Grant and I had this idea, right? We talked about it last week at family dinner."

"What idea?" Cami growled.

"Calm down," Maggie snapped. "You promised you'd listen."

"I am listening!" Cami replied with a scowl. But she then shut her mouth and motioned for Maggie to continue.

"You see, Grant and Drew have been friends forever and we just thought the two or you might hit it off—you and Drew, I mean. So this weekend was supposed to be, like, an unofficial set-up."

"What?!" Cami shouted.

Half the heads in the cafeteria turned towards her and she sank into her seat, embarrassed. But she was still scowling at Maggie through gritted teeth.

"How was it a setup if we didn't even know we were being set up? Wait… did Drew know? Was I the only one who didn't know?"

"No!" Maggie said emphatically, leaning forward in her seat. "I promise. Neither one of you were told. I wouldn't do that to you. Grant and I just kind of… pushed you two together. That was my idea, to be honest." Maggie actually had the audacity to look proud of herself as she continued. "I thought it might be awkward to let the two of you know you were being set up. Then there'd be all of this...expectation. And you would probably overthink everything."

"Not necessarily," Cami interjected.

Maggie simply raised an eyebrow questioningly. "Anyway," she continued. "We wanted you guys to be able to meet and get to know each other without any pressure or expectation. And you seemed to hit it off. I even went to bed early so that you could spend some more time with him."

"You did that on purpose?" Cami growled. "Seriously? You could have saved me from making a huge mistake."

Maggie's eyes shot up. She studied Cami closely, and Cami suddenly regretted opening her big mouth.

"Mistake? What mistake? I didn't hear about any mistake."

"That's because I didn't tell you," Cami replied grumpily.

"Well, you're telling me now!" Maggie demanded, a look of utter glee spreading across her face at the chance for fresh gossip. She looked like she was about to begin rubbing her hands now.

"The first night we were there," Cami began, "Friday night, you went off to bed early—or were pretending to, so I'd be forced to spend time with Drew. And so I did. We went for a walk on the beach and shared a bottle of wine. We'd both already been drinking and we had a little too much. One thing led to another—"

"You had sex?" Maggie interrupted, much louder than she'd probably intended.

Once again, multiple eyes turned to them.

"No," Cami whispered, leaning in for a little more privacy. "And keep your voice down! We didn't have sex. But we did make out and fool around a little bit."

"What do you mean, 'fool around'?" Maggie asked.

"I'm not giving you details, you perv," Cami muttered through gritted teeth.

Maggie sat back, looking utterly satisfied with herself. "So we were right, you and Drew *did* hit it off."

"No we didn't," Cami snapped. Maggie just lifted another eyebrow questioningly. Cami was a little jealous of Maggie's ability to speak with her eyebrows, but she continued. "It was weird…like, sometimes we'd hit it off, and he'd seem super amazing. But other times he'd act like a complete jerk. Then I realized he had a girlfriend, so…"

"Drew doesn't have a girlfriend," Maggie said confidently.

"He does too…that model chick—Analise."

Maggie actually laughed at that statement.

"Drew is *not* dating Analise. Trust me. He doesn't even like her. He just puts up with her because her dad is some important big wig. I don't know the details. But I *do* know that Drew has absolutely no interest in Analise and is completely infatuated with you."

"You do not *know* that."

"Yes, I do."

"How?"

Maggie bit her lip and looked away, as if she was debating whether or not to divulge another secret.

"Spill!" Cami demanded.

"He totally told Grant," Maggie said excitedly. "Grant called me to say that Drew confessed to him that he was practically obsessed with you. He asked Grant for your number last night and everything."

Cami paused for a second, trying to let Maggie's excited rambling sink in. It all sounded like hearsay to her. But there was a part of her that wanted to believe…that wanted to know that Drew was as fixated on her as she was on him. Yet she just couldn't. He'd been too weird, too standoffish.

"Grant did *not* say that!" she replied eventually. "There's no way Drew is obsessed with me. I promise."

"Grant never exaggerates," Maggie said. "Come on Cami, you know my brother—ever the pragmatist. If that's what he told me, then that's what Drew told him."

Cami didn't reply; she simply took the information in. It was a lot to go over—a lot to process. Drew *did* like her? How did that change things? Did it explain his actions over the weekend? Not really. Though it did make a little sense if he was trying to impress some business bigwig—even if it was still a bit of a douchey move.

"Earth to Cami," Maggie said, snapping her fingers in Cami's face. Cami sat up immediately. "Wipe that goofy smile off your face."

"I don't have a goofy smile on my face," Cami replied, though she went out of her way to make sure she was scowling.

"It's okay," Maggie said with a pleased smile. "I *knew* you two would be perfect for each other!"

"And how did you *know* that?"

"You are just like his sister Elsie in so many ways," Maggie said.

Cami's mind swept back to the altercation she'd overheard on Saturday. She really did have a lot in common with Drew's sister. Eventually, her mind registered that Maggie was still speaking.

"...and they are super close. So I knew that he'd love you."

"Wait, what?" Cami asked.

"Since Drew is so close to his sister, and you're so like his sister, I knew that he'd be into you."

Cami thought about that statement for a minute before she replied. "Isn't that a little gross?"

"No!" Maggie responded, taken aback. "That's disgusting. I just meant..." Maggie tilted her head to the side, deep in thought, before making a disgusted face. "Now that you put it like that it does seem totally weird."

"Yeah...weird."

"But that doesn't change that you guys really were perfect for each other and really hit it off, and I was right." She said every word quickly, full of self-satisfaction.

Cami just shook her head, still trying to wrap her mind around all the new information.

"But we're good now, right?" Maggie asked after a moment. "You're not mad about the set-up?"

"No," Cami replied. "But no more blind dates, whether I know about it or not! Promise?"

"There's no need to worry about that," Maggie said with a smirk. "You're with Drew now. You won't need to be set up."

"I am *not* with Drew. Trust me. He isn't going to call."

CHAPTER TWELVE
Cami

Cami was actually proven wrong on Thursday evening, when she was driving home and her phone rang with a strange number. She answered immediately, thinking that it might be someone from the law firm.

"Hello," she said as soon as the Bluetooth in her car picked up.

"Hey Cami, it's Drew. Drew Sloane—from the beach party this weekend."

"Yes…I remember who you are. That was less than a week ago and we nearly had sex… I don't think your introduction requires quite so many identifiers."

Cami winced. She didn't mean to sound so harsh, but she'd been thinking about Drew constantly for the last few days and she still couldn't decide if she was mad at him or not—and, more importantly, whether she liked him or not.

Plus, her meeting with Ken and the lawyers was tomorrow, which had her on edge. She was probably taking out her frustration on him more than she realized.

"Well, okay," Drew replied, trying to sound upbeat though she could tell he was growing more nervous. "I just called to see if there was any chance you were free tonight. But now that I'm saying it out loud, it seems silly. Of course you're not free this late. I'm sure you have plans."

Cami bit her lip, but didn't reply right away. On one hand, she really didn't want to seem desperate—and even Drew himself was admitting that accepting a date so late in the evening was a desperate move. But then again, who was she kidding? She really was longing for a company, to distract her from her dreadful thoughts.

Since her meeting was so early in the morning, her mother and she had decided that it was probably for the best that Madison just stayed over there for the night. That way, Madison wouldn't have to be woken up to be shipped off to Grandma's super early. Instead, it was a fun over-night with the grandma.

But that left Cami home alone, stressing herself out about the next day's meeting. Maggie wasn't available, and Cami really didn't have any other friends she could call up last minute. And she definitely didn't want to sit around all night, worrying.

The idea of getting all dolled up and going out on the town actually sounded nice to Cami. And the idea of getting all dolled up and going out on the town with *Drew* sounded even better. So, as much as she wanted to say no, she resisted.

"Actually," Cami said quickly, before she could lose her nerve, "I *am* free tonight."

"Really?" Drew asked, as if he didn't really believe it.

"Yeah, really," Cami replied, a smile spreading across her lips. "I'm free and I wouldn't mind getting out of the house for a little while. Plus, I could really use a drink."

"Awesome!" Drew responded. "Then drinks it is. I can pick you up in an hour."

Cami gave Drew her address and headed home for a quick shower before the date. By the time Drew arrived, Cami was dressed to impress in a low-cut blouse and a high-waisted skirt.

"You look absolutely lovely," Drew said, kissing her hand before handing her a bouquet of roses.

"Look at you, being all old-fashioned," Cami said, though there was a smile on her lips and no bite in her tone. She ushered Drew into the house while she set the flowers in a vase.

Drew paused in the living room, staring at the toys sprawled all over the place. Cami winced, regretting having invited him inside.

"You have a kid?" he asked.

"Yeah," she replied hesitantly. "A daughter. She's three. She's spending the night with Grandma."

"You didn't say anything all weekend."

"I know," Madison said, defeated. She was half expecting Drew to turn and walk back out the door any moment. "I'm sorry. I was just—"

"No, it's totally okay. I love kids. I'm just surprised. That's all. My sister has a son that age and she never shuts up about him—which is understandable. So I'm just surprised you didn't mention it."

"Usually I'm like that too," Cami said, offering him a relieved smile. "But last weekend was the first time ever where I've been around people I don't know… and who don't know about Madison. I love being Madison's mother, but it was nice, just for a few days, to be someone else as well."

"I get that," Drew replied. "Sometimes I wish Elsie—that's my sister—would try to be someone other than a wife and a mother. Sometimes I wish she'd do something just for herself."

"It's hard. Especially when you're a single parent."

"And sometimes, I wish Elsie was a single parent," he added with a cheeky smile. "But enough of the deep stuff. Let's go get drinks."

Drew took Cami's hand and escorted her out to his waiting BMW. He drove them to a swanky bar that was way above Cami's pay grade, but it was quiet enough for them to hear each other talk.

The banter was easy, just like it had been that first night on the beach. They joked with each other and laughed a great deal. Eventually though, the conversation circled back around to Madison—which it often did for Cami.

"There was another reason I didn't want to mention her last weekend," Cami admitted, looking down into her glass.

"Why is that?" Drew asked.

"My ex-husband told me recently that he's going to sue for primary custody. Which is ridiculous, because he can barely be depended upon to maintain the custody he has now—and that's only every other weekend. But he's getting married, and I think he's got it in his head that they need Madison to make them a perfect little family." It wasn't until she noticed the tears rolling off her cheeks that Cami realized she was sobbing. It was embarrassing, but there wasn't anything she could do about it. "It was still so new at the time, I knew that I couldn't talk about her without it coming back up. I mean," —she motioned to her eyes—"it's still coming up now."

Drew leaned forward in his chair across from her and reached out to take her hand, giving it a gentle squeeze.

"It's going to be alright, Cami," he said with such confidence that she willed herself to believe him.

"Oh, God," she said, swiping away the remainder of her tears. "Sorry about that. I just…our first custody meeting is in the morning. It's on my mind."

"I totally understand," Drew replied with a sweet smile. "And it's not a problem. Let's get you out of here?"

Cami nodded, though she couldn't help but feel like Drew was just ready to get rid of her after that emotional display. They were quiet in the car until he parked outside of her house.

"I'd like to see you again," Drew said, watching her from the driver's seat.

Cami stared back at him, barely believing what she was hearing. She took a deep breath and willed herself to be courageous before she replied.

"Why don't you come in," she said simply.

"Really?" Drew asked. "Even with your custody thing in the morning?"

"Especially with my custody thing the morning," Cami answered. "I need something to take my mind off it."

"I think..." Drew sucked in a shaky breath and when he spoke again, his voice was a little rougher. "I think I can give you something to keep your mind off it."

They were barely in the house with the door shut behind them before Drew's mouth was on Cami's, his tongue hungrily seeking entrance. In a reenactment of her other night—or perhaps just because of their height difference—Drew's hands found Cami's buttocks and he hoisted her up until her legs were wrapped around his waist.

They thrust their tongues into each other's mouths, both fighting for dominance. Cami couldn't help but wonder if Drew had been feeling the same pull as she had—the same desire. Had he been thinking about her as much as she had thought about him?

Eventually, Drew pulled away ever so slightly, pupils blown wide with lust as his amber eyes met Cami's.

"Is this still okay?" he asked huskily.

Cami appreciated his attempts to make sure she was really ready to do this, but more than anything she wanted to get on with it.

"This is more than okay," she promised before running her tongue along his bottom lip. "This is perfect."

For a split second, they stared at each other, and Cami watched as a predatory look spread across his face. Then he was back on her. Instead of pressing his lips against hers, however, his head moved lower, licking and nipping his way down her neck and shoulder. His hands, meanwhile, slid beneath the fabric of her skirt, stroking her soft thighs lightly.

Cami was helpless to do anything but lean into the caresses, savoring the feel of his hands and mouth on her body. But all too soon, Drew was pulling away again. He seemed to have realized that between the top tucked into the skirt and the tight belt, he wasn't going to be able to get her naked without some work.

"Bedroom," he grunted, and Cami simply pointed the way as Drew carried her towards the bed, where he dumped her unceremoniously on the comforter.

He then set about undressing her meticulously, one article of clothing at a time. He removed the belt, then slowly slid the skirt down her body and off her completely.

Reaching down to the hem of her shirt, Drew easily slid it out from underneath her and over her head. He unfastened her bra with one hand, then slowly pulled her panties down over her hips.

Cami had never experienced anything like this. It was as if Drew was slowly unwrapping a birthday present, one piece of paper at a time until finally, he was gazing down at her naked flesh. Licking his lips, he leaned towards her full, soft breast. But her hand on his chest stopped him.

"You too," she demanded, glaring at his perfectly tailored suit like it had offended her. It was a nice suit and it looked great on him, but it would look even better on the floor. "It's only fair."

Obliging Cami with a cocky smirk, Drew set about undressing himself in the same ridiculously slow manner that he had done with Cami. First, his jacket hit the floor, then his vest and tie.

Cami's eyes followed the rise and fall of his toned large muscles as he shifted and stretched to pull off his shirt. She realized she'd never actually seem him without a shirt—despite their weekend on the beach.

She reached her hand up to run it across the rippling contour of his abs as he bent down to finally wrap his lips around one of Cami's areolae.

After circling his tongue around the nipple for a minute, he began sucking and biting marks into the pale skin of her chest. She moaned and arched into his mouth, loving the way he worshiped one breast, then the other. Cami was near-delirious with need by the time Drew moved back to reassert dominance over Cami's already kiss-swollen lips. He swallowed her cries of pleasure as he ground his hard length against her bare pussy through his pants.

"Pants. Off. Now," Cami panted in between bruising kisses.

"Agreed," Drew replied, moving away only long enough to step out of his shoes and socks, then pull both his pants and his underwear down in one long motion.

Cami gasped as his swollen, dripping member was finally exposed. If possible, even more moisture began pooling between her legs at the sight. Her body throbbed with desire. She needed him inside her.

"Please tell me you have a condom," she panted as Drew positioned himself between her legs.

Drew gave her a confident smile before turning around to pull a condom out of his wallet.

"Were you counting on this?" Cami asked, though she wasn't exactly upset.

"No," he replied as he gave his leaking cock a few strokes before sliding the sheath on. "Not counting on it. Not even really hoping. Just wanted to be prepared. Just in case."

With that, the predatory gaze returned to Drew's eyes, and he crawled onto the bed beside her. He gently pushed Cami's legs even further apart, and she could feel her own juices trickling down her thighs as he pressed a large finger between the lips of her pussy, finding and then circling her clit.

Cami closed her eyes, moaning loudly as she allowed the pleasure to wash over her. She'd thought perhaps her mind had exaggerated their first night on the beach, but now she knew it wasn't so. Drew's touch was electric. It was like the first moment he'd grabbed her hand at the beach, only a million times stronger. Still though, it wasn't enough.

"Please," she begged. "I need you inside me."

Drew growled. The noise was deep and guttural and completely animalistic. It sent a bolt of electricity up Cami's spine. Suddenly, he grabbed her legs, pulled them up until they settled against his shoulders, then buried himself within her completely—in one fluid thrust.

Cami could not hold back the scream at the feeling of his thick cock stretching her open. Drew was so much bigger than Ken, and it had been so long since any man had been inside her, that it felt like she was being split in two. Only, along with the pain there was unbelievable pleasure.

Drew paused for a moment, giving Cami a chance to adjust to him. After a second, though, his patience began to wane. He slowly pulled out of her again before gently pushing back inside. He continued like this for a few moments, but soon, his thrusts were picking up speed. Before too long, he was pushing into Cami roughly, as he brought her closer and closer to release.

Cami herself was helpless to do anything but cry and writhe beneath him. She was at the edge when Drew suddenly stilled and let go of her legs. Cami didn't have any time to complain, however, before she was being flipped over onto her hands and knees. And then, Drew was back inside her, pounding into her hard and fast.

Cami quickly found that she had more control in this position and could push back against Drew. She began matching pace with him, thrusting herself back onto his ample girth.

When Drew slid a hand around her, and began to circle her clit in time with each thrust, Cami was tipped over that precipice, moaning and thrashing as wave after wave of pleasure washed over her. Drew's motions became erratic as well as he soon spent himself deep inside her.

He eventually pulled out and disposed of the condom before collapsing next to Cami. She thought that she should probably get up and get ready for bed. She should probably shower and brush her teeth at the very least. But Drew had rolled to his side and was spooning himself against her back. He felt so warm and relaxing that Cami couldn't bring herself to get out of bed. Instead, she nestled back against him and slowly drifted off to sleep.

Cami woke early with the alarm, but the spot beside her in bed was already cold. Frowning, she pulled herself out of bed and went looking for Drew.

When she realized he wasn't there, she than began looking for a note. She checked the nightstand and the dresser in the living room, the kitchen table, counter and fridge, even the coffee table in the living room.

Nothing.

Cami froze as the realization finally washed over her. Drew had left without even a note. He was just gone.

She had shared so much with him the night before—her fears about the impending custody battle, her hopes for the future. And he'd seemed genuinely interested too. But now he was gone—without even a note.

It had just been sex to him. He obviously didn't want to get involved with someone with so much baggage. Her and Madison were a package deal, after all. Well, at the moment they were. She wasn't even sure how much longer she'd have primary custody of her daughter.

Wiping the tears from her eyes, Cami went back into the bedroom to get ready. She could hope for the best, but right now, she felt like her entire world was slowly slipping away from her.

the Stubborn Suitor

BOOK TWO

CHAPTER ONE
Drew

Drew shifted in his seat uncomfortably. This was supposed to be a "casual breakfast amongst friends." In all actuality, it was a business meeting with James Cook, a potential investor in his company. But instead of a straightforward meeting in his office, Cook had insisted on this "casual breakfast amongst friends" that included his wife Nancy and his daughter Analise, neither of whom were on Drew's very short list of those he actually considered friends.

A few other investors from Cook's firm had shown up as well, and Drew couldn't help but feel restless under all of the scrutiny. The men were all deferring to Cook, laughing at his off-colored jokes and flirting with his wife and daughter just enough to be flattering.

Drew took a sip of water as he tried his best to smile and appear excited to be there. He really was, after all, thrilled about the prospect of the investment. If only it could be handled in the normal way—in boardrooms with contracts. Not here, in the baking sun of the Cooks' summer home patio, feigning interest in Nancy's latest art acquisition.

"I don't really get it," she was saying with a kind of faux-humility that Drew found pathetic. "It just looks like paint on canvas to me. But the dealer was raving about the artist. Some starving genius who'd started painting while he was homeless, I guess. I'm probably just providing him with more drug money, but what can you do? The colors really do match my drapes in the foyer."

Drew bit his cheek to keep from grimacing as polite chuckles sounded around the table. The way in which the Cooks constantly equated poverty with criminality was highly offensive to Drew, who'd grown up quite poor himself. Drew had worked very hard for his scholarship to Harvard and had then built his company from nothing into a multi-billion-dollar corporation. And in that time, he'd never forgotten his roots. In fact, a large percentage of his paycheck went to charity each month—completely anonymously, of course.

And it was his company—his baby, which he'd spent the last decade growing—that kept him quiet and in his seat while everything inside him yearned to get away from these people.

Just a few more weeks, he told himself as he took another sip of water.

"Is everything okay, Drew?" Analise's soft voice whispered in his ear as her hand came up to massage his neck.

He had obviously not been doing as good of a job at schooling his expression as he thought he was.

"I'm fine," Drew lied as he turned towards her with a fake smile. "It's just the heat. I should have worn a more breathable suit. Hadn't realized we would be dining outside."

"Oh my," she replied with an exaggerated pout. "Let's get you inside to cool off a little." Without waiting for a response, Analise stood up and faced the rest of the table. "Drew is a little warm, so we're going inside to cool off for a bit."

It took all of Drew's self-control not to hide his face in his hands.

"Of course, my dear," Nancy said with a delighted smile.

Drew then had no choice but to stand and offer Analise his arm. Cook gave Drew a knowing wink as he smiled at the two of them as well. Drew knew that the Cooks were trying to push him towards their daughter, perhaps believing that it would be easier to do business with a son-in-law. James Cook's willingness to use his daughter in order to ensure a successful business venture just reconfirmed Drew's already-existing low opinion of the man.

And it wasn't like Analise minded being used by her father. At the moment, she was leaning into him unnecessarily, so that her small breasts were pressed against his arm as she directed them into the house. Her naturally tall frame was lifted even more by six-inch heels, so that she was almost as tall as Drew himself. She *was* beautiful—Drew could admit that much. She was a model, after all—thin and lithe, with high cheekbones and delicate facial features. But she was also cold and spoiled and almost as clueless and conceited as her parents; in other words—definitely not his type. In fact, she was the opposite of his type.

Drew could not help but be reminded of the woman who *was* his type—the woman who was everything he had ever wanted in a partner. Cami was absolutely gorgeous, with a luscious petite frame he could easily lift and press against a wall. And yet she had been blessed with curves for days—large, voluptuous breasts and wide, sensuous hips. Her face was breathtaking, with large green eyes and pouty lips.

And Cami wasn't just a sexy body. Her personality was just as fiery as her long red hair. She was strong and independent and funny as hell. But she was also sweet and nurturing. She really was, all around, the perfect woman. Exactly the type of woman Drew would want for a wife.

That was the problem. Cami wasn't the type of woman you fooled around with. She wasn't a weekend fling—she was the girl you took home to meet your mom. She, herself, was a single mother, as well as a full time nurse. And she was about to begin a nasty custody battle with her ex-husband. She deserved someone who could be there for her, who could love and treat her the way that she deserved.

And—unfortunately—that was not Drew at the moment. He was so close to getting everything he'd every desired for his company and he had already sacrificed this much. He didn't have the time and energy, right now, to be the man that Cami needed, much less the man she deserved. So he'd pulled away. He'd run away, more like, without leaving so much as a note behind.

In the cool interior of the house, Drew sank onto the Cooks' overstuffed sofa, thoughts of Cami still fresh in his mind. Analise moved to settle down right next to him—a little too close to be appropriate.

"Could you get me some water?" he asked in an attempt to redirect her attention. He really didn't want to be so close to Analise, especially not while thoughts of Cami were swarming through his head. But he couldn't afford to offend her either—not with this deal hanging in the balance.

Analise nodded and headed into the kitchen, while Drew sighed and pulled out his phone. He gazed down at Cami's number. He really knew that he should leave her alone, allow her to move on with her life and find a relationship with someone who could give her everything she deserved, and more.

Unfortunately, he didn't think he was strong enough—or self-sacrificing enough—to do so.

CHAPTER TWO
Cami

Cami had awoken well before her alarm, the stress of the upcoming preliminary meeting with her ex-husband, Ken, and their lawyers, weighing heavily on her mind. Ken was trying to sue for primary custody, which was a complete joke in her opinion—he could barely be counted on to maintain the two weekends a month that he already had.

Yes, Ken had more money and more connections than Cami, but she would do whatever it took to keep primary custody of her two-year-old daughter. Ken was an alcoholic and an all-around irresponsible man. Even if he was about to get remarried, he didn't deserve any more time with Madison.

Cami rolled over in bed and stared at the rumpled pillow next to her own in confusion for a few moments before the previous evening came flashing back to her.

Drew had called her out of the blue and asked

her out to dinner. She'd been surprised to hear from him after the hot-and-cold treatment he'd given her at her best friend's beach house the weekend before. Maggie's family had been hosting a large get-together, where she and Drew had immediately hit it off.

However, when other people were around, he had turned into a completely different person—a person she really didn't like at all. Yet, despite his apparent multiple personalities, Cami had not been able to deny their chemistry. But was that enough to build a relationship on? Even after their amazing night together, she wasn't able to decide whether or not she really liked Drew.

And last night really had been amazing. They'd gone out to dinner, then she'd invited him back to her house for "drinks," which turned into earth-shattering sex. She'd fallen asleep in his arms, but—once she was thoroughly awake—Cami had realized that Drew's spot beside her in her bed was already cold.

She remained quiet for a moment, listening for any sounds of Drew in the house. When she heard nothing, Cami pulled herself out of her bed and went looking for him. The house was small, so it only took her a few minutes to confirm what she had already known: Drew was gone. And what was even worse, he'd skipped out without even leaving a note.

Now, Cami was curled up on her sofa, sobbing into a cup of coffee and feeling even worse than she had been the day before. Not only did she have the stress of her looming custody meeting in just a few hours, but she also felt used and abandoned by Drew.

"Whatever," she said aloud as she rose to get dressed and ready for the appointment. "I don't need a man in my life right now anyway—especially not one as unreliable as Drew-frikken'-Sloane. I'm better off without him. Better to use him and lose him."

She really wanted to mean those words, yet she couldn't help the sting she felt at his rejection. But she pushed that ache aside as she got ready and headed towards the lawyer's office downtown. She had enough to worry about, after all. On her list of true priorities, Drew's cowardly departure was pretty low.

Ken was an irresponsible alcoholic, but he was also extremely wealthy. He was from a prominent family and had the resources and connections to get what he wanted. He'd done just that during their divorce, getting out of the marriage without any spousal support and very little child support—even though he'd been the one to cheat on Cami. She hadn't been able to prove it and she *had* been the one to leave him, so he'd turned things around until she looked like the person "at fault" in the divorce. She'd been lucky to be awarded primary custody, though that had only been because Ken hadn't been interested in any more time with Madison.

But now he was getting remarried. And he wanted a perfect little family to present to the world. Even as he pushed for more custody, Cami knew that Ken only saw Madison as a possession, something to own and show off. He didn't want custody in order to spend more time with their daughter. She would merely be a prop used to stage a "normal"—and thus, "acceptable"—life to the outside world.

They were meeting at Ken's lawyer's firm—a large, imposing building downtown. She knew that the intimidating meeting place was just another tactic used to throw Cami off her game. And, as much as she hated to admit it, it was working.

She pulled her old, rusted Toyota into the parking lot, which was full of Porsches and BMWs, trying not to feel out of place. As soon as she stepped into the lobby, she felt underdressed. Her hair was swept back into a bun, and she was wearing a pair of dress pants and a blazer purchased at Target. The woman who entered the elevator alongside her was carrying a Chanel bag, had perfectly-coifed, professionally blow-dried blonde hair, and was wearing and a bespoke designer suit. She looked condescendingly at Cami before becoming completely fixated on her phone.

Cami couldn't help but wonder if the woman was one more obstacle purposefully placed in her way in order to overwhelm her. She shook her head slightly to get rid of the thought before it could cause her any more stress. She knew well enough from experience—that kind of thinking would just make her feel like a crazy person.

Cami's lawyer, Michael McKenzie, was waiting for her alone in the conference room and did nothing to soothe her nerves as she sat down. He looked as out of his league as she felt, shifting nervously as he rifled through some paperwork. She couldn't help but remember the subpar service he'd provided during her divorce. Yet, he was all she could afford at the moment.

"Hello," she said with a smile, trying to appear confident.

"Ms. Hendricks," he replied, offering her a fragile smile of his own. "So good to see you again, though I'm sorry it's under such circumstances."

Cami just nodded. Before she and Michael had any time to talk, Ken and his lawyer marched into the room. Cami was surprised—and more than a little upset—to see that Ken's fiancée, Natalie, was also present. Natalie really had nothing to do with any of this, in Cami's opinion. In fact, Cami blamed Natalie, in part, for this custody battle.

It didn't help that Natalie really *did* seem to fit in here. And why wouldn't she? She was tall and thin and poised. And, much like the lady in the elevator, she was wearing a perfectly tailored designer dress with a matching jacket. Her blonde hair fell around her shoulders in flawless curls, and her makeup looked like it had been professionally applied.

For those reasons alone, Cami would have had a hard time liking Natalie. But on top of all that, Natalie was about to marry Cami's ex-husband—and may very well have been sleeping with him before he and Cami had even split up. Cami couldn't help but detest the woman.

Natalie had to know all about Ken's drunken debauchery, so she was either a gold digger who didn't care if he was an alcoholic adulterer, or just as depraved as he was. Cami wondered if it was something she'd never considered before: what if Natalie was too stupid to see how harmful Ken's behavior was? Did she lack the strength of character to demand better, or was she really unable to see how miserable life with an alcoholic could become? Either way, Cami did not want Natalie around her child.

"Welcome," Ken's lawyer was saying.

He continued to talk, but Cami's eyes and attention were on Ken and Natalie, who were holding hands above the table as they sat across from her. Cami was taken aback—Ken had never been publicly affectionate while they were married. He'd never even been overly affectionate in private. In fact, Cami could probably count on both hands the times the two of them had held hands in the years they were together.

And yet, here he was now, cradling Natalie's exquisitely manicured fingers within his own as this thumb gently stroked over her knuckles. They were smiling sweetly at each other as their lawyer droned on. Cami felt like she was going to be sick, so she tried to force her attention back to the man speaking.

Gil Dubois was not just Ken's lawyer but also a close family friend. She'd gotten to know him somewhat during her time with Ken, though she'd never warmed to the man. He'd always seemed smarmy to her, and he seemed even more so now, as she sat across from him, listing all of the reasons why his client deserved primary custody of their daughter.

"My client has already been awarded primary custody," her own lawyer, Michael, began after Gil was finished. "The ruling, by a judge, has already been made and is still standing. There are absolutely no grounds to ask for a change at this juncture."

"The custody agreement, as is stands now, was only allowed because my client believed, at the time, that it was in the best interests of the child to stay with her mother. However, he now feels like the child would be better off in his care, rather than in Ms. Hendricks's," Gil retorted.

"What?" Cami cried. "That's ridiculous."

Michael placed a hand on Cami's forearm and shook his head, warning her to keep quiet. They had gone over what would be discussed beforehand, and Cami had been warned not to speak during the actual meeting. If she had something to say, Michael had advised her to speak quietly to him and allow him to talk for her. Cami wanted to say more, but instead, she shut her mouth and deferred to the lawyers.

"First," Michael replied, "it is my impression that your client was not awarded more custody at the time of the divorce because of his irresponsible and erratic behavior, as well as his dependence on alcohol."

"Although it is true that my client has struggled with substance abuse in the past," Gil replied, "he has gone through treatment, which has been documented, and has been sober for almost two years."

Cami tried not to laugh, knowing it was not true at all. She'd seen Ken drunk with her own eyes within the last year. But she kept quiet, knowing that revealing that information wouldn't help in the moment. It wasn't like she had any proof.

"Second," Michael stated, ignoring Gil's rebuttal, "as previously mentioned, the custody has already been awarded to my client, and there has been nothing to indicate that it is no longer in the child's best interests to stay with her mother."

"My client feels like Ms. Hendricks's long hours and irregular schedule are harmful to the child," Gil retorted. "As it stands now, the child is often left with the childcare provider late into the night, and on weekends. Because of this, my client believes that the best interests of the child would be to live primarily with my client and his wife, as the child would be in an environment that's both stable and constant."

Cami bit her lip. It was all she could do not to scream. The allegations were completely ridiculous, but she had expected that. Yes, since she was a nurse, her schedule featured long hours and, often, night and weekend shifts. But she took ten to twelve hour shifts in order to only work three of four shifts a week. And during that time, Madison was always with Cami's mother, not some stranger.

"Although my client's schedule is somewhat erratic," Michael replied, "she very rarely works more than forty hours a week. And during that time, Madison is with her grandmother, Cami's mother. She is still with family."

"Be that as it may, but the child is still out of the home for long periods of time, often late into the night, which disrupts her sleep schedule and her regular routine. My client feels he can provide a more consistent day-to-day life for the child. As it is obvious at this point that no conclusion can be reached today, I suggest we move forward with the trial."

Cami felt like she'd been punched in the gut at those words. She had hoped that after their lawyers had talked things out, Ken would see how unfit he was to be a father, how much better Madison was in Cami's care. It wasn't like Ken wanted Madison as anything other than a trophy, a way to prove that he had a perfect little family.

However, it was becoming apparent that he wasn't going to stop pursuing this. Cami wasn't sure if she had the finances to see things through, but there was no way she was giving up primary custody of her daughter. Instead, she turned to Michael and nodded, giving him permission to move ahead as well.

CHAPTER THREE
Cami

Cami was able to hold back her emotions—though just barely—until she was safely in her car. Still in the parking lot, wedged between two cars that each probably cost twice as much as her entire net worth, Cami finally let out a sob. That sob was followed by another until she was heaving as the tears rained down her face.

It wasn't fair that, with Ken's wealth, he could get whatever he wanted, whether or not he deserved it. He might gain primary custody of Madison simply because he had more resources and connections than she did. Cami didn't have the money for a long, drawn-out court battle. And Ken's family knew many of the judges in town—there was always a chance they would get appointed a judge that owed the Bellamy family a favor.

For the first time, Cami really began to fear that she'd lose Madison. Madison, whom *she* had raised, not Ken. Ken could barely be depended upon four days a month. She'd been there for Madison through middle of the night feedings and diaper changes, through teething and potty training. Where was Ken when Madison had a fever? Or when she'd had a bad dream and needed to be consoled and rocked back to sleep?

It wasn't just the principle; it wasn't even the fear of feeling like a failure as a mother—her whole life revolved around her daughter. Madison was Cami's everything, and she just couldn't lose her daughter.

And it wasn't only for selfish reasons that Cami feared a change in custody. She honestly didn't believe that Madison was safe with Ken and Natalie. They might have the money to take care of a child, but they definitely didn't have the maturity, commitment, or love—no matter what kind of display they were putting on this morning. Cami *knew* Ken and she knew that he wasn't man enough to raise their daughter.

"It's not going to happen," Cami said to her dashboard, willing herself to calm down. "It's not going to happen! I won't let it happen. No matter what, Ken isn't going to win!"

Cami took a few more deep breaths and focused on calming her mind. She thought about the mischievous smile, strawberry-blonde hair, and adorable freckles on her daughter's face—the daughter she would be able to go pick up from her mother's apartment as soon as she was calm enough to do so.

She reached into her purse and pulled out her phone, needing to look at the picture of Madison that she kept as her lock screen. It was strategically placed there to bring a smile to her face, and now it was a life-line. But, no sooner than she had the phone in her hand, it began to ring.

"Speak of the devil," she said, glaring down at Ken's name. She debated whether or not to answer, but he might be calling to apologize. Perhaps he *had* realized that he wasn't responsible enough to raise Madison himself.

"Hello, Ken," Cami said tentatively once she'd accepted the call.

"Cami, hey," Ken said warmly. His tone threw her off, especially considering the icy silence between the two of them during the meeting. "How are you doing?"

"I've been better," she said, though she was trying to school her voice into a confident tone.

"Yeah," he replied. "Sorry about that. Today sucked."

"Yes. Yes, it did," she agreed. "What do you want, Ken?"

"I just…I hate this…us sitting across the table, as if we're strangers. We were married for years, for God's sake."

Cami heaved a sigh of relief—the first real relief she'd felt in weeks. Ken was backing down. She had called his bluff, and now he was coming to his senses. This would all be over soon.

"Yeah..." Cami replied after a moment, her voice warming up. "It was weird. So, what do you suggest?"

She bit her lip, waiting for Ken to admit he was wrong—that he wasn't ready for primary custody. She was even willing to offer another weekend a month, if he really thought he was up for it. She could afford to be generous now that she knew this nightmare was over.

"Listen, Cami, we both know you don't have the resources for a long, blown-out courtroom drama."

"Yeah," Cami responded, willing him to get to the point—to get to the apology.

"I would just hate to see you waste any of your time or money on this."

"Me, either."

"That's why I really think we should all just be adults about this."

"I totally agree," she said, a smile spreading across her face.

"Good," he said. "I'm glad to hear that. I'm happy you came to your senses."

"What?" Cami nearly dropped the phone in confusion. "What do you mean 'come to *my* senses'?"

"Cami, you're not going to be able to afford this if it goes to court. You know I can win this."

"What are you saying?" Cami demanded, fear slowly creeping back into her chest.

"I'm just suggesting that you be reasonable—that we handle this like adults. Madison is better off with me."

"Fuck, no!" Cami replied, utterly unable to be mature at the moment. "You're the one being completely unreasonable. Madison would *not* be better off with you. You can barely deal with the custody as it is now."

"That's not true. And, with Natalie being home, Madison won't have to be carted around at all hours of the night. Plus, we can afford in-house help if we need it."

"Madison doesn't need a nanny," Cami shouted into the phone. "She needs her family. And that does *NOT* include Natalie!"

"Cami," Ken said, sounding exasperated but not nearly as upset as Cami felt. "Be reasonable. Let's be adults about this."

That was the last straw. She could not handle him telling her to be reasonable or mature one more time.

"You're right," she growled through clenched teeth. "I *do* need to be more reasonable and adult-like about this. Which is why I shouldn't be talking to you. *You* shouldn't have called me at all. And it will not happen again. Next time you have something to say to me, have your lawyer contact mine."

With that, Cami hung up the phone. She let it drop into her lap as she took deep, calming breaths. The breathing exercises were not working, however, and soon turned to panic. She now felt worse than she had before the phone call—even more hopeless and desperate. If Ken thought he could simply call her and harass her into giving up custody of her daughter, he must really think she had no case.

Her panic was interrupted by the ringing of her phone in her lap. Without a second thought she accepted the call and brought the phone to her ear.

"Listen up, you bastard," she snarled, "I am through with your shit. I do not want to hear from you again. If you have anything to say, do it through our lawyers. Do you understand me, Ken?"

The line was silent for a moment. She assumed she'd thrown Ken off with her vehement statement. He wasn't used to not getting his way.

"Um…" came a very different voice than she was expecting. "Actually, this is Drew."

Cami grimaced, suddenly extremely embarrassed. Just when she thought her day couldn't get any worse.

"What do you want?" she snapped, unable to muster up a polite response.

"Oh…um…I just—"

"You just left this morning—extremely early, I might add, as I was up by 6:30 and your side of the bed was already cold. Couldn't even leave a note either. That's fine. I'm over it. I know I'm a lot to deal with—especially right now. I'm a single mother—not really an ideal casual fling."

"And what makes you think I want a casual fling?" Drew replied, humor in his voice.

This made Cami even angrier. She'd had enough conversations with cocky men today.

"Because, as I just stated, you fled my house, practically in the middle of the night, without even leaving a note. Do I really need to explain what that implies? Or can you pick up the context clues?"

"It wasn't the middle of the night," he said, still sounding amused. "It was around five-thirty. And I'm sorry about the lack of a note. I was in a hurry. I hadn't planned on staying the night at all—I had a business breakfast I had to get to at seven. I had to go home and shower and get ready."

Cami bit her lip, suddenly feeling a little bad for laying into Drew so harshly. Maybe he really didn't flee this morning; maybe he really *did* have a reason for leaving so early. Still, it was classic Drew behavior—hot then cold, interested then indifferent, there then…gone. She was sick of riding on that particular roller coaster, no matter how hot the sex was.

"Be that as it may," Cami replied, "but I just don't have time at the moment to play games. I'm not looking for anything casual and I get the impression that you're not interested in anything serious. So I say we just call it a draw, remember the night we shared fondly, and go our separate ways."

The line was silent again for a few moments. Cami figured that the conversation was not going the way Drew intended. *Good*, she thought. At least she got the better of one man today.

"And if I don't want that?" he asked, causing Cami to pause in her gloating.

"What do you want, Drew?" she asked exasperatedly.

"I…I don't know. But I like you and I want to see you again."

"I don't think that's a good idea."

"Why?"

"I've already explained why," she said, growing more and more frustrated. "I don't want anything casual, and you don't know what you want. I can't deal with that—not right now. I have too many other things going on. I don't need this back-and-forth with you."

"One more chance. Please, Cami. Go out with me again tomorrow night. No sex, just dinner. After tomorrow night, if I'm still not what you want, I promise, I'll leave you alone."

Cami thought about it long and hard. What she was telling him was true—she wasn't just trying to bust his balls. Between raising her daughter, working full-time, and gearing up for this horrendous custody battle, she didn't have time to play games. She didn't have time to invest in anything that wasn't going to go somewhere. And Drew admitted that he didn't even know what he wanted. More likely than not, she'd end up with another broken heart, her life in even more chaos than it already was.

But, on the other hand, she *did* need a way to let off a little steam. Life was excruciatingly intense at the moment, and if she didn't have a little fun here and there, she was worried that her head might explode. Plus, their chemistry was undeniable and the sex was extremely hot. As long as she didn't let herself get too involved or attached, it might be a good thing.

"Fine," she said after a moment, trying not to sound too excited at the prospect. It was good to keep him on his toes, after all.

"Really? That's a 'yes'?" Drew was obviously not trying to dampen his excitement.

"Yes," she confirmed, allowing a small smile to stretch across her lips.

"Awesome. Tomorrow night. Seven o'clock. I'll pick you up."

"Don't bother. I'll have to drop Madison off anyway. Text me an address, and I'll meet you there."

She didn't mention that, if he did pick her up and drop her off, she'd be too tempted to ask him back into the house later. So instead she said goodbye and hung up before she could change her mind. She still felt like she was making a mistake, but she deserved some fun…especially after today.

"Just don't get attached," she told herself as she started her car.

CHAPTER FOUR
Cami

Cami's mom agreed to babysit on Saturday night, so that Cami could spend time with Drew, but Madison was not happy about that. Cami had been working all week, and Madison had already spent almost fifty hours with her grandmother. Cami could see how that could be upsetting—Saturday was usually their time. But Cami really needed this—especially after the previous day's disastrous meeting.

Madison clung to Cami and cried as they were leaving the house, begging not to be left at Grandma's. It broke Cami's heart, and she almost considered canceling her plans to spend more time with her daughter. But she'd already agreed to the date and she didn't want to appear inconsistent, since it was a trait she already resented in Drew.

I owe it to myself to see where this goes, she thought as she buckled her daughter into the car seat and attempted to soothe her with a kiss on the forehead. Besides, Cami had been under so much stress that she was worried she would unconsciously take it out on her daughter if she didn't allow herself time to unwind and decompress. She needed a little fun—it would benefit both of them. She knew that she would be a much nicer mommy if she was not constantly stressed about the custody battle. She reminded herself of all this as she drove towards her mother's house.

Unfortunately, her mother wasn't quite so understanding.

"Everything okay?" her mom asked as Cami carried a sniveling Madison into the apartment.

"It's fine," Cami replied after putting her daughter down in front of the TV, which was playing her favorite Disney movie in the background. "She's fine… just a little tired. We were at the park for a long time today, and she didn't get a long enough nap. She'll be asleep within the next hour."

"Are you sure you really want to be dropping Madison off for even more time away from you right now?" her mother asked, hands on her hips.

"You said you would do this for me," Cami replied exasperatedly.

"I did. I don't mind. I just mean…with all of the custody issues and the accusations Ken is making, are you sure now is a good time to be going out with your friends?"

Cami sucked in her breath and debated whether or not to tell her mother about the date. On one hand, it would make her mom ecstatic. On the other, she would never stop nagging Cami for more information. She decided to go the honest route.

"I'm not going out with friends," she finally admitted. "I have a date."

"In that outfit?" her mother asked after scrutinizing her for a moment.

Cami took a deep breath, willing herself not to allow her mother's words to bother her.

"Yes, Mom, in this outfit," she replied, looking herself over in the mirror.

She wasn't dressed poorly, she just hadn't gotten all made up. She wore a pair of nice jeans and a blouse, with her hair back in a ponytail, and very little makeup on. She still looked pretty, she thought—just not like she was trying too hard.

She'd had to deal with a fussy Madison all evening. Plus, she didn't want to give Drew the wrong impression. She was definitely not going to sleep with him tonight. If he couldn't deal with her in her natural state, the relationship didn't need to go forward. Tonight was a test in so many ways.

"I just think that there are better options. You know that dresses better flatter your figure, since you won't lose weight. Those jeans just accentuate your hips and butt, you know."

"I love my hips and butt," Cami replied angrily.

She didn't add that Drew had already seen her body completely naked and also seemed to love her curves. Instead, she turned and marched towards the door.

"I won't be back late," she promised as she shut the door behind her, not giving her mother a chance to reply.

She really did love her body, but that didn't make her mother's words sting any less, and she was in a bad mood by the time she made it to the restaurant, which happened to be much fancier than she was expecting, and she began questioning her casual appearance.

Drew didn't seem to mind, smiling warmly at her as he met her in the lobby of the restaurant.

"You look lovely," he whispered into her ear as he leaned over to kiss her cheek. "Our table isn't ready yet," he said a little louder, glaring at the hostess, who was within hearing distance.

"That's fine," Cami replied, both to Drew and the hostess. She was trying her best not to start the date off in a bad mood.

"Your table will be ready in just a moment," the hostess replied with a polite smile.

"I had reserved a specific table," Drew told Cami, still loud enough to be heard. "But due to some slight *incompetence*—" he emphasized the word with a glare towards the hostess stand—"it was given to someone else. They are taking forever to get another one ready."

Cami, who had waited tables in college and understood what it was like, cringed. She offered the hostess an apologetic smile and didn't reply to Drew's biting words. It wasn't the poor girl's fault, after all, and Drew taking it out on her was embarrassing—and slightly out of character for him. She'd never seen him be outright rude to anyone.

But, she reminded herself, she had seen him laugh at the elitist jokes she'd overheard at the Emerson's beach party. She had never heard him say anything condescending or rude himself, but the comments and jokes of others hadn't seemed to offend him either. She'd thought he was a stuck-up snob at the time. Perhaps her first impression had been correct. He obviously thought he was better than the poor girl working at the restaurant. Maybe she should have just stayed home with Madison.

Before she had the opportunity to turn and flee, however, the hostess was approaching them.

"Your table is ready," the girl said with a smile, leading them towards the back of the restaurant.

"I asked for a table by the window," Drew growled as the hostess stopped at a table in a corner.

"I'm sorry, sir. This is what we have available."

Drew opened his mouth to argue, but Cami stepped in front of him and smiled at the girl.

"This will be fine," she said. "Perfect, in fact. Very private and romantic; right, Drew?" She turned towards Drew with her eyebrow raised.

"If you like it, that's all that matters," he replied, pulling out a seat for her.

Cami sat in silence for a while, staring at the wine list.

"See anything you like?" Drew asked in a more gentle tone.

"I'm not really much of a wine connoisseur," Cami replied curtly.

"How about I just order a bottle for both of us?"

"Fine, whatever," Cami answered.

She knew she should try a little harder to be polite or the entire date was going to be miserable, but she just couldn't help herself. She was too upset over the way he'd treated the hostess. In that moment, he'd reminded her a lot of Ken—just another spoiled rich guy who thought he was so much better than the working class.

Cami buried her head in the menu and barely paid attention as Drew ordered their wine from the server. She did note, however, that he was much more polite to the server than he had been to the hostess. He'd probably picked up on her distaste and was trying to get back into her good graces. But she didn't want him to treat people well just because of her… she wanted him to do it because it was the right thing to do.

If this date really was a test, he'd already failed.

The waiter brought the wine, and Cami had to fight the urge to chug the glass in front of her. She and

Drew sat in tense, awkward silence for a few minutes, each sipping their wine. She hadn't eaten since breakfast, and it was quickly going to her head. When the waiter returned a few minutes later to take her order, she had finished her first glass and was halfway through her second.

"Ready to order?" the man asked with a smile.

"Give us a minute," Cami replied, feeling bold. Once the server had left, she leaned forward and continued speaking to Drew. "Listen—maybe we should just leave. I can pay for the wine and have the rest corked to go. We can just call it a night and go our separate ways."

"What?" Drew replied, surprised. "No! Why?"

"This is awkward, and we both seem miserable," she stated.

Drew took a large sip of his own wine, practically finishing off the glass, before he replied.

"Look…I'm sorry. We got off to a bad start. But I like you a lot and I want this to work."

"It doesn't seem that way right now. Why did you even ask me out? We're just sitting here in silence."

"I asked you out because I like you…a lot. And then the stuff with Claudia made it all awkward and weird. I'm sorry…let's start over. I like you. I like you a lot."

There were a lot of confusing things about that statement, so Cami decided to take them one at a time.

"Why?" she asked.

"Why?" Drew repeated, obviously confused.

"Why do you like me?" Cami clarified. "Because sometimes, it seems like you like me, but other times, you seem pretty apathetic. You're hot and cold. It's confusing. So I want to know why you think you like me."

"I don't just think I like you. I know I do," Drew assured her while finishing off his second glass of wine. He topped them off before continuing. "Listen, I don't really date often. No…that's not true. I never date. Not anymore. In fact, I haven't dated anyone since my divorce."

"You were married?" Cami asked. This was news to her.

"Yeah. It's been about four years now, since the divorce."

"Why didn't you say anything, when I was talking about my ex?"

"I didn't want to impose on your problems. And…I just don't like talking about it."

"Why? What happened?"

Drew winced and finished off his third glass of wine. The server was hovering in the corner, waiting to take their order, so Cami ushered him over in order to give Drew a moment to organize his thoughts. Drew also ordered another bottle of wine, which Cami was totally okay with. They were going to be there a while—they'd have plenty of time to sober up.

Drew was so much more open when he was buzzed.

"So…" Cami prompted once the server was gone.

"I really did think we were in love," Drew admitted, staring down at his napkin. "We began dating right after my company started making money. That should have been the first clue. She said she wanted kids—that she wanted to start a family with me. But after we were married, it became apparent that she really only wanted to spend my money. She didn't even like children, as it turned out. And children were something I couldn't imagine my life without. We started arguing and, eventually, we split up. It was pretty ugly there at the end. It was so weird. You think you know someone—love someone—then they just become this whole other person."

"Sometimes, I think they were always that person," Cami said, "and we were just too blinded by love to see it."

"Yeah," he said with a sad smile. "You're right. I mean, take Claudia, for example…the hostess."

"You know the hostess?" Cami asked, confused again.

"Yeah…she's my ex's best friend. She was really rude to me before you came in. She purposefully "lost" my reservation and sat us back here in the corner out of spite. And I don't even know why… Gwen—my ex—came out on top in our divorce. I thought Claudia and I were friends. Who knows what Gwen has said about me? I really don't see any of our old friends anymore."

Cami thought about the altercation with the hostess in a new light now, grimacing at the way she seemed to have stuck up for the woman that was treating Drew poorly. Reaching out, she squeezed Drew's hand.

"I don't really talk to anyone from my old life with Ken," she admitted. "But I'm okay with that. I've made new friends. I didn't really get any money in the divorce, which was okay—I got Madison. But our mutual friends didn't really have much to do with me after I was no longer on their income level."

Now it was Drew who was squeezing her hand.

"That, to answer your question, is the reason why I like you. One of them, anyhow."

"What is?" Cami asked.

"That you don't care about money. I don't get the sense that you're only after me for my money. I mean, I haven't really talked about my business with you, and you haven't asked. I'm sure you know a little bit from Maggie, but you haven't been trying to impress me or anything. You're never anything but completely yourself and I really appreciate that about you."

Cami felt the smile spread across her face at those words. She still had some doubts—this didn't explain his erratic, hot-and-cold personality—but he definitely seemed sincere in the moment.

The food arrived before they could say much more, and they ate in comfortable silence.

"So," Drew said after a while, "how did the meeting go yesterday?"

All of the calm and contentment Cami had evaporated at once as her mind went back to the distressing reality of her life. She let out a little sigh.

"Awful," she replied after a moment. "Just awful."

"I'm sorry to hear that," Drew said, voice soft and gentle. "Do you want to talk about it?"

Cami wasn't sure she did, but the mood had already been ruined, and she wasn't going to be able to get it out of her head now anyway, so she nodded.

"It was so weird, sitting across from Ken and his new fiancée. It's like we were talking about before—you think you know someone so completely, then you find yourself sitting across from a stranger." Drew nodded in understanding, so Cami continued. "You know what was really awful?"

"What?" Drew asked.

"He was holding Natalie's hand—that's his new fiancée. She was there, and he was being so sweet and comforting towards her. He'd never been like that for me. And I can't help but wonder if it was me…if he was capable of love and compassion, just not with me, you know? And it didn't help that Natalie is younger and thinner and taller and all around more perfect."

"You're perfect," Drew replied.

Cami was about to tell him to quit flattering her because it wasn't helping, but when she looked up, the utter sincerity and passion in his eyes cut her off short. So she only smiled and looked away again.

"So, what happened? What was decided?"

"Absolutely nothing was resolved," Cami said with a sigh. "Which means we'll have to go to court. Which will waste a lot of time and money, and he'll have the upper hand. Ugh…and that isn't even the worst part."

"What's the worst part?" Drew grabbed her hand and gave it a soft squeeze.

"He called me right afterwards, while I was still in the parking lot. We didn't say one word to each other during the meeting, then he calls me five minutes later. And he was so warm and friendly, and I thought maybe he'd come to his senses. In fact, I was completely convinced that he was calling to tell me he was dropping the case. He was going on and on about being mature and reasonable and handling things like a couple of adults, and I agreed. So then he was, like, 'Good, so you're just going to give me primary custody.' I was, like, 'What? No!' I ended up telling him not to contact me except through my lawyer and hanging up on him."

"Good," Drew said, still holding Cami's hand. "Is that when I called? You were a little upset on the phone."

"That's an understatement," Cami said with a laugh, thinking of the way she'd chewed Drew out before she realized he wasn't Ken. "Sorry about that. It's just really frustrating to know that he thinks I have such a bad case that I'll just give up and give in without a trial. It really undermines my confidence."

"That's probably exactly what he's doing," Drew told her. "Maybe he's scared. Maybe he doesn't actually think he has much of a chance, which is why he called and tried to intimidate you into giving up custody."

Cami considered what Drew was saying. She thought about the steps Ken and his lawyer had taken to intimidate her. Perhaps they were only relying on such techniques because they knew they didn't actually have much of a case. For the first time in weeks, Cami felt better.

"Maybe you're right," she said. "I just need to remain positive. I'm a great mother. There's no way I'm going to lose custody."

"That's the spirit," Drew replied with a smile.

The rest of dinner passed easily, with no more serious conversation. Drew kissed her on the cheek as they left, promising to call her the following day.

Cami was in such a good mood that she even put up with the annoying questions her mother bombarded her with when she went to pick up Madison.

Perhaps things were going to be all right, after all.

CHAPTER FIVE
Cami

Cami didn't really expect Drew to call the next day. Following the pattern of the way that things had worked with Drew so far, Cami almost expected a cold shoulder. That had really been Drew's MO since she'd met him.

Upon first meeting, they'd clicked and spent an hour flirting, then he'd turned into a complete snob. They'd spent a passionate—albeit drunken—night on the beach, then the following morning he'd practically ignored her for some skinny model.

She'd seen him be sweet and compassionate with his sister, only to witness him being rude and cold later—laughing at jokes about the poor. Then they'd spent a ridiculously hot night together, then he'd fled in the morning without even leaving a note.

So yes, their date last night had been fantastic, but Cami was still unsure. She was waiting for the other shoe to drop. In fact, she pretty much expected not to speak to him for another week or so.

Which was why she was thrown for a loop when, right after she'd put Madison down for her nap the following day, she received a call from Drew.

"Hello?" she'd said hesitantly into the phone, almost unsure whether he'd meant to call her or not. She was half expecting to find he'd dialed her accidentally.

"Hey, Cami. How are you today!"

"Good," she replied, slightly caught off guard and surprised to hear his voice. "Just put Madison down for a nap, which is why I'm talking quietly. In case you were wondering."

"And how is Madison?" Drew asked, surprising Cami even further. He had never asked after her daughter before. He'd asked about the custody suit, but never about Madison herself.

"She's good. We stayed at my mother's last night, since I got back so late. Then we all went to brunch this morning, then to the park. She's had quite a day."

"Sounds like it," Drew replied with a laugh. "I haven't had nearly as exciting of a day. I spent the morning doing paperwork, now I'm returning emails."

"Sounds boring," Cami offered.

"It is," Drew replied. "But at least I'm talking to you, so that's something, at least."

Cami didn't know how to respond. She was flattered, but still unsure.

"I had a lot of fun last night," Drew said after a moment of silence.

"Me, too," Cami agreed, thankful that Drew couldn't see the goofy smile on her face.

"So…does that mean you would be interested in seeing me again?" he asked.

That was the problem. Cami had agreed to last night's date because she'd told herself it was just a bit of fun—that she wouldn't get attached. After last night, Cami knew that wasn't possible.

On paper, Drew seemed absolutely perfect. He was rich and handsome, sweet and funny. And, most perfect of all, he wanted a family. But in reality, he was unpredictable and unreliable, and moving any further in the relationship would mean Cami would end up heartbroken.

"I don't know," she said after a moment. She could hear Drew deflate over the phone.

"But," he began, "I thought you had a good time yesterday. You said you'd give me a chance, and I thought I made it up to you."

"Last night was great, Drew. It really was. But, like I've said before, I'm not really looking for anything casual. And I don't really know if a relationship with you is a good idea."

"Why not?" Drew asked.

"I'm just not sure," Cami replied. "I know that's not much of an answer, and I'm sorry. But I just need a little more time. Give me a day or two to think it over, okay? Just a few days."

"Okay," Drew replied. "I really hope you decide to see me again, Cami."

"I'll let you know, Drew," she said before hanging up the phone.

She sat in silence for the rest of Madison's nap, deep in thought. Things had just become much more complicated. Drew seemed like he really wanted things to become serious, but could she be in a relationship with someone if she was always waiting for something unexpected to happen? She just wasn't sure.

Thankfully, Madison woke up not too long afterwards, pulling Cami from her thoughts. It was almost impossible to be contemplative with a three-year-old in the house. So Cami spent the rest of her weekend ignoring the Drew dilemma as well as the impending custody battle and simply enjoying life with her daughter.

Monday was extremely slow in the ER, leaving Cami, Maggie, and Ashley loitering at the nurses' station with nothing to do. After Maggie finished telling the girls about her exciting weekend in New York City, she turned to Cami.

"So," she said, her face turning serious. "How was the meeting?"

Cami didn't even have to ask in order to know exactly what meeting she was talking about. It must have shown on her face, because Maggie responded without waiting for an answer.

"That bad, huh?"

"Yeah," Cami said, struggling to be positive so she didn't break into tears at work. "The meeting itself was awkward. Ken and I didn't say one word to each other. And Natalie was there."

"Ugh…why?" At least Maggie looked appropriately upset by that news.

"No clue. And they were holding hands the entire time and were all lovey-dovey."

Ashley made an angry noise, shaking her head.

"Sam brought his new girlfriend to some of the divorce hearings too. I think he was just trying to intimidate me."

"Yeah, I'm pretty sure that's what Ken was doing," Cami replied. "And, afterwards, he called me all warm and friendly like."

"That's weird," Ashley said.

"I thought so, too," Cami agreed. "Until I realized he was trying to talk me into backing down and giving up primary custody of Madison without a fight."

"That bastard," Maggie proclaimed a little too loudly. One of the doctors looked at them funny and the girls couldn't help but giggle before turning serious again.

"Maybe he's doing all of this because he knows he can't actually win in court," Ashley offered.

"Yeah, that's what Drew said."

The words were out of Cami's mouth before she could stop them, and she saw Maggie's eyes grow wide.

Oh well, she thought. She'd been debating asking Maggie for advice anyway, so she might as well spill.

"Who's Drew?" Ashley asked before Maggie could speak.

"Drew is the guy I was telling you about," Maggie said, giving Ashley a nudge.

Cami raised her eyebrows questioningly at the mention of the two other women discussing her private life without her, but it wasn't like she could be critical. She and Maggie had talked about Ashley's love life—or lack thereof since her divorce—plenty of times. So she let Maggie continue.

"You know, the guy she had a torrid affair with at my parents' beach house," Maggie said.

"It wasn't a torrid affair," Cami said, giving Maggie a playful push. "We met. He was hot and cold. One minute, he liked me, the next, he was an ass."

"They had sex on the beach," Maggie said in a whisper.

"We did not!" Cami insisted. "We just made out… and stuff."

Ashley raised her eyebrows at the "and stuff," but thankfully didn't comment.

"And you've been talking to him?" Maggie asked. "Told you he'd call!"

"Yes, you were right!" Cami finally admitted.

"So, spill," Maggie continued. "You've talked on the phone. Have you been on a date? Ooh, have you slept with him?"

Cami thought about lying, but she knew that the blush on her cheeks was giving her away.

"Oh, my God!" Maggie continued. "You slept with him. When?"

"He called me Thursday. You were out of town, and I needed something to take my mind off that Friday's meeting. Madison was staying at my mom's, and I was lonely. So we went out, had some drinks, and one thing led to another."

Both Maggie and Ashley giggled.

"And?" Maggie prompted.

"And I woke up the next morning, and he was gone. No note or anything." Maggie and Ashley both looked murderous, so Cami quickly continued the story before they could hunt Drew down and kill him. "He called later, after my meeting. I guess he'd had a super early meeting of his own and hadn't meant to stay the night. He was running late and forgot to leave a note."

"Ohhhh," both women cooed.

"That's so sweet that he called later to make sure you didn't feel abandoned," Ashley said.

Cami refrained from telling her that she'd already felt abandoned by the time she'd heard from him.

"So was that it?" Maggie asked, an almost manic look on her face as she pressed for every last detail about her interactions with Drew.

"No," Cami admitted. "I was mad when I talked to him on Friday. It was right after that call from Ken.

But I agreed to go out with him the following night, so we went on a date Saturday."

"And have you heard from him yet?" Ashley asked.

"Yeah," Cami said. "He called the next day."

"Guys never call the next day," Ashley replied, a surprised look on her face.

"Drew did," Cami responded.

"So, when are you seeing him again?" Maggie asked.

"I'm not sure," Cami admitted. This was the part she really wanted the women's advice on, but she also knew that it was going to be hard to explain her reticence to Maggie, who was a little too invested in Cami's love life. "I'm not sure if I'm going to see him again."

"What?" Maggie asked, confused. "Why?"

"He called the next day," Ashley added, still seemingly in shock about it. "Guys never call the next day. He really likes you."

"That's just it," Cami said. "Sometimes, he *does* seem to really like me. But other times, he ignores me and spends all night flirting with skinny models."

"I did notice that," Maggie confirmed, then turned to Ashley to explain. "At the beach house, there was this girl Drew kept flirting with. Or, more honestly, who kept flirting with Drew."

"And he was letting it happen," Cami countered. "He was letting her hang all over him. He even started ignoring me when she joined us for breakfast."

"Who was she?" Ashley asked with a frown.

"I don't know her very well," Maggie replied. "She was the daughter of some right-wing business guy my dad knows. I really didn't talk to her much. But Cami is right, Drew was definitely encouraging the attention."

"See," Cami said emphatically. "He says he really likes me, that he wants to continue seeing me. But he's been so unpredictable that I don't really know what to believe. I have a daughter to think about and a lot going on right now. I don't really have time to play games. And I really don't want to get hurt again."

Ashley nodded understandingly. Cami knew that Ashley had never really gotten back into the dating field after her nasty divorce.

"I'm going to get to the bottom of this," Maggie stated, a mischievous look on her face. "I'll figure out what's going on."

"Please don't," Cami replied. "I told you this because I want advice. I don't want you to meddle. Things are already complicated enough without you sticking your pretty little head in the middle of it."

Maggie looked torn for a minute, but finally nodded in agreement.

"Fine," she said with a pained sigh. "But if you change your mind, I can talk to my brother. I know Grant and Drew were, like, best friends in college. They aren't as close now, but Grant can find out what's going on in Drew's head."

"I'll let you know if I change my mind," Cami said with a smile. "But don't hold your breath."

"As for now," Ashley said, "I think all you can do is see where it goes. Try not to get attached, and just wait and see."

"Yeah," Cami replied.

Don't get attached. That was so much easier said than done.

CHAPTER SIX
Cami

Despite her apprehension, Cami slowly allowed herself to picture a life with Drew. He seemed to genuinely like her, at least during their last few dates. In fact, the leaving-without-a-note incident aside, he hadn't given her the cold treatment since their time at the beach house. And he'd more than explained his note-less absence the morning after they'd slept together. Plus, he did want a family after all, and Cami came ready-made with a family—as long as she didn't lose primary custody of Madison.

Maybe, Cami thought, *just maybe, this could turn into something real.* And so Cami decided that, next time Drew called, she would tell him as much. Well, she might not tell him that she was picturing them growing old together or anything like that, but she *would* tell him that she was more than happy to see him again.

Of course, it was once Cami had decided to give Drew a chance that he didn't call. Cami had at least talked to him every day since Thursday, so she'd just expected him to call Monday evening. But he didn't. He didn't call Tuesday either.

Maybe I was too difficult, she thought. Maybe, when she had told him that she needed more time to think things over, he'd taken it as an insult. He was used to women throwing themselves at him, after all. He had said that it was only because of his money, but if he had women like Analise hanging on his every word, he definitely didn't need to wait around for Cami to make up her mind about him.

Every day on each of her breaks Cami would diligently check her phone, hoping for a missed call, or even a text. Yet there was nothing. By the end of the week, Cami was disappointed, but not surprised. She tried to remind herself that she'd been waiting for the other shoe to drop—that she hadn't really expected him to follow through—but still, she was disappointed.

When her phone did ring on Friday, Cami's heart leapt for just a second—still refusing to give up hope completely—until she realized that it was her lawyer's office on the phone.

"Please tell me you have good news," she said.

"Actually, Ms. Hendricks," Michael said, sounding slightly flustered. "I have some rather distressing news."

Panic began to creep into Cami's heart at those words.

"What is it?" she demanded.

"Well," he began, "I received a notice from your ex-husband's attorney today. It appears that he is filing for full custody."

"What does that mean?" Cami knew, but she didn't want to admit it.

"It means that, if your husband wins the case, you will no longer be allowed any custody of your daughter. Meaning you would not get to see her at all."

Cami felt sick. This was much worse than anything she could have foreseen. Now she wasn't in jeopardy of losing primary custody—she was in jeopardy of losing her daughter altogether.

"Can he do that?" she asked in a broken voice.

"He can try," Michael replied. "We still have a strong case. You're a good mother and he is a documented alcoholic with past reckless behavior on his record. Plus, full custody is a very extreme way to go. This may encourage the judge to rule against the request for full custody even if he would have approved a petition for primary custody."

May was not a very comforting word, and the lawyer didn't seem very confident even as he was trying to assure Cami. She quickly got off the call before she collapsed into sobs with Michael still on the phone. Throwing her phone across the room, she swooped down and picked up her daughter, cuddling her close to her body.

"Mommy isn't going to lose you," she said into her daughter's hair.

"Lose?" Madison asked innocently, having no idea what was going on, but sensing her mother's fear and sorrow. She gently stroked Camis cheek and hugged her back, muttering incoherently under her breath.

Cami really didn't know what to do or where to go from there. Not for the first time that week, she wished Drew would call. Drew had always been so comforting when it came to the custody battle, confident and reassuring. She could use some reassurance at the moment. But Drew hadn't called, and he probably wasn't going to. So she put that thought out of her mind and focused on what she *could* do. She got Madison situated with some toys and a movie playing, then she called Maggie.

"Hey there," Maggie said, answering on the first ring, even though it was a Friday afternoon. One more reason why she loved her best friend. "What's up?"

Cami found that she couldn't speak, now that she was on the phone. All the fear and panic began whirling inside her and all she could do was sob into the phone.

"Oh, honey, what's going on?" Maggie asked.

"Sorry," Cami was finally able to stutter between her sobs. "I just…I…" But she couldn't bring herself to get any of it out.

"Don't worry," Maggie said. "I'm on my way over now. I'll be there in fifteen minutes. Just hang tight."

Cami nodded, even though Maggie couldn't see her over the phone. She opened her mouth to speak, but before she could respond verbally, Maggie had ended the call.

Thank God for Maggie. Just the knowledge that her best friend was on her way was enough to help calm Cami's nerves. At least she wasn't in this completely alone.

True to her word, Maggie showed up less than twenty minutes later, a large bag from the liquor store in hand.

"I figured you could use a drink," she said by way of explanation.

"It's three in the afternoon," Cami replied.

"So? You need this. And we're not going to get wasted or anything. I'm just making you a cocktail to calm your nerves."

With that, she turned and headed into the kitchen, where she made herself at home as she mixed up a couple of extra-strong vodka-cranberries. Cami collapsed onto a stool in the kitchen, where she could still keep an eye on Madison in the living room, and watched Maggie work.

Maggie let Cami take a few long drinks of her cocktail before launching into an interrogation.

"What's going on?" she asked, taking a sip of her own drink. "Is it Drew?"

"No," Cami replied. "I mean, he still hasn't called. But that's not why I'm upset. I heard from my lawyer today. Ken is suing for full custody."

"I thought you already knew that," Maggie said.

"No. He was suing for *primary* custody. Like what I have now. I would still get Madison on weekends, or whatever. Madison would just live primarily at his house. Full custody would mean that I'd never get Madison at all. I would lose my baby girl."

With that explanation, Cami once again dissolved into tears. Almost instantaneously, Maggie was off her stool and hugging Cami.

"Shhh," Maggie whispered, careful not to alert Madison. "It's okay. It hasn't happened yet. It *won't* happen. That bastard isn't getting full custody of Madison."

Once Cami was calm, Maggie moved back to her seat.

"I don't know," Cami said after a moment. "On one hand, I think 'That *can't* happen… There's no way I'm losing custody of Madison!' But then I think about all of Ken's resources and connections. Half of the judges in this town are personal friends of his family. He pretty much gets whatever he wants. How do you think I ended up with nothing in the divorce?"

"You *agreed* to nothing in the divorce, because all you wanted was Madison. You didn't fight it the way you're going to fight this now."

"Yeah," Cami replied. "But my lawyer sucks."

"Then get another one. I can loan you some money."

"I can't take your money," Cami said simply.

"You will if you have to," Maggie insisted. "When it comes to Madison, you will do whatever it takes."

"You're right," Cami replied. "Hopefully it won't come to that, but if it does, I'll let you loan me some money. And thank you…for everything."

"Of course," Maggie said with a smile. "That's what best friends are for! But there isn't anything we can do tonight, so let's just relax, drink our cocktails, and talk about why in the fu—" Maggie looked at Madison guiltily but the little girl was not paying attention to them. "…fudge, Drew hasn't called you back."

Cami offered the first genuine smile she'd been able to muster all afternoon, and nodded. It was better to focus on the smaller of her two problems, after all.

Maggie stayed late into the evening, making more cocktails, then dinner, trying her best to keep Cami's mind away from serious things. And she did a good job of that. Cami was calm and happy for most of the evening.

But later, after Madison was safely tucked for the night and Maggie was long gone, Cami lay in bed, staring up at the ceiling, thinking about everything. Just a month prior, she was relatively happy. Yeah, she was single and slightly lonely, but she wasn't about to have to fight for the right to take care of her daughter and she wasn't having her heart played by a guy who constantly sent mixed signals.

When did her life become so chaotic?

CHAPTER SEVEN
Cami

It had taken hours to fall asleep the night before and, although she hadn't actually drank much the previous evening, Cami felt hung over when she was jarred awake by the three-year-old jumping on her bed.

"Mommy!" Madison squealed. "Breakfast!"

Cami groaned but she pulled herself out of bed. Sleeping in was a luxury one didn't have when dealing with a toddler. Ignoring her headache, she pulled Madison into her arms and held her tight as she made her way into the kitchen. She got Madison situated into her highchair with some Cheerios before she started coffee and set about making a more substantial breakfast.

After eggs, toast, and coffee, Cami was feeling a little more alive. She knew that she needed to hold herself together for Madison. She couldn't afford to fall apart, no matter how much stress she was under. And the only way she was going to be able to keep herself from falling apart was to keep busy.

Cami was able to take a relatively relaxing shower while Madison was distracted with Saturday morning cartoons. Even though she didn't feel like it, Cami blow-dried her hair, did her makeup, and chose a cheery sundress with brightly colored flowers on it. She then wrestled Madison into an outfit and got them both out of the house.

Cami really didn't have any plans for the day—she just knew that she had to keep moving. So they went to the park, then the farmers market, and then stopped for lunch at a kid-friendly café. She thought about calling her mom, but she knew that her mother would ask about Drew as well as the custody dispute. She really didn't want to have to discuss either of those things today, so she kept to herself.

After a full day out on the town, Cami let Madison help her make a delicious dinner full of fresh veggies they'd bought at the market earlier. Having skipped her nap, Madison was ready for bed by early evening. She didn't even fuss when Cami put her in the bath, and stayed calm while Cami slipped her favorite jammies on her.

Cami curled into Madison's tiny bed with her and began to read a goodnight story, but Madison was asleep less than halfway through. She continued to read aloud, just to distract herself, until the story was finished. Rising from the bed, she made her way back into the living room.

There was nothing else to distract her now. She was alone with her thoughts. Making herself a cocktail with the leftovers from the night before, Cami tried to relax on the couch. Even with a drink in her hand and her feet up, she was finding it hard.

There was no way that she was going to lose her daughter, she told herself. Things would work themselves out. Still, she couldn't seem to keep the panic at bay. She was just about to work herself up into a full-blown anxiety attack when there was a knock at the door.

Frowning, Cami looked at the clock. It was nearly eight o'clock, and she wasn't expecting anyone. She assumed it was Maggie, back to check on her, so she kept the cocktail in her hand as she headed towards the door. She answered with a smirk on her face, ready to tell her best friend that she wasn't as fragile as Maggie thought she was. But the smirk was wiped clean off her face and replaced with one of surprise when she found herself facing Drew, not Maggie.

"Um…hi," Cami stammered ineloquently.

"Hi," Drew said with a timid smile. "Sorry to stop by unannounced, but I wanted to see you. Can I come in?"

Cami shook her head. She really didn't know what to make of Drew's appearance, but she was still angry after the silence all week and just wanted to forget all about him. Leaving her drink on the shelf in the entry hall, she stepped out onto the porch and closed the door behind her.

"Madison's asleep inside," she told him curtly, crossing her arms in front of her. "I don't let men I'm dating into the house while she's home."

"I thought I was the first man you'd dated since the divorce," Drew said with a smirk that made Cami even angrier.

"It was a theoretical rule until recently," she replied coldly. "But now it's more applicable than ever."

Drew's grin faded quickly, and he gazed down.

"Look," he began after a moment of silence. "She's asleep, right? I'll be quiet, I swear! And if she wakes up, I'll leave before she can see me. I just want to talk to you. Just for a few minutes."

Cami debated for a second. On one hand, she was pissed that she hadn't heard from Drew all week. But, on the other hand, he hadn't promised he'd call on a certain day. And he would be a welcome distraction right now from the anxiety that was constantly hounding her. Finally she nodded and opened the door, walking through it and leaving it wide for him to follow.

She grabbed her cocktail on her way into the living room and sat on one side of the sofa, looking at him expectantly. Closing the door behind him, Drew took a seat on the other end of the sofa. He looked down at his hands for a moment, obviously nervous.

"Well?" Cami prompted eventually.

"Look," Drew began, finally looking up and making contact. "I know that I'm supposed to be waiting for you to make up your mind. And I do realize that, since I haven't heard from you all week, your mind is probably already made up, and you really don't want to see me anymore. But I thought, instead of just waiting for your call—if it ever comes—I would be proactive. So I'm here."

Cami just stared at Drew for a moment. *He* had been waiting for *her* call? Her mind went back over their last conversation. Had she given him the impression that she was going to call him? She hadn't said as much, she knew she hadn't. He'd always been the one to call, so she just assumed he would continue to do so.

She suddenly felt a little silly, pining all week, waiting for his call. Why hadn't she considered calling herself? Pride, she realized. She didn't want to seem like the one doing the pursuing. And yet she *had* told him that she needed time to think. It totally made sense that he was waiting for her call.

She didn't say any of this, however, not wanting to admit her mistake. Instead, she offered him a small smile.

"I'm sorry I haven't called," she said. "It's not that I don't want to see you again. It's quite the opposite, actually. And I thank you for giving me the time to come to that decision. I've just been really distracted lately—with new custody issues."

"Oh no," Drew said, his face turning into a grimace. "What's happened now?" He looked genuinely upset and it made Cami's heart flip a little. He really did care about her and what happened to her daughter.

"My asshole of an ex-husband is now suing for full custody." Cami didn't even try to keep the anger and frustration out of her voice as she spoke. "If he wins the case, I will lose my daughter completely."

"That's not going to happen," Drew said confidently.

"You don't know that," Cami replied. "Ken has money and connections. He has a habit of getting pretty much whatever he wants. Hell, he has two years of *documented* sobriety according to his lawyer, while I know for a fact that he hasn't been sober for even a year. I wouldn't be surprised if he isn't sober now."

"If that's the case, he can't hide it forever," Drew said hopefully.

"With enough money, you can hide anything forever," Cami responded dejectedly. "He's a shitty father and he's going to win simply because he has the means. I can't even afford a half-decent lawyer."

Cami could no longer hold back the tears that had been threatening to fall all evening, and she turned her head away as she sobbed against her arms. She could feel the cushions shift as Drew scooted across the sofa towards her, then warm, strong arms were wrapped around her, holding her tight. Instinctively, she turned and buried her face in Drew's muscled chest, seeking comfort in the firm grip.

Drew didn't try to shush her or calm her down. He just let her cry. Eventually, she was calmed by the steady beat of his heart and the hands rubbing soothing circles against her back. When she was all out of tears, she finally pulled away. She was embarrassed to see a wet spot on his shirt where she'd been crying.

Cami quickly excused herself and slunk to the bathroom to clean herself up. Just a few hours ago, she'd completely written Drew off, and now, she was sobbing on his shoulder and leaving tear stains on his clothing. She shook her head, finding that she was too worn out to muster up too much mortification over what had just happened. Instead, she focused on splashing cool water on her face and adding a little foundation to her blotchy skin.

When she finally headed back into the living room, Drew was sitting comfortably on the middle of the sofa where she'd left him, looking at his phone. He put it away as she approached and smiled at her sweetly. But he didn't move back to his side of the sofa, leaving her to squeeze in next to him, their bodies still pressed together.

Once she was situated, he wrapped his large arm around her again, pulling her in even closer. Cami knew that she should say something—that she should establish some boundaries and create some distance between them. But the closeness was just too comforting, and she felt herself move into it.

"I've missed you this week," Drew whispered against her hair as he kissed the top of her head.

Cami closed her eyes and let out a contented sigh. "Me too," she admitted.

"You've missed you too?" he joked. "You really must be under a lot of stress if you've lost yourself in the process."

"You know what I mean," she said, playfully slapping his chest.

She went to move away slightly, but Drew's large hands were suddenly cupping the sides of her face, and then they were kissing. His lips were hesitant at first, soft and questioning, as if he was seeking consent before taking things further. Cami moved into the kiss, pressing her lips against his hungrily. That was all the consent Drew needed. He was suddenly sliding his tongue against her lips until she opened for him, then began to sensuously circle it around her own.

Cami let out a little moan, only to catch herself.

"Madison," she whispered against Drew's lips.

"I can be quiet," he assured her, moving his mouth down to kiss and lick her neck and jaw.

When his tongue found the sensitive skin behind her ear, Cami had a hard time keeping quiet. She bit her lip as she arched up into his embrace.

Cami felt herself pressed back down against the sofa as Drew crawled on top of her, until his long, muscular frame was above hers, pushing her down into the cushions. It felt delicious, and Cami bit her own cheek to keep from crying out as Drew thrust his hips into her. She could feel his growing erection through his jeans, which were rubbing against the bare skin of her thigh. She could feel her little dress getting hiked up as Drew's greedy hands began to explore her thighs.

"No," she whispered, pushing her dress back down.

"Sorry," Drew replied, pulling away slightly. "I really didn't come here for sex. I'm fine just spending time with you."

"No!" Cami said, a little louder than she meant to. But the fire between her legs was not going to let her be satisfied with simply sitting next to Drew on the sofa. Especially not when she could still feel his hard cock pressed against her leg. She needed him inside her, and soon. "No, this is good. Just not here. In case Madison wakes up."

Cami wiggled out from under Drew, leaving him sprawled out on the sofa. He looked so sexy and debauched that it took Cami's breath away. His dark hair was sticking up in every direction, and his lips were swollen and bruised. His eyes were blown wide with lust, and the tent in his jeans left very little to imagination.

Cami took a deep breath, savoring the rhythmic pulsing between her legs as she looked at this man.

Her panties were already completely wet, and she could feel her own juices trickling down her thighs. Unable to wait any longer, she held out her hand to Drew.

He rose from his position and took Cami's hand, allowing her to lead him through the small house and into the bedroom. She ushered him there, where he stopped to look around while she shut the door. He eyed her up and down, his look full of lust. He grinned wolfishly as he stared at her for a moment. Cami wondered if she looked as messy and hungry as he did. She sure felt like she did.

"Remember," she whispered as he stalked towards her. "We have to be quiet."

"Oh," he whispered back. "I can be quiet."

With that, he grabbed her and whipped her around before tossing her across the bed. She lay there, limbs splayed out, completely at his mercy. She knew that her little sundress was up around her waist and her panties were visible.

"So wet for me already," he growled as he leaned over and stroked her thighs, which were gleaming with her juices.

"Yes," she whispered.

"It was so hard saying goodbye to you after our last date," Drew whispered into her ear as his fingers began to stroke her through her wet, clinging panties. "All I wanted to do was take you home, tie you to my headboard, and take you hard, until you screamed."

"Yes," Cami moaned a little too loudly, pushing against his hand.

"No, no," he chastised, taking his hand away. "You have to be completely silent for me. If not, you're not going to get what you need. Can you be silent for me?"

Cami nodded.

"Good girl," he breathed against her neck. "Now, not a word, or we'll stop completely."

Cami bit her lip to keep from crying out as his hand slipped beneath the black lace to circle her clit. She thrust down against his hand as he brought her closer and closer to the climax. She was right at the brink, ready to tip over into complete bliss, when the hand disappeared.

Cami almost let out a whine of complaint, but she swallowed it down at the last moment. Drew must have noticed, because he leaned over and offered another breathless "Good girl!" into her ear. He then stood and slowly began undressing. He pulled off his sweater first, then his tie, which he ran through his hands for a moment, as if he was thinking about something. After a second, he crawled back onto the bed with a mischievous glint in his eye.

"I know you've had a really stressful few weeks," he said in barely a whisper as he grabbed both of her hands and pressed them against the comforter above her head. "So I want you to simply relax and let me take care of you. Can you do that?"

Cami nodded. She couldn't see what was going on above her head, but she could feel the silk of his tie sliding along the flesh of her wrists as he bound her arms above her head. Cami let out a deep breath, closing her eyes and sinking back into the mattress. For a little while at least, she could relax and relinquish control, let someone else take care of her for a change. She was liking this game.

Eyes still closed, Cami felt Drew's hands run down her body to the hem of her dress and pull it up over her head. He slid it to the end of her arms, where he left it caught against her tethered wrists. He then quickly removed her bra. The cold air stung at her exposed nipples deliciously, causing them to harden and ache.

Again, she had to fight to remain silent as Drew's hot, rough tongue laved at one nipple, than the other. The heat of his lips, followed by the stinging chill of the hair, caused waves of sensation to dance through Cami's body. She pulled her thighs in tight and rubbed them together, trying her best to relieve the throbbing pulse of need that bordered on painful.

"Uh-uh," Drew chastened breathily.

He slid her panties down and off before grabbing each ankle and pulling them apart. Much like with her nipples, the sudden chill on her most sensitive area sent an almost-painful thrill through her body. Drew then placed her legs back on the bed—still spread wide—and stepped away.

After a few moments without Drew's touch, Cami opened her eyes in confusion. She smiled when she saw his bare chest, as Drew unzipped his pants and quickly slid them down his muscular legs. His cock was hard in his tight black boxer briefs, which featured a wet spot that betrayed Drew's obvious enjoyment. At least Cami knew she wasn't alone in this.

Realizing that he had an audience, Drew slid his underwear down his legs in a much more leisurely pace, slowly revealing inch after inch of perfectly toned skin.

His throbbing manhood slapped up against his stomach when it was finally free—swollen, red, and dripping angrily. Cami licked her lips and felt another wave of need wash over her as he slowly stood and stroked himself for a few moments, watching her. She wanted to whine or beg, but she knew she would get in trouble. She settled on releasing a long, distressed breath.

Drew smiled, obviously getting the message. He reached down into his pants and pulled out a condom, slowly and sensuously sliding it on. He then gave himself a few more strokes, just for show, before crawling back over her.

"It's okay, baby," he whispered in her ear. "I've got what you need. You just have to remember to be quiet, okay? And I'll take care of you."

Cami nodded in agreement, trying to communicate her need with every look, instead of the sounds and touches she wasn't allowed to make. Finally, Drew settled back on his knees and pulled her towards him by the hips. He lined them up and didn't even wait before sliding completely into her. It had only been a little over a week since they'd had sex, but she still felt the stretch and burn of his massive length and girth as if it had been years.

Unlike last time, Drew didn't give Cami a moment to acclimate to his presence before pulling almost completely out of her body and slamming back in. He continued in this way, thrusting into her furiously.

Cami had to bite the side of her cheek to keep from crying out. Somehow, the need to remain silent seemed to heighten everything else. The hunger and the pleasure were almost unbearable and it didn't take Cami long before she was right at the edge once again. This time, however, Drew let her go over, thrusting into her feverishly as her entire body was wracked with pleasure. It felt like it was tearing her apart, yet she never wanted it to end.

When she finally came to, Drew was shaking above her as he found his own release deep in her body. She held him through it, hoping he experienced even half of the pleasure she had.

Eventually, Drew rose and disposed of the condom. He then untied her hands and pulled her clothes all the way off before rubbing and kissing each wrist. He helped her slide under the comforter and, to her surprise, crawled in with her.

"I'll be gone before Madison wakes up," he whispered into her ear. "I promise."

Cami couldn't really bring herself to care one way or another as she nestled back against him and drifted off to the deepest sleep she'd experienced in weeks.

CHAPTER EIGHT
Cami

"Cami!"

Cami rolled over in her sleep, willing the voice away, fighting to stay in the calm, comforting world of her dreams.

"Cami, wake up."

She slowly surfaced from sleep to the sensation of a warm hand rubbing her naked back and shoulder. She blinked awake and stared into the face of Drew, who was sitting on the bed beside her, fully dressed.

"What time is it?" she asked. A smile spread across her lips as last night's memories slowly came back to her.

"It's early," he replied. "I just wanted to wake you up before I left. I know you were upset that I didn't do that last time. I'll be leaving on a business trip later today and I'm not sure when I'll be back, so I wanted to say goodbye."

Cami's smile grew even larger as she slowly sat

up. The sheet slid down her body, revealing her large, naked breasts. Drew sucked in a loud breath.

"God," he said, "if only I had a little more time."

"There will be time," Cami assured him. "There will be plenty of time later."

"Later," Drew repeated with a grin of his own.

He leaned forward and pressed his mouth to hers. Cami leaned in and opened to him, morning breath be damned. Drew groaned as he deepened the kiss, then pulled away with a regretful sigh.

"I'll call you once I'm back in town," he said.

"You do that," Cami replied.

"I'll let myself out," Drew told her, standing. "I would hate for you to have to put on clothes." Cami just offered him another smile and wave as he left the room, then promptly lay back down and drifted back to sleep.

* * *

Cami didn't expect Drew to call for the next few days, but when she hadn't heard from him by the following weekend, she began to worry. The next week grew so stressful, however, that she didn't have any time to waste worrying about Drew. She received her first bill from her lawyer. He'd gone through what she'd paid him on retainer quickly, gearing up for what looked to be a nasty custody battle. Even being the cheapest lawyer in the phone book, the man was expensive.

Cami looked down at the bill hopelessly. She'd already spent most of her measly savings on the retainer, and now she was going to have to shell out another thousand dollars quickly, or she'd soon find herself without representation.

Tucking the bill inside her purse, she loaded Madison into her car and headed towards her mother's. She was already working overtime—close to sixty hours a week—so there wasn't much more she could do.

"Everything okay?" her mother asked as Cami carried Madison into the apartment, obviously detecting the stress Cami was feeling. Her mom had been oddly supportive lately, not even harping on Cami's weight or relationship status. "I mean, besides all the crap you're already dealing with," she clarified when Cami shot her a look.

"Got a bill from the lawyer's office today," Cami replied. "Almost a grand."

"Damn!" Mom said before catching herself.

"Gramma said bad word!" Madison said. "Bad word!"

"Yes, she did," Cami replied, looking at her mother with an exaggerated "angry" face. "That's rude, Gramma!"

"Yes, it is," the older woman replied. "And I'm very sorry."

Madison seemed to take this as punishment enough, as she turned and teetered into the living room to play with her toys.

"So," her mom said quietly once Madison was out of hearing range, "what are we going to do?"

"I'll figure something out," Cami replied tiredly. "I will have a big paycheck next week. I've been working overtime a lot lately. And I can try to pick up some more shifts. Madison is at Ken's this weekend, so I can work four shifts in a row."

"Goodness, child, you'll pass out if you work yourself to the bone like that."

"What else can I do, Mom?" Cami asked, heavy emotion in her voice. "I need the money."

"*We'll* figure something out," her mom said, wrapping her arms around Cami. "Together."

Cami just nodded, leaning into the hug for a moment before pulling away.

"I have to go," she said. "And I'll be late again. I'm working another half shift on top of my own, picking up for a girl who wanted the early evening off."

"Okay," her mother replied, smiling sadly. "Have a great day!"

Cami went to kiss Madison goodbye before heading to the hospital.

The ER was busy, which made Cami even more worn out, but also helped the time go by faster. Cami found that it was almost easier to function in an exhausted mode when things were busy. Only when things were slow was when she would start to nod off at the nurses' station.

It was after midnight by the time Cami made it back to her mother's house. She let herself in quietly, expecting both Madison and her mom to be sleeping at this late hour. But, to her surprise, her mother was up at the kitchen table, a cup of tea in her hands.

"Hey," Cami said. "You're up late."

"You too," her mom responded, offering another one of her sad smiles. Cami was beginning to hate that smile. "Want some tea?"

"No thanks. I'm just gonna grab Madison and go."

"Why don't you stay here tonight?" her mother asked. "I can throw your scrubs in the wash and I have plenty of clothes for Madison. That way you don't have to go all the way home only to turn around and drop her off back here in the morning. Then you can sleep in a little and spend a bit of time with your daughter."

Cami was too tired to argue, so she just nodded.

"Then I'm going to shower and head to bed," she replied.

"One more thing," her mom said, rising from her chair and moving to her purse on the counter. She pulled out an envelope and handed it to Cami.

Cami opened it, her breath catching in her throat as she noticed the crisp hundred-dollar bills. There were ten of them…exactly a thousand dollars.

"Where did you get this, Mom?" Cami asked in a cracked voice.

"I sold a few things of your grandmother's," her mom said, face betraying no emotion.

Cami couldn't hide her own feelings, though. Her mom had held on to her own mother's jewelry since her death nearly two decades prior. Even at their poorest, when her mom had been working two jobs just to put a roof over their heads and food on their table, she'd never even considered selling any of her mother's jewelry.

"Mom..." Cami said, tears welling up in her eyes. "I can't believe you did that."

"We've got to do what we've got to do," she said with a determined air. "That will pay for this round of bills, and I still have some more jewelry I can sell. And I'll be able to get more than that for it. I could have gotten more than a grand for the pearls I sold if I hadn't been in such a hurry. But we needed the money now, so what can you do?"

"Thank you, Mom," Cami said through tears, pulling her mom close. "I love you."

"Don't worry," her mother whispered into her ear. "We won't let them take Madison. I promise."

Cami just nodded before pulling out and moving towards the bathroom, more grateful for her mother than she'd ever been before. When she got out of the shower, the washing machine was running, and there were some sleep clothes laid out for Cami on the sink. She dressed quickly and then went to curl up next to Madison in the guest bedroom. She was so exhausted that she fell asleep almost instantaneously.

Cami had to leave early the next day in order to meet with her lawyer. Thankfully, she was able to bring a check with her, so that his services were guaranteed for a little while longer.

She sat across from him in his small, stuffy office. It was a far cry from the office of Gil Dubois, Ken's lawyer. Cami hated to be here… It reminded her of how much things were stacked against her. Ken had the best lawyers money could buy, as well as family connections, while she had a second-rate lawyer with a small, dank office.

"So," Michael began, "things are at a stalemate right now. He has filed the petition for full custody, and we have countered that. We have not been able to come to a satisfactory agreement—obviously, Ken's lawyers have stated that he will now only be happy with full custody, which is out of the question for you—so now we're moving on to court. Our first court date is set for early next month."

"What happens then?" Cami asked, not trying to think about how expensive his fees were going to be once they were actually going to court.

"Well, first we need to find character witnesses that can speak about Ken's poor skills as a father as well as his substance abuse problems."

Cami grimaced, hating the idea of allowing the fighting to get so dirty.

"I'm going to start looking into past arrests and old acquaintances, trying to find as much dirt as possible."

Cami knew that all of those hours wouldn't come cheap and, worst of all, Michael didn't even seem confident in his ability to find much. In fact, as the weeks had progressed, Michael seemed less and less confident. At one point, he'd even asked if she would be willing to give up primary custody of Madison if that would mean being able to see her at all. Cami had almost punched him at the time.

"What should I be doing?" Cami asked.

"Well, I want you to think of anyone who may be willing to testify against your ex-husband. I also want you to write down all incriminating information about him that you can remember. Other than that, just spend as much time with Madison as you can."

Because you may not have her for much longer. This went unsaid, but Cami knew it was there. She knew she had to do something. Even if it meant selling her house and moving in with her mother, she needed to hire a better lawyer. If she thought it would move fast enough to get a lawyer soon, she'd do just that.

She was sitting in her car, debating whether or not to call Maggie and take her up on her offer to pay for a better lawyer, when her phone rang. Cami pulled it out of her purse and did a double take. It was Drew calling. After the first week of waiting, she'd pretty much given up on hearing from him again. This week, she hadn't even had the time or energy to think about it. And yet, here he was.

Cami was tired and upset and debated letting the call go to voicemail. But she knew that if she did that, she'd never call him back. At least she could talk to him now and get closure.

"Hello," she said after the fourth ring.

"Cami, hey! How are you?" Drew sounded warm and happy to hear her voice—not like he'd been radio silent for the greater part of two weeks.

"Okay," she lied. She really didn't want to talk to Drew about her emotions. That was, in fact, the last thing she wanted to do right now.

"You don't sound okay," he said. "Is everything alright? Is it the custody battle?"

"I really don't want to talk about it right now, Drew," she said in an icy tone. "What do you want?"

"Oh…um…I just wanted to talk to you, I guess. I just got back from my trip and I was hoping I'd be able to see you this weekend."

"I don't know, Drew. I haven't heard from you in nearly two weeks, and now you're just back and expecting me to be at your beck and call."

"Listen, Cami, I'm sorry I haven't called. This trip was extremely exhausting. I didn't really have a moment to myself. But I missed you. A lot. One of the things that kept me going was the knowledge that I would get to see you when I got back."

He sounded so sincere that Cami felt her heart begin to thaw a little bit. Maybe he really had been on a business trip for the last two weeks and hadn't been able to call. That was the thing…there was always a reasonable explanation, but it continued to happen. He continued to disappear every time things started to get good. He was inconsistent and unreliable.

"Please," he pleaded.

Cami had half a mind to refuse him, but the truth was, Madison was going to be at Ken's all weekend, and if she didn't have anything to occupy her mind, she'd just sit around depressed and moping.

"Fine," she said after a minute. "I'm free tomorrow night."

"Awesome!" he replied, sounding ecstatic. "I'll pick you up at six."

Cami agreed and hung up the phone.

"What am I getting myself into?" she asked herself as she pulled out of the parking lot. Still, she couldn't stop the smile spreading across her face.

CHAPTER NINE
Cami

Cami couldn't help herself. Even knowing that she shouldn't get attached when it came to Drew, she was ecstatic at the idea of seeing him tonight. Madison was at her father's all weekend, so Cami had ample time to get ready. She took a long hot bath and spent hours shaving and scrubbing herself all over. She wanted to look perfect for their date.

It wasn't just the prospect of seeing Drew again that had her excited. The truth was, she hadn't been able to stop thinking about the sex they'd had last time they were together. Yes, she'd been too busy this week to mope and pine after the man, but sometimes, in the wee hours of the night, she couldn't help but think about the way he'd whispered commands softly into her ear, taunting and teasing her. The way he'd tied her hands, held her down, and pounded into her. Even now, her body shuddered at the thought.

Cami had never thought she'd be the kind of girl that liked "kinky" sex, but she was realizing now this may only have been because Ken was such a pathetic excuse for a lover. She couldn't even picture her ex-husband holding the thrall over her that Drew did in the bedroom. She couldn't help herself...she wanted more. What did Drew have planned for her tonight?

She had her hair blown out and curled to the pinnacle of sexiness and her makeup done up like a vixen, and she was just trying to decide what outfit to wear when her phone rang. She smiled to herself when she saw it was Drew. Perhaps he wanted to move the date up a little bit. She could be ready in just a few minutes, she reasoned.

"Hello there," Cami answered in the most sensual voice she could muster.

"Hey," Drew said in a subdued tone.

"Everything okay?" she asked.

"Not really," Drew admitted. "I really hate to do this, but something came up, and I absolutely have to cancel our date tonight."

"What happened?" Cami asked, suddenly worried.

"Nothing I can really talk about," Drew said. "I'm sorry. I'll make it up to you, I swear. I'm really sad to have to cancel but I have something I just can't get out of. Again, I am so sorry."

Cami was more than a little pissed that Drew wasn't even willing to explain why he had to cancel. He'd gone out of his way to talk her into the date in the first place, only to cancel less than two hours before they were supposed to get together—it all made her even angrier. Any worry she'd had a few minutes ago had completely flown out the window.

"Whatever," she replied. "Don't even worry about it." Then, without giving him the chance to reply, she hung up the phone.

Cami felt absolutely ridiculous. Her hair was done up to high heaven and she had way too much makeup on. She was exfoliated and waxed to perfection. And now she was going to sit around all night feeling sorry for herself.

Maybe not, she thought. She knew it was last minute, but she decided to give Maggie a call and see if her best friend was available before completely collapsing in on herself.

"Hey girl, what's up?" Maggie said as she answered the phone.

"Drew just canceled our date," Cami replied angrily.

"Ouch," Maggie said.

"Yeah…less than two hours before we were scheduled to get together."

"That sucks, Cami…but I'm sure he had a good reason."

"He wouldn't even tell me why," Cami snarled angrily. "He just said he was sorry and would make it up to me…like that made everything okay. I'm so over that asshole. He's so hot and cold."

"I'm really sorry, Cami. But I know Drew is a nice guy. I'm sure he has a good reason."

"Honestly," Cami replied. "I really don't give a fuck at this point. He can shove his reasons up his ass. I'm over it."

"Um…okay then," Maggie said.

"But I'm not calling just to bitch. I'm all made up with nowhere to go. What are you doing tonight?"

"Oh…well…" Maggie paused for a second before continuing. "I actually have a date tonight. But it's a casual thing. I can cancel."

"Oh my God, of course you're not going to cancel," Cami cried. "But I can't believe you didn't tell me you were going on a date. I want to know all about it. Who's the guy? How'd you meet? Is this the first date? It better be, or I'll be pissed that you're holding out on me!"

"Listen, Cami," Maggie began when Cami finally paused to breathe. "This thing is kind of new, and I'm not really sure about it yet, so I don't really want to say."

"Okay," Cami replied, taken aback. Her best friend had never *not* wanted to spill about her love life. In fact, Maggie normally wouldn't shut up about whatever guy she was seeing at the moment. "Okay, I guess."

"Thank you so much for understanding, Cami," Maggie said, obviously relieved. "And I really will tell you eventually. I promise. I love you to death, but I have to go now 'cuz he'll be here soon. I'm really sorry about Drew."

"That's fine. Have a great night," Cami said, trying to sound more cheerful than she felt. "Bye!"

"Bye!" Maggie called as she hung up the phone.

Cami tossed her cell on the couch cushion next to her and slumped over, feeling somehow even more dejected than she had before she'd called Maggie. It wasn't that she didn't feel happy for her best friend, because she did. She might've been slightly jealous that Maggie had a date when she didn't, but not enough to hold it against her. And it wasn't like Maggie didn't deserve her privacy. She really did.

But, after all of Drew's shadiness, Maggie's secrecy just rubbed her the wrong way. Why was everyone being so weird all of a sudden? First Ken, with his ridiculous custody demands. Then Drew, with his weird hot-and-cold attentions. And now Maggie, and her secret boyfriend.

Cami got up and opened a bottle of wine, not even caring that it wasn't yet five o'clock. It was a Saturday, she was off work, and she'd had a rough day… week…month, really. She deserved to get hammered while her daughter was at her scheming ex-husband's house, probably cuddling up to his perfect Barbie doll of a new fiancée.

Cami was slumped over on the couch, three glasses of wine deep and watching *Sex and the City* reruns when the doorbell rang. She sat up, confused, then wandered towards the door. She opened it to find Drew standing in front of her. He had a bouquet of sunflowers in one hand while the other held a bag.

"Hi," he said sheepishly. "Can I come in?"

"I don't know," Cami replied, hands on her hips. "I don't know if you deserve to come inside."

"Probably not, but I came to make amends for canceling so abruptly earlier. Look. I'm really sorry. And I brought flowers." He held the sunflowers out, and Cami took them from him.

"They're my favorite," she admitted begrudgingly.

"I know," he replied with a proud smile. "I also brought you a bottle of merlot and burgers from Downtown Grill."

Cami eyed the bottle of wine—which just so happened to be her favorite brand. And, of course, Downtown Grill was her favorite place to eat.

"How did you—"

"Maggie," Drew answered before Cami even had time to finish her question. "And I really owe her because she answered and talked me through everything, even though she was on a date."

All the resentment Cami had been feeling towards Maggie immediately melted away, replaced by warmth. She felt guilty and promised herself that she'd do something nice for her best friend very soon. Reluctantly, Cami stepped away from the door and allowed Drew into the house.

Drew headed straight towards the dining room, where he began pulling delicious-smelling burgers out of the bag.

Cami came up behind him and slid into a seat, watching him work. He moved around her kitchen with ease, making himself at home as he searched out everything he needed. Eventually, they were both sitting across from each other, with plates stacked high with burgers and fries in front of them, two generous glasses of wine next to the food.

"So," Drew started after they'd both begun eating. "I think I owe you an explanation about earlier."

"You don't have to explain," Cami replied, though she really did want to know.

"My sister Elsie has been in a horrendous marriage. Her husband Robert is an abusive alcoholic. Well, she called me earlier today in tears because she'd seen Robert shake their four-year-old son, Robbie. She finally realized she needed to leave him and she was asking me for help. I really couldn't say no to that. It took a lot longer than I expected, hence the canceled date. But they're all set up in my apartment right now, and when I admitted to her that I'd canceled a date to help her, she insisted I go. And, since I've been waiting to see you for weeks, I could hardly put up a protest. So…a quick call to Maggie and here I am."

Cami didn't admit that she'd overheard Drew and his sister having a serious conversation about said marriage while at the beach house a few weeks ago. She didn't want him to know that such a private moment had been witnessed. What she did do was offer him a large, sweet smile.

"You're an amazing brother," she told him. "I wish I'd had someone like you during my divorce."

"Well," he said with a smile of his own, "you have someone like me now."

Cami smiled at that, feeling bold with the mixture of wine and Drew's own confession.

"I've missed you too," she admitted. "I haven't been able to stop thinking about you…stop thinking about our last night together."

Drew's smile went from sweet to lascivious in a matter of moments.

"Oh, really?" he asked, his voice growing a little deeper. "And what couldn't you stop thinking about?"

"You," Cami replied. "You, holding me down, tying me up, telling me what to do." She couldn't believe she just said all this aloud.

Drew was looking at her with a gaze so intense that Cami thought she might explode. Her body was already responding, and she could feel desire beginning to build between her thighs. He licked his lips before standing and walking towards her side of the table. He offered her a hand, which she took, and he pulled her up and out of the kitchen. Their food was left half-eaten on the table as he directed her towards the bedroom.

Drew was the epitome of calm control as he led Cami to the bed.

"Strip," he commanded as he stood next to her.

There was no hesitation in his tone, and Cami knew better than to question him. Instead, she slowly slipped off the t-shirt she'd donned when she'd realized that she'd be spending the night alone, then the unflattering sweatpants she'd also been wearing. Thankfully, Cami had forgone underwear of any kind out of laziness and she was soon standing in the middle of her bedroom completely bare. Drew stood still for a moment, silently devouring her body with his eyes, before he moved forward and pushed Cami until she fell against the mattress.

Like last time they had been together, Cami sprawled out against the comforter and watched Drew slowly undress himself. Once he was down to his boxer briefs, which were tented and wet with his excitement, Cami couldn't control herself anymore. She rose to her knees and crawled to the foot of the bed, where she pressed her palm against his hard length through the thin fabric of his underwear.

"No," he commanded her. "No touching. Just like last time. I want you to simply lay back and enjoy it while I take you apart. Let me take care of you." He pressed her firmly against the mattress again, pulling her hands up over her head. "I'm not wearing a tie today, so I will need you to practice restraint and keep your hands right where I put them. But you don't have to be quiet this time sweetheart. In fact, I want you to be loud. I want to hear you."

Cami clutched the comforter above her head and nodded. Drew stepped back and pulled his underwear off. He was swollen and dripping—even more excited than the last time they'd been together. Cami moaned with desire as he crawled on top of her, rubbing his erection against her wet thigh, mixing his juices with her own as he began to suck and nip at her hard nipples.

Drew ground down against Cami's thigh, but that wasn't enough. She needed more friction. Without thinking, she reached down and grabbed his tight, muscled ass and pulled him towards her aching core. He immediately pulled back and crawled off her, pinning her hands to the bed above her head once again.

"Sorry," Cami replied sheepishly. "I forgot."

"I understand," Drew said soothingly. "But it's not going to happen again, do you hear me?"

"Yes, sir," Cami answered, feeling herself shudder at her own response. She didn't know where it had come from, but she'd loved the feeling of it slipping from her lips.

Leaving one hand on her wrists above her head, Drew used the other to flip Cami over in one fluid movement, so that she was sprawled out on her stomach. Cami let out a sharp, needy cry, thrusting her ass in the air in an attempt to find some sort of friction.

"You've been very naughty," he said in her ear. "I know exactly what you need."

With that, he brought his large, strong hand down roughly against her raised ass. The sharp sting of the contact caused an unexpected swell of pleasure within Cami, and she felt herself grow even more excited.

"You liked that, didn't you?" Drew asked with a chuckle. "I thought you would."

Quickly, another slap was brought down on Cami's ass, even harder than before. Cami moaned and pushed her buttocks higher into the air in encouragement. Then more smacks came down, one after the other, until Cami's ass was stinging pleasantly, and she'd lost count of the number of time's she'd been struck.

She'd never been spanked like this before and she would have never guessed that she would like it, but a thrill of pleasure shot through her with each point of contact. Soon, her ass felt like it was on fire, only matched by the burning heat between her legs. Cami closed her eyes and let go, allowing her insecurities and tendency to over-analyze to go as she let the sensations to wipe through her body and completely relinquished all control.

She lost track of time, and it wasn't until Drew's strong hands began to massage her hot, throbbing buttocks, that she realized the spanking was over. Drew squeezed and rubbed for a few minutes, stopping every few moments to bend down and kiss one cheek, then the other.

"Your ass looks so pretty with my hand marks," he crooned, his voice thick with his own desire.

After a few more minutes of massage, one hand began to slide lower, slipping between her legs, and Drew slid three fingers in and out of her aching core. By the time that he started to use his thumb to circle her clit, Cami was a crying, writhing mess.

"Please," she sobbed.

"Please what, sweetheart?" Drew asked, using his other hand to stroke her hair as he continued to play with her pussy.

"Fuck me," Cami pleaded, though it came out as barely a whisper, her voice growing hoarse with need.

Drew smiled and stood up, bending to pull a condom out of his pants pocket. Like last time, he wrapped his hand around himself and gave his shaft a few slow jerks before pushing the sheath on his swollen member.

Cami turned back away from him, burying her head in the comforter as she lifted her hips again in invitation. She felt strong hands grip her sore buttocks, pulling her towards him. One of those hands moved to her hip as he used the other to line up his cock, rubbing against her clit a few times before pushing it into her burning body.

They cried out in unison as he filled her completely, thrusting himself to the hilt in one fluid motion.

The delicious feeling of Drew's cock, stretching Cami open and filling her up, had her keening and pressing back against him almost instantaneously. Bringing his other hand up so that they were both gripping her hips so tight they would leave bruises, Drew began to pound into her hard and fast. He set a punishing pace, driving into her without mercy. Cami was helpless to do anything but cry out as she pushed herself back onto his cock. She was so overcome with need that she could barely think.

Through the cloudy haze of desire, Cami felt one of Drew's hands leave her hip and move down between her legs to circle around to her clit. He began moving his fingers with the same vigor with which he was fucking her, causing pleasure so intense it was almost unbearable.

It didn't take much longer for Cami to completely lose control. A few more harsh thrusts, and Cami was overtaken by wave after wave of pleasure that pushed everything else out of her mind.

When she finally came back to her body, Drew's own movements had become erratic. Then, with a loud cry, he stilled above her. Cami could feel his cock pulsing as he spilled himself deep within her.

In that moment, Cami regretted the latex between them. She wished that she could feel his seed deep inside her. That was Cami's last coherent thought before she collapsed onto the bed and passed out.

CHAPTER TEN
Cami

Cami slowly blinked awake, rolling onto her back and cringing at the sting of her bottom as it rubbed against the cool sheets. The sensation brought a smile to her face as she remembered the night before, and the vigorous spanking she'd received. In fact, she didn't even remember crawling between the sheets. Drew must have tucked her in after she'd fallen asleep.

He had really proven himself last night. He'd shown up like a knight out of a fairy tale and whisked her off her feet with her favorite food, wine, and flowers before pulling her into the bedroom for some very kinky—and not to mention steamy—sex.

At the thought of dinner, however, her stomach began to growl. They'd left their dinner half-eaten on the kitchen table last night, too caught up in each other. Now, however, she was regretting it.

Perhaps she'd make Drew take her to brunch today. It was Sunday, after all. Surely he was free. He'd just gotten back from a business trip that had lasted almost two weeks. He deserved a little R&R. Perhaps afterwards, they could come back here for another roll in the hay.

Drew was no longer in bed, but his side of the sheets was still warm. Cami climbed out of bed and set out to find him, not even bothering to put on clothes. Perhaps she could talk Drew into coming back to bed for round two *before* they went to brunch.

In the kitchen, Cami was surprised to find the table completely cleaned off, all the food from last night disposed of and the dishes washed and put away. Something deep inside of her stomach began to curl into a knot, however, when she noticed the note in the middle of the kitchen table.

Cami,

Something came up and I had to run off early this morning. I'll explain later, but didn't want to leave without a note.

Drew

Cami grimaced. It was *always* something with him. He seemed so sincere and into her in the moments that they were together, but he was always dashing off as soon as those moments ended. He was so unreliable.

She hated feeling like she wasn't his priority. Helping his sister out of a horrible situation was totally understandable...but what about the other times? He'd never spent the night at her house and actually been there the following morning to eat breakfast with her. There was always something more important to do—somewhere else he needed to be. And it wasn't like the last few times had been week-days, either. They'd been Sundays, and yet Drew had still run off at the crack of dawn.

Cami started thinking back over all of his excuses. She knew that he was telling the truth about his sister—she'd seen it with her own eyes. But what about the other times? A business breakfast, a business trip, now something had simply come up, dragging him away from her. The knot in her stomach became even tenser as a new idea began to work its way into her mind.

What if Drew wasn't as sincere as he seemed? What if he had been lying to Cami the entire time? For all she knew, he could be in a relationship with another woman—that tall, skinny model from the beach, perhaps. Cami could be *the other woman.*

After having had her husband cheat on her, that thought made Cami sick to her stomach. Now that she thought about it, though, it made perfect sense. The erratic behavior, the change in personality around certain people, constantly dashing off for vague reasons.

Cami sat at the table for a long time, staring off into space, until she heard her phone ring in the other room. It was Maggie's ringtone, and she still felt indebted to Maggie for the night before, even if Drew turned out to be a cheating asshole.

"Hey," she said once she'd answered the call.

"Hey, girl. You and your beau want to roll your sorry behinds out of bed long enough to join my brother and me for brunch?" Maggie chirped.

She was entirely too perky, which was surprising for Maggie. Perhaps her date had gone extremely well.

"I don't have a beau," was all that Cami said in response.

"Oh…" Maggie replied. "I thought…Drew called me last night. Did he not show up?"

"Oh he showed up, all romance and hot kinky sex. Then he crept out in the night, or the early hours of the morning. Who knows? He only left a vague note about something coming up."

"I'm sorry, honey," Maggie replied, her voice soothing. "Come join us for brunch and we can talk about it. Grant and Declan will be there. They know Drew well… Maybe they'll be able to shine some light on the situation."

Cami agreed to meet them at a local café in half an hour, so she jumped in the shower to wash all of the funk from the night before off. She felt halfway decent by the time she joined the already-sitting group at the table. Once they'd ordered and had steaming cups of coffee between them, Maggie turned towards Cami.

"Spill," she demanded.

Cami eyed Grant and Declan wearily.

"Oh they won't care. And I'll make sure nothing you say here will get back to Drew. They can probably help. So, spill."

"There's nothing really left to say. He showed up late last night with a bottle of my favorite wine, a bouquet of my favorite flowers, and takeout from my favorite restaurant. I hear that I have you to thank for that, by the way—so, thank you! And it was amazing. And he told me all about how he'd played the knight in shining armor to his distressed sister. He wined me and wooed me until I willingly allowed him to pull me into bed."

"Don't act like it takes all that much wooing before you allow him to take you to bed," Maggie said with a smirk.

"Shut up," Cami said with a blush as the two men at the table chuckled. But she couldn't really deny that either, so she just chose to move on with the story. "So…then I woke up alone. There was a hastily scribbled note on the table vaguely stating that something came up."

"That doesn't sound too bad," Declan volunteered. "At least he left a note, right?"

"That's better than you do, right, Declan?" Maggie joked, punching him playfully.

Cami couldn't help but notice that Maggie's hand didn't leave Declan's arm even after her punch had landed. She continued to touch him as she smiled at him brightly. Cami was a little thrown off…

This was definitely Maggie's flirting behavior, yet it was Declan. He was practically her brother. Not to mention that he flirted with pretty much anything with boobs. Shaking her head, Cami tried to veer her obviously over-reacting mind back to the conversation at hand.

"It wouldn't be that bad if it were the first time it had happened," Cami replied dejectedly. "I mean… it was the first time he left a note. The first time we actually slept together, I woke up alone with no note or anything."

Both men at the table grimaced and Maggie nodded knowingly. She'd already heard that story…more than once.

"We've slept together three times," Cami said, deciding not to have any shame or hold anything back from these guys if it would help her get to the bottom of what was going on with Drew. "And all three times, I've woken up alone. The second time he had the decency to wake me up and say goodbye. He told me he would be going on a short business trip and would call me soon."

"That doesn't sound bad," Grant offered.

"I didn't hear from him for almost two weeks," Cami replied with obvious frustration in her voice.

"Oh…" Grant said, looking a little disappointed to hear that. "Listen… I know Drew is going through some things right now, but he's a really great guy."

"I know he's a great guy…when he wants to be. He can be so sweet and caring—like he's really into me. Then he'll disappear for a week or two. He's completely inconsistent. Even at the beach house he was like that. One minute, he'd be totally into me, the next minute ignoring me while some stuck up model clung to his arm and he laughed at really snobbish jokes. His behavior is so erratic, I've come to the conclusion that he's cheating on me. Or…not cheating on me. I don't even think we're in an exclusive relationship. But I think he's cheating on someone else *with* me. I'm the other woman."

"Cami, calm down!" Maggie said, leaning over to place a soothing hand on Cami's shoulder. It was only then that Cami realized that she was hyperventilating.

"I'm sorry," she said to the others. "I'm just under a lot of stress right now, with the custody battle. I'm a little more sensitive than usual. I know I'm over-reacting."

Maggie opened her mouth to speak but was interrupted by a server with a large tray, which carried heaping plates of pancakes, waffles, and omelets. For a while, conversation died down, and the group ate quietly.

Throughout the meal, Cami kept an eye on Maggie and Declan, who were constantly stealing food off each other's plates and pushing one another playfully. It was like Maggie was looking for any opportunity to touch Declan. And Declan seemed to be reciprocating—not that it was surprising, the guy had always flirted with anything that moved.

But Maggie had never shown any interest in the man before, other than fraternal affection. Cami couldn't help but remember Maggie's secret date from the night before. Could it have been with Declan? Or had her date gone so poorly that she was searching for some validation? That seemed more likely, in Cami's opinion. She shook her head and decided to let it go. It was probably nothing, after all, and Grant didn't seem to notice or care.

"Listen, Cami," Grant began after a while, "Drew is my best friend…no offense, Declan."

"None taken," Declan replied before turning back towards Maggie, with whom he was arm-wrestling for the last sausage. "You guys have known each other much longer."

"Yes. Yes, that's true," Grant said. "Anyway," he continued, turning back towards Cami, "I've known Drew for over a decade. We've been through a lot together. He's like a brother to me. What I'm trying to say is, Drew isn't the type to cheat."

"No," Declan agreed. "Not at all." He turned back towards her to resume their wrestling match.

Grant just rolled his eyes and continued talking. "I know he isn't seeing anyone else. In fact…and I probably shouldn't tell you this—don't let him know I've told you or he'll kill me—but you're the first person he'd slept with since his divorce."

"What?" Cami asked skeptically. He'd said she was the first person he'd dated since his divorce, but with the women throwing themselves at him, she found it hard to believe that he hadn't had a fling or two. "There is no way that's true."

"It's totally true," Declan confirmed. "The man has the self-control of a…I don't know. Something that has a lot of self-control."

"Good one, Declan," Maggie chimed in, laughing.

Declan laughed too for a moment, then turned towards Cami seriously. "All joking aside," he said, "Drew really is a great guy. And he would never cheat."

"And he really likes you," Grant added. "He's got a lot going on at the moment—things pulling him in opposite directions. He can't really be himself right now. But he likes you, and once he deals with some of this stuff, which I believe will be quite soon, I know he'll be an ideal boyfriend."

"I don't understand," Cami said. "What do you mean that he can't really be himself right now? Why not? What kind of stuff does he need to deal with? Because from the vague way you're talking, it does sound like he's in a relationship that he's trying to get out of, which would mean that he is cheating on someone with me."

"No! It's not that, I promise," Declan said. "He's—" Before Declan could finish his sentence, Grant had placed his hand on his shoulder and was shaking his head. Declan shut his mouth and nodded in understanding.

"Look," Grant said, "we can't really talk about what Drew's up to right now. It's his private business, and he'll tell you when he's ready. However, I can promise you that it's nothing shady. He's not in any kind of relationship—other than the one he has with you—and he's doing absolutely nothing illegal. I know that it sounds bad, but I promise you, it's not. You just have to trust me."

Cami nodded. She did trust Grant. She knew he would never purposefully lead her into something harmful. But what if he didn't know Drew as well as he thought he did? And even if Drew wasn't doing anything shady, Cami was obviously not very high on his priority list. He seemed to genuinely care about her when he was with her—but not enough to stick around afterwards.

Cami decided to let the topic of Drew drop and went back to eating her breakfast in quiet. The rest of the brunch passed smoothly, with continued bickering and flirting between Maggie and Declan keeping Grant and Cami entertained.

When they got up to leave, Grant walked beside Cami.

"I know I've already said a lot, but I just want to reiterate that Drew is a great guy. And I know for a fact that he is head-over-heels for you. He's going through some stuff, but it's almost through. If you can stick it out for just a little bit longer, it will be worth it. I promise."

Cami nodded, though she didn't know whether or not she was agreeing with him. She just wasn't sure anymore.

CHAPTER ELEVEN
Cami

By the time Cami got back from brunch, she still had hours ahead of her before she was scheduled to pick up Madison. She debated going over there early, but she knew that it wouldn't be received well. And she didn't want to deviate from the set custody schedule at the moment and thus give Ken even more merit in his demands.

Cami tried to keep her mind calm and away from any of the massive problems dogging her life that she could currently do nothing about. She decided that the best way to keep her mind clear was to keep her body busy. And so she started to clean.

She cleaned her entire house from top to bottom. She straightened Madison's room and washed all of her toys, then vacuumed under her bed.

She did load after load of laundry, including the sheets from her own bed, which were definitely in need of a wash. Pulling the bedding from her mattress brought her thoughts back around to Drew… and what they'd done the night before.

God, the sex had been good. Not just good—amazing. She'd never had sex anywhere near as good. And they'd only slept with each other three times. That was hard to believe, given the way that they moved together with ease. She'd slept with Ken for years, and they'd never been as attuned to each other's bodies as she and Drew seemed to be.

The harder she tried not to think about Drew, the more adamantly he seemed to bludgeon his way into her thoughts. The conversation at brunch had both helped and hurt Cami's opinion of the man. All of Declan and Grant's praise reminded Cami of just how sweet Drew actually was.

She thought about the scene she'd witnessed at the beach house between him and his sister. Drew had come upon his sister and his sister's abusive husband. He'd sent the husband packing and had then held his sister while she cried, all the time whispering sweet encouragements in her ear. And then, yesterday, he'd helped her and her son escape the drunken asshole for good, taking them into his apartment. Cami only wished she'd had someone that supportive during her own divorce.

Then there'd been the way he'd always inquired after her custody battle, offering encouragement and advice. It was as if she really did have someone supporting her, like she'd always wanted.

But he was so erratic and unreliable, and this was reconfirmed—though not on purpose—by Declan and Grant. The ambiguous "things" that Drew was dealing with, that neither man could actually explain, just validated what Cami already knew about Drew's hot and cold personality.

Even if the "things" Drew was dealing with weren't shady or illegal, they still seemed to be of much higher priority than Cami herself. She didn't know if she could handle being in a relationship with a man who didn't see her as his top priority.

Yes, things would come up from time to time—that was life, and Cami realized that. And it wasn't like Cami expected to be Drew's number one priority this early in the relationship. But his never staying at her place in the mornings, his not choosing her over the other "things" in his life—made her feel like she'd never be that priority to him.

Cami ran those facts back and forth through her mind until it was time to go pick up her daughter. She felt sick during the entire drive across town to the wealthy neighborhood where Ken lived. It wasn't that she didn't want to see her baby. She was super excited to pick up Madison. She just really didn't want to have to face Ken at the moment.

He'd picked her up from Cami's mother's house on Friday while Cami was running errands. She hadn't seen him since their icy, silent meeting with their lawyers weeks ago and hadn't spoken with him since the phone call directly after.

Cami wasn't sure if she was angry or relieved when she pulled down the long driveway to see that Ken's BMW wasn't there. It meant she wouldn't have to deal with him, yes. But it also meant that she'd have to deal with Natalie instead. Natalie had never been anything but perfectly polite to her, but Cami couldn't help but hate her anyway.

Natalie opened the door with Madison on her hip, clinging to her like a monkey. Of course, Natalie looked perfect, with her blonde hair curled just right and her white pants and tank top without even the smallest stain. Cami offered her a weak smile.

"Hey, sweetie," Cami crooned as she reached to take Madison out of her arms.

"No," Madison replied, clinging to the other woman. "I want to stay with Daddy and Natalie."

Cami visibly cringed. Madison had always been excited to see her and ready to go home after weekends at Ken's. Now she was clinging to the step-monster and demanding to stay.

"I can keep holding her for a few more minutes," Natalie told her, like she was doing Cami some big favor. "We're not completely ready to go yet anyway."

With that, Natalie turned back into the house, Madison still in her arms, but not fast enough to hide the wide, self-satisfied smile that had spread across her face. Cami had never hated her more than in that moment. She wanted more than anything to demand that Natalie hand over her daughter, but she didn't want to cause a scene in front of Madison.

"Sorry. We were just packing up her stuff when you arrived."

Her use of the word was driving Cami insane. It was as if she was implying that she and Madison were a team—a *we.* But they weren't. Madison and Cami were the team—they were the *we.* Cami curled her fists into balls and didn't speak as she followed Natalie through the enormous, pristine house—it was even larger than the one Cami had once shared with Ken. It appeared that Natalie lacked any ability to reel in Ken's spending.

Cami had never been beyond the front foyer. She'd never been invited, and she didn't understand what was going on now. At least, she didn't understand until they headed up the stairs and into a large bedroom.

The room was completely decked out as an ideal nursery, with everything a baby could want. A pink princess bed, almost the size of Cami's own, was pressed against one wall, a gauzy net hanging down from the ceiling to cover it in translucent purple. There was a Barbie house full of dolls and a matching Barbie car large enough for Cami to drive. The walls were covered with pictures of Disney princesses and the closet door was open, revealing an array of extremely expensive-looking girl clothes.

Cami didn't know when this room had been built, but she knew it hadn't been here long. She also realized why Natalie had brought her up here. It was to show Cami how much better she believed they could support Madison—how much better Natalie believed Madison's life would be here. And perhaps, it was another intimidation tactic as well. By showing Cami this room, Natalie was letting her know that she and Ken fully believed they would win the custody battle. In fact—they were already prepared for it.

The thought made Cami sick. She knew it wasn't true. She knew that stuff wasn't what would make Madison happy.

With Madison still on her hip, Natalie was leaning down and scooping up the clothes and toys that came from Cami's house. They paled in comparison to the clothes and toys in this room—but that was just the point Natalie was trying to make.

As soon as the last article had been deposited in the bag, Cami yanked it from Natalie's hand.

"I'll take my daughter now," Cami said, prying Madison from her clutches.

Madison whined for a moment, asking for one of her dolls.

"These toys are for this house, Madison," Natalie said. "Your mother has other toys for you at your other home."

Other home. Cami wanted to scream that this was not Madison's home—that Madison had one home, and it was with her. But she didn't. She simply carried her daughter out of the room and down the stairs, not waiting to be shown out.

Madison was still fussing, calling for Natalie and a dolly Cami knew nothing about. Cami didn't care. All she cared about was getting out of this house as quickly as humanly possible.

She had to force herself not to run through the living room and out the door. She leaned into her car to buckle Madison in, then noticed Natalie was at the house's entrance, still smiling her nauseatingly sweet smile.

"Bye, Madison, my love," she called. "See you soon."

"Bye, Natalie," Madison called with a wave even as Cami was slamming Madison's door and getting behind the wheel.

Cami only got a few blocks away before she had to pull over and dissolve into tears. How was she supposed to compete with *that?* She couldn't. She didn't have the means. Even if she won the custody battle, which was looking less and less likely every day, Ken and Natalie would be able to win Madison over by the sheer amount of stuff they were willing to purchase for her.

It might not matter much to a three-year-old, but it would sure as hell matter to a thirteen-year-old. By the time Madison was old enough to decide for herself, she'd be old enough to be bribed and wooed away from Cami with promises of the most expensive clothes and the coolest gadgets, tropical vacations and a new car on her sixteenth birthday.

No! Cami told herself. *It will never be like that!* She would make sure that Madison grew up knowing what to value. She'd make sure that her daughter realized that money and material goods didn't make people happy. By the time that Madison was old enough to choose, she'd know what really mattered. But that would only happen if she won this lawsuit.

Wiping the tears from her eyes, Cami tried to focus on something else for a little while. There was absolutely nothing she could do, at the moment, to affect the outcome of the trial, so it would be better if she invested her time and energy in stressing about something she did have some power over.

Her mind once again drifted to Drew. She really did like him more than she was willing to admit. If he was more constant, she'd probably be in love with him already. Even with his erratic behavior, she knew that it wouldn't take much to make her love him.

But she didn't want to be with someone who only saw her as an afterthought. She had been there and done that with Ken already. And now Madison was even drifting away from her. She would not invest in one more person who didn't see her as his number one priority.

"We're through," Cami said aloud, making up her mind once and for all. "Drew and I are over."

the Stubborn Suitor

BOOK THREE

CHAPTER ONE
Drew

As he watched Sylvester Kenton sign his name on the contract, making the sale final, Drew Sloane felt his entire body relax. Stress and tension he'd been carrying for months slowly began to seep from his body, making him feel lighter and younger all at once.

It was over. It was all over. The sale of Drew's company had been finalized—for two and a half billion dollars, at that—and he was finally free to do what he wanted with his life. He never had to work another day.

Of course, he *would* work. Drew had no delusions about that. A life of leisure just wasn't for him. But now he didn't have to slave away in the corporate world, working twelve to fifteen-hour days and falling all over himself to impress people he couldn't stand. Instead, he could focus on developing his philanthropic foundation. There was so much he wanted to do with his wealth—so many people he could help.

Drew shook Kenton's hand, then the hand of James Cook, Kenton's chief investor and the man Drew had been falling all over himself to impress over the last few months. Although Drew had wanted to sell his company, he had refused to do so until he could ensure that all of his employees' jobs would be secure. Kenton was not willing to sign the deal until Cook approved of it. And so, Drew had spent the last few months convincing Cook that keeping on every single one of the over five-hundred people employed by his company, as well as ensuring that they retained their healthcare and other benefits, was a good investment for the corporation.

Drew had succeeded eventually, though it had been a difficult process. Cook only really cared about profits and looked down his nose at those he perceived to be below his social sphere. Drew had to convince him that happy, grateful employees provided much better return for their investment than those who resented the company they worked for.

After looking at the numbers—how Drew had been able to build the company from nothing into a multi-billion dollar corporation—the man was finally convinced. Though it had involved months of misery on Drew's part, all of that hard work had paid off.

"It's been a pleasure getting to know you, son," Cook said warmly as he grasped Drew's hand. Drew couldn't help but chuckle slightly, because the man really didn't know him at all. "I'm sure we'll see each other again soon. Analise speaks very highly of you and I know she'll want to have you over to the house again soon."

Drew just nodded in reply, though he recoiled inwardly at the thought. He knew that Cook and his wife Nancy had been pushing their daughter, Analise, at him in the attempt at creating a more permanent type of business venture. Drew loathed that Cook was willing to sacrifice his daughter's happiness in order to ensure the sale of the company. His wife Nancy had also encouraged the match, though Drew thought it was only because she wanted her daughter to marry someone as wealthy as they were.

Drew had played along as he'd worked to get Cook's approval of the employee retention and benefits clause in the contract of the sale. The truth was, he was in no way interested in Analise Cook. She was beautiful, yes, in a generic way—tall and thin and cold. But she had nothing that interested Drew. The truth was, Drew already had someone of interest—someone he couldn't get off his mind, even now. Especially now.

After the meeting was adjourned, Drew hurried to the car that was waiting outside to take him to the airport. He'd been in New York City for the last week, finalizing the sale of the company. But it was over now and he could finally go home to Cami.

Cami Hendricks was his ideal woman, fiery and passionate, and beautiful beyond compare. Unfortunately, up to this point, he'd been unable to treat her the way that she deserved. He'd met her at the most inopportune period in his life, during the last few weeks of the sale of his company. He simply did not have the time to properly devote to her.

But now, he did. And Drew was going home to do just that—woo Cami, and sweep her off her feet. He just hoped it wasn't too late.

He looked down at his phone with a frown as the thought stuck in his head. He really did hope it wasn't too late. In fact, he hadn't heard from Cami in almost two weeks. The last time he'd seen her, they'd spent an incredible night together—which had included some of the hottest sex Drew had ever experienced.

Unfortunately, he'd been called away in the early hours of the morning by an emergency. His sister, Elsie, who was currently in the middle of a nasty divorce, had called because her soon-to-be-ex-husband had shown up outside of their house and had refused to leave. Drew had to go home and physically throw him off the property so that their son wouldn't have to see his father taken away in handcuffs.

It just so happened that it had been the third time in a row that Drew had to dash early after spending the night with Cami. And it may have proved to be once too many. Since then, Cami had refused to answer his calls or return any of his messages. He'd even shown up at her house once and, though her car was in the driveway, no one had answered her door.

Now, though, Drew was free. His sister was safe from her ex-husband, protected by a restraining order, and his company was now in the very capable hands of Sylvester Kenton. He had all of the time in the world to give Cami exactly what she deserved. And he vowed to make it up to her. He was going to go home and make her fall in love with him. He didn't care what it took. He was prepared to do anything.

He *would* win the heart of Cami Hendricks.

CHAPTER TWO
Cami

It had been a rough weekend for Cami. In truth, it had been a rough few months for Cami, but this particular weekend had been particularly hard. Since her ex-husband had petitioned for primary and then full custody of their three-year-old-daughter Madison, Cami's life had been in upheaval.

The fact was, Ken wasn't even capable of taking care of Madison for two weekends a month, but now that he was engaged again, he seemed to have it in his head that he needed a trophy child to go with his new trophy wife. And, although Ken was a completely unfit parent, he had the money and resources to get what he wanted, which is why Cami was worried.

To make matters worse, last time Cami had shown up to pick her daughter up from Ken's house, she had been clinging to Ken's fiancée Natalie, not wanting to go home with Cami. It had been the first time Madison had ever behaved in such a manner and it broke Cami's heart.

When Natalie had invited Cami in under the pretense of needing to finish packing Madison's bag, Cami had realized exactly why her daughter wanted to stay with her father. Natalie and Ken had spent top dollar to build Madison a nursery that looked like something out of a Disney movie.

Of course, at that moment, it hurt to see Ken and Natalie giving Madison all of the things that Cami herself would never be able to afford. But Cami had quickly reminded herself that Ken and Natalie would never be able to give Madison the things she really needed—the things Cami was able to provide. Cami was able to give her daughter the love, support, and stability that Madison couldn't get from them, no matter how many toys they could buy her. Ken was immature and irresponsible and—Cami didn't care how much Ken' lawyer argued the opposite—her ex-husband was a roaring alcoholic.

That didn't mean that Cami was happy with letting her daughter go over there and get spoiled. She knew Madison wasn't old enough to think about what was really important in parents. And so Cami had spent the weekend worrying.

Her best friend Maggie was busy with a mysterious new relationship, and Cami didn't want to burden her mom any more by unloading on her. Her mother had already sold some of Cami's grandmother's precious jewelry to help pay for a lawyer. Cami spent the weekend lounging around and feeling sorry for herself, burying her sorrows in long bubble baths, counting down the hours until she could finally pick up her daughter.

Before dropping Madison off at Ken's house, Cami had promised her daughter that, after picking her up on Sunday, they would go do something fun together. Cami had to admit that she was probably looking forward to spending a fun night with her daughter as much as Madison was.

When it was finally time to head across town, Cami was so excited that she practically skipped to her car with a big smile on her face. The smile quickly fell, however, when she went to start her car, and it would barely turn over. She spent a few minutes trying again and again, each time praying frantically for it to work, before finally dropping her head to the steering wheel.

"Dammit!" she said, trying not to cry. "Could things get any worse?"

Because, of course, this would happen right at the moment when she was supposed to go pick up her daughter. Now, no matter what she did, she would be late. Not only would that disappoint Madison, it would also be giving Ken and Natalie even more "proof" that she was unfit to care for Madison. God knows how they would twist it to their advantage in court. They could say she was flakey and unreliable, or they could claim that she was so poor that she couldn't even afford a working car.

She could call her mom, who would come pick her up and take her to Ken's place, but it would take her mom twenty minutes to get here at least, so she'd still be late in picking up her daughter.

Cami was debating her options and trying not to panic when, out of the corner of her eye, she saw another car pull up in her driveway next to hers. She turned to that side and immediately recognized the sleek, black BMW.

"Why did I have to question whether or not things could get worse?" she said out loud, cursing herself, because things definitely had just gotten out of control.

With one last surge of hope, Cami tried to start her car again, praying that it would work and she could drive away before Drew had a chance to get out and try to talk to her.

But, as her luck would have it, her car just made a pathetic puttering sound and shut down again. Cami closed her eyes and once more tried to bury her head in her steering wheel.

She hadn't talked to Drew since the last time they'd slept together, nearly two weeks prior. Before she awoke he'd already gone, leaving her with a vague, ambiguous note. They'd slept together three times now, and each time he'd fled before the crack of dawn. The third strike was it for Cami. She realized that she wasn't a priority for him and, with everything else going on, didn't really want to deal with his games.

He'd called several times the first week, but she hadn't answered or called him back. He'd even shown up at the house once, and she'd refused to open the door. She'd told herself it was because Madison was home and awake and she never let the men she dated around her daughter. But the truth was, if she faced him, it would be near impossible to keep her resolve. And so she'd ignored him. He'd obviously gotten the message as, after the first week, he'd left her alone.

And yet, here he was. In her drive way. In fact, she didn't even have to look up in order to know that he was tapping on her window. As much as Cami wanted to remain there, like an ostrich with its head buried in the sand, she still needed to call her mother and go collect her daughter. And so she raised her head and looked at Drew.

Over the last two weeks, she'd been able to convince herself that he wasn't nearly as good looking as she'd remembered. She'd told herself she was exaggerating his sex appeal out of desire to be with someone. But now, staring into his large, whiskey colored eyes, she knew how wrong she'd been.

Drew was easily the most handsome man she'd ever seen, with dark, disheveled hair and deep sparkling eyes. He smiled at her, revealing the dimples she'd been trying to make herself forget. He was bending down in front of the driver's side window, waiting for her to open the door. Not ready to relinquish the bit of steel between them, she rolled down the window instead.

"Hi," he said, crouching down so that his face was the same height as hers.

Cami tried not to shudder at the sound of his voice—so deep and rich that it sent a tingle of longing through her. She'd remembered thinking, when they'd first met, that the voice reminded her of butter. Now it just reminded her of sex.

"Hi," she replied, trying to steer her mind away from that direction.

"Car trouble?" he asked, still smiling.

It was making her frustrated, that confident, joyous smirk. Cami was feeling anything but joyous at the moment.

"What do you think?" she snapped. To her frustration, it did nothing to erase the smile on Drew's face. In fact, he only grinned wider. "I'm glad you find this funny. I, on the other hand, am screwed. I'm supposed to pick up Madison in fifteen minutes. I'm going to have to call my mom and by the time she shows up, we'll be late to Ken's house. God knows he won't let us forget it… He'll probably use it to his advantage. And…oh God, I have no clue how I'm going to pay for this."

It wasn't until a sob escaped that Cami realized she was crying. She looked up, expecting to see the smile still spread across Drew's lips. Instead, there was a look of distress on his face and compassion in his amber eyes.

"I'm sorry," he said. "I'm just really happy to see you. I've missed you a lot. I'm not trying to make light of the situation."

The confession made Cami hitch her breath. She felt like a bushel of butterflies had been released in her stomach. Drew hadn't been able to stop thinking about her! She focused on the problem at hand to keep a stupid grin of her own from spreading across her face. She still needed to figure out the Madison situation, after all. Plus, she'd already decided that she and Drew were over.

"It's fine. But, as you can see, I'm busy. So, if you'd please excuse me, I need to go inside—because I forgot my phone—and call my mom to come and get me."

Without waiting for Drew to move out of the way, she unlatched her door, purposefully opening it into him and striking his leg.

"Cami," Drew called, finally stepping away from the car but quickly following her towards the house. "Cami, wait."

She tried to shut the house door in his face, but Drew put his arm out, easily preventing it from closing. Cami couldn't help but notice the ripple of muscle revealed beneath his short-sleeved t-shirt. She hadn't even noticed what he was wearing—she'd been too distracted by the car and surprised to see him.

But now that she noticed, she couldn't look away. He was wearing well-fitting jeans and a shirt that hugged his chest in just the right way—especially as he flexed to hold the door open. She'd never seen him so dressed down and she had to admit that he looked damn good.

"I don't have time for this," she said, purposefully making herself look away.

"You're right," Drew agreed, smiling down at her again. "You don't have time to argue with me right now. You need to go pick up your daughter, and you need to do it now. So, put Madison's car seat in the back of my car, and let's go."

"What?" Cami asked, shocked. It took her a moment to realize what he was implying. "No! That is a horrible idea!"

"Why? Do you have a better one? Wait for your mom and be late?"

"Yes…it's my only option," Cami replied stubbornly.

"Why?"

"You know I don't let Madison fraternize with the men I'm dating. Or *have* dated." Cami emphasized the past tense to remind Drew—and herself—exactly where they stood as a couple.

"Fraternize?" Drew asked. "She's a three-year-old. She doesn't even know what that word means, much less how to do it." The smile once again slipped from his face as his voice grew serious. "Listen, I know we have a lot to talk about. I know that there are things we need to work through. But right now, you need to pick up your daughter—and not be late doing it—and I am your only option. We don't have to tell Madison who I am. She most likely won't even remember me tomorrow. And if she does, we can worry about it then. Right now, we need to go."

Cami stood in the doorway for a moment, biting her lip and debating her options. Drew had taken his hand off the door, giving her the ability to slam it in his face. But then she'd have to call her mom and wait for her to get here. If she left with Drew within the next five minutes, she wouldn't be too late. Plus, she couldn't help but think about the way Drew had talked about their relationship in the present tense. To him, at least, things weren't over. Cami didn't know why that made her feel so giddy inside.

Eventually, Cami nodded in consent and followed Drew back towards the cars, locking the door behind her. She knew that this was probably a bad idea, but, at the moment, Cami couldn't bring herself to care.

CHAPTER THREE
Cami

The drive to Ken's place was awkward. Other than sparing a few words to give Drew directions, Cami sat in silence. Drew opened his mouth to speak a couple of times, but obviously decided that it was better not to try and embark on an inevitably heated conversation on their way to Cami's ex's house.

Cami, for her part, was overwhelmed by emotions, each battling for a place at the forefront of her mind. She couldn't help but think about what Drew had just implied and wonder about the state of their relationship. Was she going to give him another chance? Should she? On top of that, he was about to meet her daughter. Even if it was simply out of necessity, it was an enormous step.

On a completely different note, Cami was anxious to see Ken and Natalie. Last time she'd picked up

Madison had been a disaster. She really didn't want a repeat performance.

When thinking about things in that light, she couldn't help but be glad that Drew was there to support her. Her arrival at Ken's house in a BMW, driven by a tall, dark, sexy man, made her feel a lot less pathetic. She wanted Ken to see her moving on—to know that he wasn't the only one who thought that they'd traded up since the divorce.

"Wait here!" she commanded as Drew steered his BMW right up next to Ken's own Beemer.

Cami couldn't keep the smile from her face when she realized that Drew's was a much newer, nicer model. She knew that she was being petty, but she couldn't bring herself to care.

"Sure thing," Drew said with a wink.

He offered her a wide smile, complete with dimples. His dark eyes seemed to dance in the late afternoon sun and she had to remind herself to breathe as she got out of the car and made her way towards the house.

Cami didn't even have to ring the bell before the door was opened and Madison was barreling into her arms.

"Mommy!" the little girl cried as Cami knelt to scoop her daughter up in a tight hug.

"I've missed you, sweetheart," Cami whispered into Madison's hair as she kissed her daughter's head.

"Missed you," Madison repeated, returning her hug.

"New car?" Ken's voice interrupted her blissful moment, and Cami looked up with a glare over Madison's shoulder.

She hadn't talked to her ex since he'd called them after their first custody meeting and tried to talk her into giving up primary custody without a fight. He had since filed a petition for full custody and, if it weren't for the presence of their daughter, Cami would have to fight not to claw his eyes out because of it. Instead, she just smiled.

"No. It's my boyfriend's," she replied.

She didn't know why she lied. Her and Drew's relationship was way too complicated to be using such terms. And it was none of Ken's business anyway. But she relished the shock on his face as he looked across the driveway. Cami turned to see Drew staring back, glaring murderously at Ken. Cami wasn't sure why, but it made her like Drew all the more.

"Not that it's any of your business," Cami continued, grabbing Madison's bag from Ken's hand. "Now say goodbye to your dad Madison!"

"Bye, Da!" Madison called, but didn't reach back to hug or kiss the man goodbye.

Cami couldn't help but wonder whether she would have reached for Natalie, had she been the one at the door. Cami shook the thought out of her head and turned towards Drew's car.

"Boyfriend!" Madison shrieked as Cami opened the back door to get her situated in the car seat.

Cami cringed and avoided Drew's questioning glance.

"What happened to 'not telling her who I am'?" he asked with a smile as she slid into the passenger's seat next to him a minute later.

"I didn't tell her that," Cami said, which was really only half a lie, as she'd told Ken that, not Madison. "Ken made an assumption."

"Good." Drew simply replied.

Cami opened her mouth to argue, but Madison's little voice from the back seat interrupted her.

"Something fun, Mom?" Madison asked.

Cami's heart sank. She was hoping her daughter hadn't remembered the promise she'd made on Friday.

"Not today, sweetheart. I'm sorry. I know, I promised, but Mommy's car is broken. That's why Mr. Drew is giving us a ride. As soon as it's fixed we'll do something fun. I promise."

"Mr. Drew!" Madison cried, seemingly having stopped listening after Cami had mentioned him. "Boyfriend."

Cami cringed again. She was still turned towards the backseat, watching her daughter, but she could see the look of delight on Drew's face out of the corner of her eye.

"We can go do something fun!" Drew offered. "I don't mind. I don't have any plans."

"I don't think that's a good idea," Cami said, but Madison's shrieks from the back seat interrupted her again.

"Something fun! Something fun!" the little girl was squealing with delight.

As much as Cami wasn't sure about having Drew spend time with Madison, she really didn't want to disappoint her daughter. And so she finally heaved a deep sigh and relented.

"Fine," she said, trying not to sound too nervous. "We can do something fun."

"Awesome!" Drew replied, sounding just as excited as Madison. Cami had to bite her lip to keep from smiling at his reaction. "So," he continued. "What does one normally do for fun with a three-year-old? I take my nephew to Chuck-E-Cheese a lot."

Cami couldn't hold back the smile as she pictured Drew at Chuck-E-Cheese, running around behind a five-year-old version of himself.

"Chuck-E-Cheese is fine. We go there sometimes," Cami replied.

"Chuck-E-Cheese!" Madison repeated from the back-seat, though Cami doubted the little girl actually knew what they were referring to.

It had been a while since they'd had an opportunity to go. Money had been tight because of the custody battle. Lawyers were expensive, and Cami had been picking up overtime at the Emergency Room, where she worked as a nurse, and she was still struggling to get bills paid. Still, she could splurge tonight. Madison deserved some fun, and so did she.

As soon as they were inside the door, Cami was able to see her fantasies acted out in real life. She ran around with Madison and Drew for a while before sitting back and just watching as the man played with her daughter. He helped her win at ski ball and miniature basketball, and Cami couldn't help but laugh, even though she was sure that he was technically cheating.

They used the tickets they had won to get tiaras, which both Madison and Drew wore around the restaurant. He helped her down the slide, never leaving her side. It made Cami's insides melt in a way that let her know that she was in trouble.

When their food came, Drew held Madison on his lap and helped her eat pizza. It was sort of disconcerting, seeing the man that was usually so poised and put together—whom she had only seen dine at five-star restaurants—bounce a baby on his hip as he ate slice after slice of greasy pizza. His dark hair was in complete disarray, sticking up in every direction under the little pink tiara that sat jauntily on his head. She waited to see a sign of exasperation or annoyance on his face, but he really seemed to be having as much fun as Madison.

In fact, Drew almost looked like a completely different person, Cami realized. The tension that had always seemed to be in his shoulders was gone. He appeared to be completely relaxed and looked years younger than he had last time she'd seen him, less than two weeks prior. There was color in his cheeks and his dark eyes were sparkling with energy.

Cami barely had Madison buckled back into her car seat before the little girl was out, like a light. They'd stayed longer than Cami had meant to, especially considering Madison already had an over-stimulating weekend with her father. But she didn't want the night to end. Madison was having too much fun. And, though Cami was loath to admit it, she had too much fun as well.

The drive home was silent for a few minutes before Drew's deep voice broke Cami out of her thoughts.

"I had a lot of fun tonight, Cami," he said. She didn't know how to reply. She still wasn't sure if she was ready to give him another chance. What if he just ditched out on her again? "Listen," he continued when she didn't respond. "I know we have a lot to deal with. I have a lot to make up for. I realize that. And you have every right to be mad at me. But I've changed. I promise. I've been going through something recently, but it's over now. Things will be different."

Cami wanted to believe him. She really did. But she just wasn't sure if she could. He'd acted like this in the past. In fact, every time they'd been together, he'd acted like she was the most important thing in his universe. But then something else would come up, and he'd dash away without a second thought, revealing what his true priorities were.

"I don't know," was all Cami was able to say.

Thankfully, they were soon pulling into her driveway and she was saved from any more conversation before she'd had time to think.

Cami hurried from the car as soon as it was parked, gently unbuckling Madison and sliding her from the car seat.

"I've got to get her to bed," she whispered to Drew as she carried her daughter towards the house. She fumbled with her keys, which Drew caught and used to open the front door. "Once she's tucked in, I can come unbuckle her seat from your car. Or, if you can figure it out, you're more than welcome to do it yourself. That way you don't have to wait. Just leave it inside the door."

Without a second glance, Cami headed down the hall towards Madison's bedroom. She tenderly removed Madison's clothes and dressed her in a nightgown before tucking her into her bed. It was a testament to how much Drew had worn her out that she didn't even wake up at all.

Instead of hurrying back out to help Drew, she sat down at the edge of her daughter's bed. She told herself that she just wanted to make sure Madison was asleep before she left her side. The truth was, she was hoping Drew would take the hint and unbuckle the car seat himself—that way she wouldn't have to face him again tonight. Without the buffer of Madison there, she knew they'd have to have a serious conversation, and she just wasn't sure if she was ready.

Watching Drew spend time with Madison tonight had really done a number on Cami. All of the reasons not to date him were slowly slipping out of her mind. She'd pictured so many more days just like this one, and before she knew it, her mind went unbidden into the scariest territory: her secret dreams. Lazy Sundays where Madison didn't have to go to Ken's—where they could all wake up slow and make a big breakfast, Drew helping Madison stir the pancake batter. She thought about a wedding where Madison was the perfect little flower girl, all dressed up in a frilly white dress. She thought of Madison as a big sister, cradling a baby brother or sister in her arms as Drew looked on adoringly.

Catching herself, Cami shook her head, trying to rid her mind of such unrealistic and painful fantasies. She knew that she couldn't afford to think about things like that. When Drew had promised that things were going to be different, she had really wanted to believe him. But Cami just didn't know if she did—or *could*.

In all honesty, she didn't know if she'd ever be able to fully trust him. Even if they did work things out, Cami was pretty sure that there would always be a part of her that was waiting for the other shoe to drop—waiting for Drew to lose interest or disappear again.

And with Madison involved, things became even more complicated. Madison obviously adored Drew, and he appeared to feel the same way about her. But what if he didn't, really—not enough to stick around, at least. What would she tell her daughter then?

It was best to shut this down before it even had a chance to go downhill, Cami concluded—before Madison even had a chance to get hurt. Cami was already going to be hurt in the equation. She knew that fact undeniably. Just seeing Drew with her daughter had sent Cami over the edge. If she hadn't been attached before, she was now. But she had to think about what was best for her daughter.

So, like a coward, she hid out in her daughter's room until she was sure he was gone. She had heard the door open and close, then waited five more minutes just to be sure before heading out into the living room.

To her surprise—and a mixture of horror and relief—Drew was still there. He was relaxed on the sofa, typing something out on his phone. When he noticed she was there, he looked up and smiled at her. Cami looked away, too caught up in conflicting emotions to deal with that smile at the moment. Then she noticed the empty hallway and frowned.

"Where's the car seat?" she asked.

"I left it in the BMW," he replied.

"Oh...was it too hard to figure out? I guess I'm just used to dealing with it. Here...I'll go get it out. Sorry I made you wait."

"No," Drew said, rising and walking towards her. He grabbed her hand and placed something in it. It took Cami a moment to realize that it was a pair of keys. "I'm leaving the car with you for now, so that you'll have something to drive tomorrow. You have to get to work, after all."

"I can't let you do that," she said sternly. She wasn't going to let him leave his car with her.

"It's already done," he replied with confidence. "And I've arranged for a tow truck tomorrow morning before you head off to work. They'll pick up your car and take it to the garage I always use. These guys are top notch. I'll make sure you get the best maintenance."

"No," Cami replied, though she was now less sure of herself. She was also trying not to delight in the fact that he obviously knew her work schedule. "That's too much. Really. I'm sure I can have somebody come look at it tomorrow."

"Like I said, it's already been done. I have a car on the way to pick me up already. It's probably almost here."

"Drew," Cami replied, her voice barely more than a whisper. "I can't let you do this. *I* can't do this. Not with Madison. It's not—"

Drew squeezed her fingers gently, and Cami was suddenly all too aware that he was clutching her hand in both of his.

"I know you don't have any reason to trust me. Not yet. But I'm going to make it up to you. I'm committed to this—committed to you—I swear. And I'll prove it. Like I said before, I've been going through some stuff. But it's all over now. And I'll explain everything to you. Tomorrow night. I'm going to come back over and cook you and Madison dinner. And I'll tell you everything. Everything you want to know. And I'll start making this right."

Drew's deep voice rang with sincerity, and his whiskey-colored eyes were full of passion and what almost looked like love. Cami didn't want to believe that that was even a possibility, but she could feel her resolve slipping all the same. Drew must have noticed her hesitation, as his hands left her own and he slowly brought them up to cup her cheeks. His softly stroked her face with his thumbs, looking at her with an even more loving expression than he had only seconds before.

"Trust me. Please." he whispered before leaning forward to press his lips to hers.

The kiss was soft at first, hesitant and gentle. But his lips were so warm and enticing against hers that Cami leaned into them against her own will, deepening the kiss. Drew took that as all the consent he needed, moaning as his lips pressed more firmly against hers and his tongue licked its way into her mouth. Cami moaned as well, savoring the taste and feel of him.

Drew pressed into her, pushing her back against the wall beside the door. She could feel his body responding, hardening inside his pants. Cami herself was now growing hot and hungry as the kiss intensified. She was reminded of their last time together—the last few times, to be exact—and she felt her body pulse with need at the memories.

Just when Cami expected things to escalate even more, Drew pulled back with a sigh.

"My ride is here," he whispered against her lips before leaning in to kiss her one last time. "Goodnight, Cami. See you tomorrow."

Cami didn't even reply. She just nodded and slumped against the door once he'd shut it behind himself. She brought her fingers to her lips, touching the place where she could still feel the ghost of his mouth and the taste of his tongue against hers.

Cami realized that she was probably making a huge mistake, but she also knew that she was too far gone to fight the thing that was developing between them. Whatever happened was going to happen—she was helpless to fight it anymore—so she might as well enjoy the ride.

CHAPTER FOUR
Drew

Drew slumped against the back of the town car, closing his eyes with a sigh as the driver took him to his house.

The night had gone better than expected. He'd thought he'd maybe run into Cami—if he was lucky—and they would argue. He'd assumed things wouldn't be resolved easily, but he'd at least get to—hopefully—see her beautiful face and let her know that he was still around and not planning on going anywhere.

Instead, he'd found her in need of assistance and he'd been able to play the knight in shining armor, swooping in and being exactly what she needed. It wasn't everything she would need in order to feel secure in their relationship again—if she ever had—but it was a start. It was way more than he could have hoped for.

And he'd had way more fun than he'd thought he would while spending time with Madison. Drew had always known that he loved children—and he spent a good amount of time with his nephew Robbie—but Madison had been a delight that he hadn't been expecting. She was just as spirited and lively as her mother. She had her intelligence as well. Despite the short amount of time he'd been around Cami's daughter, he found himself feeling as attached to her as he was to her mother.

As they had played together and then eaten together—with Madison perched happily on Drew's lap—he couldn't help but imagine what it would be like if they were a real family; if both Cami and Madison were *his* family.

One day, he told himself. One day that dream would be a reality—he would ensure it. As he'd watched Madison pick up her daughter earlier in the evening, he'd stared daggers at the man who currently called himself Madison's father. Even before Drew had the pleasure of getting to know Madison, he had known that Cami's ex was complete scum—undeserving of the title of a father. And Drew was going to make sure the man didn't carry it for long.

His home was brightly lit when Drew got home, which was still surprising. Drew wasn't used to having a house full of people. Not that it was *full* per se, but Robbie was such a handful that he made it feel full all on his own.

"Uncle D," came a screech from the boy in question as Robbie threw himself at him, assuming that he would be caught before he hit the ground.

And, of course, Drew lunged forward to scoop his nephew into a tight hug. "I'm surprised you're still up, little man," Drew said, raising an eyebrow at his sister, who had followed her son into the room.

"Yeah, I guess his uncle had brought him some candy from New York City, which he ate in one sitting, without telling me," Elsie replied, raising an eyebrow of her own. "He's all yours to put to bed, since this is your fault."

Elsie smirked, and Drew couldn't even find it in himself to complain. It had been so long since he'd seen his sister smile—years, really, after her marriage had started taking a drastic turn for the worse—and he was powerless against it now. Instead, he carried his nephew into the room that had quickly become the boy's bedroom. There were already superhero posters all over the walls, and the bed was shaped like the Bat-mobile.

"I can't believe you're wearing Spider-man pajamas," Drew teased as he set Robbie down on the bed. "How can you even live with yourself, crawling into the Bat-mobile in Spider-man pajamas? What would Batman say?"

"Batman and Spiderman are friends," Robbie replied, launching into a long-winded, sugar-fueled tale about Batman and Spiderman's crime-fighting adventures.

Drew wasn't even really listening, though he nodded and gasped at regular intervals as if he was. Instead, he simply marveled at the excitement in his nephew's eyes—excitement that hadn't been there a month ago.

Since Elsie had left her abusive husband, Robbie had flourished. While both Drew and his sister had expected the boy to take it hard, crying and asking for his father at regular intervals, Robbie had proved them wrong. The shy and mostly silent child had become a rowdy, rambunctious boy.

Drew couldn't imagine the trouble he and Madison could get up to together. He couldn't wait to schedule a play date between the two of them. He also wanted Cami and Elsie to get to know each other—they both had similar stories.

Elsie probably felt like she already knew Cami, given how much Drew had been talking about her. He had expected his sister to give him a hard time—she'd never liked his ex-wife, after all. But Elsie had been nothing but supportive, listening patiently as Drew rambled on and on about the woman who had captured his heart.

Eventually, Robbie's energy petered out and Drew kissed him on the forehead before leaving him to drift off to sleep—probably still fighting crime with the superheroes in his head.

When he made his way back into the living room, Elsie was still up. She motioned for him to sit next to her on the sofa and handed him a glass of wine.

"So?" she prompted once he was comfortable.

"So?" he repeated, playing dumb.

"I take it that, since you weren't back twenty minutes after you left, you at least got to see her."

"Yeah," Drew replied, unable to stop the smile that spread across his face as he thought about the night he'd just had.

"C'mon, tell me all about it."

"I actually got there right in time. Her car wouldn't start, and she needed to pick up her daughter from her ex's house. So I gave her a ride."

"Did you get to meet the scumbag?" Elsie asked excitedly, having heard all about Cami's custody battle.

"No," Drew moped. "But I glared at him from the car. I couldn't help myself."

"Down, boy," Elsie replied, patting his head as if he were a dog. "So, then what?"

"Well, I guess Cami had promised Madison that they would do something fun when she picked her up, but without a car, she was at a loss. So I agreed to chauffeur them. We went to Chuck-E-Cheese."

Elsie's entire face lit up at the news.

"You got to spend time with her daughter?" she gushed. "That's a big deal. Huge!"

"I know," Drew replied, the dopey smile on his face getting even bigger. "And it was great. Madison was great. She's so much like her mother—fiery and intelligent. And watching Cami with her daughter, oh my God—it made me love her more, if that's possible."

Drew suddenly realized that he'd used the word *love* and slammed his mouth shut, but it was too late. Elsie had noticed. Her eyes got wide and soft.

"Ohhhhh," she cooed. "That's so sweet. So things are good between you two now?"

Drew took a deep breath, thinking his answer over before he replied.

"Not yet—not completely, at least. But I think they will be. I'm going over there tomorrow night to cook them both dinner. And, honestly, I could use your help. I have no idea what to make for a three-year-old."

"Oh, don't sweat it. Just make lobster mac-and-cheese. Kids love it, and Cami will appreciate that you made the meal sophisticated enough with the lobster. I have a recipe, in fact. Trust me, you can't go wrong."

"Thanks, Elsie," he replied as he rose. He leaned down and kissed his sister on the forehead. "I'm glad you're here."

"Me, too," she replied with a slightly sad smile.

Later, Drew lay in bed awake for a long time, mentally planning the meal he would make the following evening. His mind then shifted to what it would be like if he, Cami, and Madison were a real family. Outings like the one they had gone on tonight would be a regular occurrence.

They'd make dinner together, take vacations together—Drew smiled at the thought of Madison at Disney World. She'd be even more exhausting than she'd been tonight, but it would be so worth it to see her face light up and hear her squeals of delight. Drew wasn't sure how his mind had moved from planning a dinner to planning their future together, but he knew that it would happen.

He just needed to play his cards right tomorrow night.

CHAPTER FIVE
Cami

Just as Drew had promised, a tow truck arrived the following morning at 7:30 sharp. The men were quick and skillful at their job, and in only a matter of minutes, the car was all hooked up and ready to go.

"We're taking her across town to Executive Motors," the driver said, handing her a business card that listed the auto mechanic's address and phone number.

She tried to offer the men a tip, but they both assured her that they'd already been well taken care of. Cami wondered how much Drew had already spent on her but tried not to think about it in the moment. She'd find a way to pay him back—though it might not be until after her custody trial.

A quick Google search revealed that Executive Motors was the most well reviewed—and most expensive—auto shop in town. As with the tow truck, Cami forced the worry from her mind, knowing that

Drew would most likely pay for everything and she would think of a way to pay him back later.

Nervously, Cami then loaded Madison into Drew's BMW and headed towards her mother's house. She'd never driven a car half as expensive and, at first, she was convinced that she'd do something to ruin it. However, she soon relaxed and began enjoying the smooth, quiet ride. It wasn't until she was behind the wheel of a luxury car that she realized how poorly her ten-year-old piece of junk performed.

"I didn't hear you pull up," her mother said as Cami carried Madison inside.

"Um…" Cami replied, not sure how to tell her mom the truth.

Instead, she busied herself with getting Madison situated. When she came back into the living room, her mother was standing in the open door way, hands on her hips, looking at the BMW with a raised eyebrow.

"You better start explaining—and that explanation better not include the robbery of a car dealership," her mom said, though there was humor in her voice.

"Actually," Cami said as she walked towards the car, "it's a little more complicated than that."

"I'm listening!" her mother replied.

"So…I was heading out to go pick up Madison from Ken's last night when my good-for-nothing car wouldn't start. I was about to call you to come pick me up when Drew pulled into the driveway."

"I thought you'd ended it with that boy," her mom stated, though she was smiling.

Cami knew her mother thought she should have tried harder to make things work with Drew, if only for his money. Cami rolled her eyes.

"I tried. And I hadn't heard from him in a week. Turns out he'd been on a business trip and had just returned. He ended up taking me to get Madison and he left me his car until mine is fixed."

She left out the part about dinner and about being half in love with him already. But she knew her mother could see it in her face, as she was beaming at her daughter with a knowing look.

"Isn't that nice."

"I'll pay him back," Cami said, trying not to smile in return. "Now I have to leave or I'm going to be late. I won't be late tonight. I'm not picking up any extra time so I'll be here at five."

"See you then," her mother said, still smiling as she turned back into her house.

As soon as she was out of her mother's view, Cami finally let the dopey grin she'd been suppressing spread across her face. Fight as she might, she couldn't keep it off her face throughout her entire shift.

She thanked her lucky stars that Maggie didn't usually work Mondays as her best friend would have known something was up. Ashley continued to give her odd looks, but thankfully didn't ask. Ashley was much better about knowing when Cami wasn't ready to talk about something yet.

* * *

WHEN HER SHIFT WAS OVER, she almost got confused in the parking lot, looking for her own car. She was a little self-conscious as she climbed into the sleek vehicle and looked around to make sure none of her coworkers had seen her. She really didn't want to answer any questions.

"Stay for dinner," her mother said as soon as Cami was through the door.

"I can't," Cami replied. "I have plans."

"Plans, huh?" her mother asked. She seemed a little too happy at the news. "Anything to do with that fancy car you've got outside?"

"No, Mom," Cami deadpanned. "I don't have plans with a car."

Her mother didn't answer, just continued to smile as Cami readied Madison and headed home. To her surprise, she was home less than ten minutes when Drew pulled up in her driveway. He was driving a classic Thunderbird, painted baby blue, which had its top down.

"A little ostentatious, don't you think?" Cami asked as Drew pulled a few bags of groceries from the back seat.

"Yeah," Drew said a little sheepishly, though Cami had only been joking. "That's why I don't actually drive it much. But someone else has my other car."

Now it was Cami's turn to look sheepish.

"I'm sorry," she said. "You can have it back any time."

"Don't be ridiculous," Drew replied, following her into the house. "I'm happy to loan it to you. And my baby out there doesn't get driven nearly enough. I'm sure she's excited to get out on the road."

"She?" Cami asked as Drew moved ahead of her into the kitchen and placed the bags on the counter. "The tow truck guys from this morning referred to my car as a she as well. What's with that?"

Drew just shook his head, feigning disappointment.

"Women never understand," he muttered under his breath.

Cami opened her mouth to respond, but was interrupted by a little body shooting past her.

"Drew!" Madison squealed as she wrapped her tiny arms around Drew's leg.

Cami swallowed and tried not to melt as she watched the man in question bend down and scoop her daughter up.

"Hey, you little rascal. Have you had a good day?"

"Yep," Madison replied, bringing her hand up to pat Drew's cheek. "Chuck-E-Cheese?" she asked hopefully.

"Not today, kiddo," he replied. "I'm going to make dinner tonight. Do you like macaroni and cheese?"

"She loves it," Cami assured him as he began to unpack the groceries, Madison still in his arms.

"Good," he said, "because I have an awesome recipe for homemade mac and cheese that you'll love as well. He shot Cami a warm smile over Madison's head and any attempt on Cami's part not to melt failed.

"Can I help?" she asked, trying to keep her wits about her.

"Nope," Drew replied as he pulled a bottle of wine—Cami's favorite, of course—out of the bag. "You just sit and relax. Madison and I have got this."

Drew sat Madison on the counter next to him, making sure she was safe and secure as he opened the wine and poured Cami a glass. Madison on his hip, he methodically scoped out her kitchen, opening cabinets and pulling out drawers until he knew exactly what she had and where it was located.

Feeling not needed—and not minding it one bit—Cami finally sat down at the counter and sipped her wine as she watched Drew and Madison make dinner. Though Drew obviously knew exactly what he was doing, he constantly asked Madison's advice and let her help whenever it was safe for her to do so. The sight was almost too much for Cami to endure.

She couldn't help but think about how this would work permanently. She could come home every night to the sight of this man cooking her dinner as he carried her daughter around on his hip. Cami felt her throat constrict at the thought as she tried her best to push the images out of her head.

To combat her wayward imagination, she continued to remind herself that she couldn't trust Drew. He was hot and cold. That was his MO. Sure, he was all about Cami and Madison right now, but he'd already proved that they weren't his top priority. She couldn't let herself get attached and she shouldn't be allowing her daughter to get attached either.

By the time they sat down to dinner, Cami was deep in her head, caught up in her own conflicting thoughts. Drew had to have noticed her change in mood, but he didn't say or act any differently. When she was slow to respond, he would simply turn to Madison and speak to her instead.

Drew eventually handed Madison off to Cami to get situated in her highchair while he plated up their meals and brought them to the table. Cami had to admit that the food was amazing. Everyone had a healthy portion of homemade macaroni and cheese.

"This is amazing," Cami gushed after she swallowed her first bite of the creamy pasta. "I've never had it home made before. I don't think I'll ever be able to eat the boxed kind again."

"Glad you enjoy it," Drew replied with a sheepish smile. "I have to admit, it's my sister's recipe. I wasn't quite sure what to make for Madison."

"Well," Cami said, forgetting her reticence, "you did a great job."

Dinner was a warm affair after that. Cami was surprised—though by now she probably shouldn't have been—to see that Drew paused his own meal to help Madison eat just as much as Cami herself did.

After the meal, Cami excused herself to bathe her daughter and put her to bed. Drew told her to take her time, as he had a huge mess to clean up.

"Don't worry about it," Cami told him. "You cooked. The least I can do is clean."

"I don't mind," Drew said. "You just take care of your daughter."

Madison did not want to say good night to Drew and it was a fussy bath time. Thankfully, however, she'd tuckered herself out and was asleep before Cami could even finish one bedtime story.

Cami sat at the foot of her daughter's bed for the second night in a row, too reluctant to go confront the man in her kitchen. But, Cami was under no delusions that Drew would leave if she hid out in Madison's bedroom here long enough.

What was he expecting? Did he think they were going to have sex? *Were* they going to have sex? Did

Cami want that? Her body was screaming yes, reminding her of their last few passionate trysts together. But, in her heart, she knew it was a bad idea.

Deciding to take each moment as it came, she eventually headed back towards the kitchen. To her surprise, the kitchen was spotless, with all the food put away and the dishes clean. But Drew was nowhere to be seen, so she wandered into the living room.

Drew was sitting at one end of the couch. On the coffee table before him was the bottle of wine, with both of their glasses topped off.

Hesitantly, Cami made her way into the living room and perched at the other end of the couch. Drew leaned forward, picking up her glass and handing it to her. But then, instead of staying close to her as Cami had been expecting, Drew returned to his end of the couch, leaving a good bit of distance between them.

"So," Drew began. "I promised you an explanation." Cami didn't say anything, so Drew continued. "I know I've seemed distracted lately and haven't been able to give you the attention you deserve. But that's all changed now. I promise."

Cami wanted to speak up, tell him that damn right, he hadn't given her the attention she deserved, and to demand answers. But, instead, she remained silent, giving Drew a chance to speak his piece.

"For the last several months, I've been in the middle of trying to sell my company. When we met, at the Emersons' beach house, I was only there because I was trying to impress an investor. The man—James Cook—was there with his awful wife and daughter. You met his daughter, remember? We had breakfast together. Her name was Analise… She wouldn't shut up about herself."

"I remember," Cami replied.

Her mind went back to that weekend. She knew exactly the moment he was talking about. Cami and Drew had been having breakfast together the morning after they'd fooled around on the beach. He'd seemed to really be interested in her—until Analise had shown up. Then Drew had shifted his attention solely to the conceited model. Cami had been hurt and confused at the time but, if he was trying to impress her father, his actions made a bit more sense.

"Anyway. The man that was offering to buy my company, Sylvester Kenton, he didn't want to finalize the deal until *his* investor—Cook—signed off on it. And Cook didn't want to sign off on the contract that I had insisted upon. You see, I was stipulating that none of my employees be terminated. I couldn't bring myself to sell unless they were all secure. But I didn't want to hold on to my company anymore. Too much stress. Too many long hours. I wanted to settle down, start a family. So that's where my focus has been for the last few months. That's why I've been busy and unable to treat you the way you deserve to be treated. But the deal was finalized on Saturday. The company is sold. I'm free to take care of you now and I want to do that."

"Why," Cami interrupted, genuinely bewildered, "why didn't you just tell me that? It would have been so much easier than acting all hot and cold around me."

"I'm sorry," Drew said, looking down at his hands. "I should have. I guess that was just my own insecurities getting the better of me. I told you about my ex-wife, right? Pretty much every woman I meet is just after my money. I think I was scared to tell you that I was about to sell my company for two and a half a billion dollars until I was completely sure that you liked me for me."

"Have I ever given you the impression that I was after your money?" Cami asked indignantly.

"No!" Drew assured her. "I know you aren't like that. I think I've always known. That's why I've been into you since the moment I met you. Well, one of the reasons. I was just being insecure. I know that now and I'm sorry."

Cami thought about her own insecurities. Perhaps if she wasn't constantly waiting for Drew to ditch her, perhaps if she wasn't always waiting for the other shoe to drop, things might have gone a little more smoothly too.

"I think I just needed to be sure," Drew continued. "And I'm sure now. In fact, I've never been more sure of anything in my entire life."

Those words—and the promise they contained—sent a chill down Cami's spine. She suddenly felt sure of something as well.

"I understand," Cami said after a moment, offering him a reassuring smile. She then placed her wine glass on the table and crawled across the couch to give him a soft kiss on the lips. Drew leaned into the kiss, deepening it for a moment. But he soon pulled away.

"I should probably go, if you want," he replied, moving to stand.

"No," Cami said, standing herself. She offered him her hand. "Stay."

"Okay," Drew replied. He placed his hand in hers and let her lead them towards the bedroom.

Every other time they'd been together, Drew had been in charge. And Cami loved that. She really did. But this time, Cami wanted to be the one to show Drew just how much she appreciated his honesty. She felt the need to prove that she wasn't just after his money—that she cared about him.

This was why, as soon as the door to the bedroom was locked, Cami stopped. She turned towards Drew and pushed him onto the bed. Even though he was tall and strong, he was caught off guard and went toppling back against the blankets. Cami smirked at his puzzled expression as she leaned to pull a condom out of the nightstand, tossing it onto the bed next to him.

She then climbed onto the bed. He moved to sit up, but Cami stilled him with a hand against his chest.

"Not tonight," she said with a smile. "Tonight, it's my turn to take care of you."

"But—" Drew began.

"No buts," Cami interrupted. "Your only job is to lay there and enjoy yourself as I take care of you."

Drew looked like he wanted to argue, but eventually, he relented and relaxed back against the bed. Cami moved to the foot of the bed and began by pulling off his shoes and socks. She then straddled his waist as she ran her hands up and down his chest, first outside of his shirt, then below it. He shivered as her nails raked along his flesh. Cami allowed herself to settle down against him, grinding her body against his hardening flesh.

"I see you're already enjoying this," Cami replied as she pulled his shirt up and over his head.

She spent a few minutes gliding her hands against his hard, muscular chest, exploring it first with her fingers, then with her mouth and tongue. When Drew was a moaning mess, Cami finally crawled off him, unfastening his fly before pulling both pants and underwear off in one fluid motion.

Cami couldn't stifle the moan of her own as his swollen, dripping erection popped up against his stomach. Drew reached down to grope himself, but Cami stopped him.

"Nope. No touching, remember? Two can play this game," she said, smirking at his glare.

Oh, how the tables had turned. Making sure not to touch him herself, she climbed off the bed and slowly began to undress as sensually as she could.

Drew moaned at the sight, his cock twitching and leaking pre-cum across his stomach as he unconsciously thrust his hips into the air. Cami remembered being in the exact same position when he'd teased her. It made her smile. Once she was naked, she crawled back up the bed, rubbing her hands along his legs, thighs, and hips, but avoiding the spot he wanted her to touch the most.

Eventually, Cami grabbed the condom, opening it with her teeth while her other hand finally reached out and grasped his throbbing erection. Cami had planned to slip the condom on right away, but found that she loved the feeling of him, hot and heavy in her hand. And so she spent a while sliding her fingers up and down his cock at a teasingly slow pace.

After only a few minutes, Cami's hand was wet with his excitement and she could feel her own juices trickling down her thighs. She didn't think *she* would be able to wait much longer. And so, at an agonizingly slow pace, she slid the condom over his rigid length.

Once the sheath was secure, Cami didn't waste much more time before straddling Drew and guiding him against her aching pussy. Then, her self-control shot, she pushed down onto him, completely enveloping him in her hungry body.

This position allowed him into her deeper than ever before and she had to pause for a moment to acclimate to his substantial size. She couldn't bring herself to wait too long, though, and was soon rocking back and forth as his massive cock pulsed within her.

He looked beautifully debauched beneath her, face twisted in pleasure and pupils wide with desire. She could see his eyes on her bouncing breasts and, having a little mercy, reached down to grab his hands, placing them on her aching nipples.

Drew took this as permission to participate and squeezed her mounds roughly as he thrust up into her body. Cami, driven half out of her mind at the sensation, ground down on his cock in earnest. He pushed up to meet her with just as much vigor, their bodies slamming together as Cami felt her orgasm building within her.

"I'm not going to last much longer," he panted huskily.

The sound of his voice, combined with the confession itself was enough to send Cami over the edge.

"Come for me," she commanded as she rode Drew through her own climax, wave after wave of pleasure pulsating through her, extended by the sight and sensation of Drew losing himself beneath her.

Spent, Cami collapsed against Drew's chest, panting heavily. They lay there for a long time, Drew still inside her, as they both regained their breath. Eventually, Drew slid out from under her, disposing of the condom and helping her under the covers. He crawled in next to her and nestled against her back.

"I'm not going to stay the night," he whispered in her ear, which made Cami tense for a second. "Relax," he continued, obviously sensing her distress. "I just don't want to confuse Madison by being here when she wakes up. But I'll come back over tomorrow night. I can make the two of you dinner again. If that's okay with you, that is."

"That's perfect," Cami replied with a smile before letting herself drift off to sleep.

CHAPTER SIX
Cami

The following week went by quickly. "Time flies when you're having fun," Cami's mom had always said. Cami was realizing now, more than ever, how true that saying really was.

Drew came over most nights and made dinner for Madison and Cami. Most evenings, he stayed late to make quiet but passionate love to Cami while Madison was asleep, though he never spent the night. On the nights that he didn't come to their house, they had been invited over to his.

Cami was getting to know Drew's sister, Elsie, whom she had taken to liking right off the bat. She could see what Maggie meant when she'd said that the two of them would have a lot in common—and not just abusive ex-husbands and small children they were raising practically alone. Elsie was funny and smart and fun to be around. And Robbie and Madison had taken to each other well, despite the slight age difference, and were now as thick as thieves.

As much as Cami had enjoyed getting to know Drew's family and having Drew bond with Madison, when he mentioned that his sister and nephew would be out of town for the weekend visiting a friend, Cami made plans for Madison to have an overnight stay with her grandma. She wanted to be able to spend an evening alone with Drew—and to make love to him without having to worry about how loud they could get.

After dropping Madison off with her mom, who gave Cami another one of her knowing smirks, Cami made her way across town to Drew's house. Although his house was just as large and nice as Ken's, he was in a much less ostentatious neighborhood. It was actually situated on a small plot of land near the edge of town.

As she pulled into the long driveway—which separated the house from the road—Cami imagined what it would be like to come home to this view every day. The three-story house sat in a little clearing, surrounded by trees. There was a large deck on one side and a pool in the back, which was enclosed by a fence to keep the children from accidentally falling in.

Since up until very recently, Drew had spent almost all of his time at work, he hadn't put a lot of effort into landscaping. Cami imagined what it would be like with flowerbeds and a vegetable garden. They'd get a dog or two. Hell, they were even far enough outside of town to get a pony for Madison when she was older.

Cami shook her head, trying to get her mind away from such thoughts. She and Drew had really only been an actual couple for less than a week. Yes, so far he'd been consistent and reliable. But she still wasn't one hundred percent sure that she could trust him.

Drew had the door open before Cami had even stepped up onto the porch. He was wearing a bright orange apron over jeans and a t-shirt. His feet were bare, his hair a complete mess, and there was dark stubble along his jaw. He looked relaxed and happy and Cami didn't even try to fight the urge to lean in and kiss him, running her hands through his dark locks.

"Hi," she said against his lips.

"Hi," he replied with a smile as he led her in.

The house was as magnificent on the inside as it had been on the outside, though just as bare. According to Drew, Elsie had brought a lot when she'd moved in, so Cami couldn't imagine how empty it had been before. Apparently, he'd had the house custom built for his ex, thinking they would have a large family, and when she'd left, she'd taken almost everything with her. Drew said he didn't mind. Now that he had free time, he could work on making this house a home.

He hadn't outright stated that he wanted her help in decorating because he wanted it to be her home too, one day, but it seemed the assumption was there. And Cami wasn't sure how she felt about that. She was still waiting for something bad to happen, she realized. Good things didn't happen to her, after all.

"How was your day?" Drew asked as he took her bag and set it on the couch in the living room. He led her into the kitchen, where he handed her an already poured glass of wine.

"It was good," Cami replied. "With all the custody stuff going on, I've gotten to where I really value my weekends with Madison more than ever. We went to the park and the farmer's market, then out to lunch."

"Oh," Drew replied, looking uncertain. "You didn't have to leave her with your mom tonight, since you don't get to spend every weekend with her…at the moment." Drew's confidence in Cami's chances at winning the custody battle always made her feel better.

"No," Cami replied, trying to assuage his guilt. "We had a great time. Now she's having fun with grandma. I needed this. Trust me."

"Okay," Drew replied, pressing up against her for another kiss before he moved back towards the stove, where dinner was simmering.

"What's for dinner?" Cami asked, coming up behind him and resting her head on his shoulder to look over him at the stove.

"Fettuccine Alfredo with chicken," he replied with a proud smirk.

"Well, I can't wait. It smells amazing."

"Thanks."

"What did you do today?" Cami asked as she pulled herself up onto the bar stool away from where he was cooking.

"Not much," Drew admitted. "After I saw Elsie and Robbie off, I did a little bit of paperwork for the philanthropic foundation I'm trying to start, but there's not much I can do on a Saturday."

"Tell me more about the foundation," Cami prompted.

He'd mentioned it in passing a few times, but the only time they'd had away from Madison in the last week had been spent making love, so she still didn't know the details.

"It's going to focus on fighting poverty in the U.S. I want to partner with local food banks and Habitat for Humanity chapters, things like that. As much as I can, I want to work with existing institutions instead of reinventing the wheel. You know what I mean?"

Cami nodded. Drew looked so excited when he talked about the foundation that it made Cami excited as well.

"I also want to work with inner city schools, funding after school programs and tutoring for underprivileged and at-risk youth."

"That sounds awesome!"

"Yeah," Drew replied. "I'm pretty excited."

"Is there anything I can do to help?" Cami asked. Drew stopped what he was doing and looked at her for a moment, tilting his head questioningly.

"You'd really want to help?" he asked, as if anyone *wouldn't* want to help with a project like that.

"Of course!" Cami said. "I don't really know what I could do. I guess I could use my medical expertise. Maybe we could work on setting up a free health clinic in a low-income neighborhood."

Even as Cami heard herself speaking, she knew it was a bad idea. She didn't need to get this involved this fast. But she couldn't help herself. And Drew obviously didn't think she was being too forward, as he shut off the stove and moved towards her with a goofy smile on his face.

He took the wine glass out of her hand and set it on the counter beside her before moving between her legs and pressing his mouth against hers. She wrapped her legs around his hips as she perched on the stool, opening to him as he deepened the kiss.

"That's amazing," he whispered between kisses. "*You're* amazing. I don't know what I did to deserve you, but I'm so grateful I get to have you just the same."

Cami couldn't help but think that the exact opposite was true. Drew was the amazing one. He was the one who hardly seemed real, now that they were together. He was wealthy and handsome, sweet and caring. He wanted to spend time with her daughter and he planned on spending the rest of his life helping the poor. Not to mention that he was amazing in bed.

That's why she was waiting for things to get bad again—because Cami was never able to keep good things. She was the girl that bad things happened to, not the girl that got to marry Prince Charming.

But, as Drew ran his fingers through her hair and bit her lip hungrily, those thoughts were being pushed from her mind by the desire building in her body. She was about to suggest they put dinner on hold for a while and head upstairs—or just have some fun on the kitchen table—when her phone rang. She tried to ignore it, but it was the creepy theme from *Halloween*, the ringtone she'd downloaded specifically for her ex-husband. The phone went to voicemail after four rings, but soon rang again.

"That's Ken," Cami said, pulling away from the kiss.

Drew let go of her and stepped back, frowning. "Your ex-husband? Why would he be calling? I thought he wasn't supposed to contact you except about his weekends with Madison."

"He's not," Cami said, confused. "Should I answer it?"

"Yes," Drew replied, going to fetch her purse from the living room for her. "It may be important if he keeps calling."

By the time Drew was back with her phone, Ken was calling for the third time.

"Hello?" Cami answered, now feeling worried.

"Took you long enough," Ken snarled. "Having sex with your new boyfriend or something?" Cami cringed, not letting Ken know how accurate his accusation was. "In front of our daughter, no doubt. That's disgusting. You're disgusting."

Ken words were slightly slurred, letting Cami know that he'd been drinking. Her apprehension soon turned to fury.

"You're disgusting to even entertain that possibility," Cami replied, not bothering to keep the anger out of her tone. She knew that Ken's accusations weren't any less repulsive because he was drunk. "I thought you stopped drinking, Ken," Cami growled. "What do you want?"

"I want to know why you're having sex with that guy in front of our daughter."

"You know what," Cami replied. "I don't have to deal with this. You know you're not supposed to contact me this way."

"Well, you won't have to deal with me much longer. Pretty soon, Madison will be all mine and you and your stupid little boyfriend can forget all about her."

"Not going to happen," Cami replied with all of the confidence she could muster.

"Yes it will. Natalie wants a child, I'm getting her a child."

"What?" Cami asked, suddenly enraged. "This is about Natalie? What Natalie wants is completely inconsequential. Cami isn't Natalie's daughter and she never will be."

"Oh yes, she will," Ken jeered. "We both know I'm going to win this. Then Madison will be all ours. Natalie will have the daughter she wants, and you'll have what you deserve: nothing."

Cami, unable to handle another minute of this conversation, hung up the phone and let out a frustrated growl.

"What?" Drew asked, having only been able to hear her side of the dialogue.

"He was drunk and being an asshole. I think he was calling just to intimidate me, but he let it slip that this whole custody battle is Natalie's idea. He doesn't even want Madison. He's just doing this because his fiancée wants children and can't have any of her own."

Cami felt tears of frustration slip down her face, but she couldn't stop them. She was so upset that she could barely contain herself. She wanted to punch something. She wanted to punch Ken, if she was being honest, and Natalie too.

Drew didn't reply. He just stepped forward and pulled her into a tight hug.

"You know the worst part?" she asked.

"What?" he said softly, gently rubbing circles against her back.

"They're going to win."

"No, they aren't," Drew answered quickly and confidently.

"Yes, they are. My lawyer is complete shit. He's the reason I got nothing in the divorce."

"Then why are you still letting him represent you?" Drew asked, pulling away slightly to look at her, his eyebrows raised.

"Because I can't afford anyone else," she sobbed. "I can barely afford this. I'm picking up overtime at the hospital and my mom is selling my grandma's expensive jewelry and we're still barely covering the bills."

"Oh, Cami," Drew said, pulling her back into his arms. "Why didn't you say anything?"

"Why would I? It's not your responsibility."

Drew didn't reply to that, he just continued to hug Cami until her sobs slowly subsided. He then helped her to the sofa in the living room. He left her there and returned with another glass of wine a second later.

"Rest here for a little bit, and drink this. I have something to attend to. I'll be right back."

Cami was a little annoyed that he would leave her while she was so upset, but she reminded herself that this wasn't his problem and she wasn't his responsibility. She was a grown woman and couldn't rely on others to take care of her.

And so she took deep breaths between sips of wine and tried to will herself into calming down. A few minutes later, Drew returned to the living room, his phone in his hand, and sat down beside her.

"I just got off the phone with Norman Michaels," he informed her. "He's the best family lawyer in the state. He's taking care of my sister's divorce right now and it's going incredibly smoothly. He's agreed to take you on."

"Drew, I can't—" Cami began but he interrupted her.

"You can and you will, Cami. This is your daughter we're talking about. We need to fight this with everything we can." The word *we* sent waves of warmth through her body, allowing her to finally calm down a bit. "We can't let Ken win. And now, with Michaels, we won't. Trust me, when Michaels is done with him, your ex won't even have partial custody. If he's the drunk, abusive asshole he just proved himself to be over the phone, Madison doesn't need to be anywhere near him…ever."

Cami just nodded, still unable to wrap her mind around the rapid change of events that had just gone down.

"So Michaels is available to meet with you first thing on Monday morning. I told him you could be there at eight. That may make you slightly late for work, and I'm sorry. But it's best to get this ball rolling as soon as possible."

"No," Cami said, still a little stunned. "I mean, eight is fine, no need to be sorry. My boss will understand."

"Great. As soon as you meet with Michaels and sign the paperwork, his team will notify your old lawyer that he's lost a client and begin building a case against Ken. Trust me, these guys are efficient. We'll hopefully have this entire thing dealt with and over in just a couple of weeks."

Cami nodded, more tears slipping down her cheeks. This time, however, they were tears of joy. She hadn't felt this confident in a long time.

"Thank you," she whispered, pulling Drew into another hug.

"Of course," Drew replied as he held her tight. "I just wish you'd mentioned your financial difficulties sooner. We could have had this thing dealt with weeks ago. Are you okay now?"

"Better than okay," Cami answered honestly. "I'm happy that Ken called. I'm more than happy to take some drunken verbal abuse if it leads to a victory in court."

"You know," Drew replied, "I doubt it will even make it to court at this point. Especially not if Ken is still drinking. All we need to do is prove it."

"But how?"

"That's the lawyers' job. Let's leave it to them and go finish dinner."

Cami nodded, allowing Drew to help her up and usher her towards the kitchen. Reclaiming her perch on the bar stool, she watched the amazing, brilliant, gorgeous man in front of her finish dinner, hardly believing that this was her life.

CHAPTER SEVEN
Cami

Cami excitedly told her mom all about the new lawyer when she arrived to pick up Madison the following morning. If possible, her mom was even more excited than she was. Cami assumed this was not just because Cami had a new lawyer and thus the outcome of the custody battle was a lot more certain, but also because Cami now had a wealthy man in her life who could take care of her. That was the part of the equation that made Cami cringe and feel guilty, not sure how she would ever be able to pay Drew back. But Drew had been right—Madison was more important than Cami's pride. Even if Cami was still constantly waiting to wake up and realize it was all just a dream.

Despite her insecurity and inherent pessimism, Cami dropped her daughter off with her mother extra early on Monday morning and made her way over to the nice part of town. Cami was quite happy to realize that her new lawyer's office was in the same area as Ken's. She felt like it finally put her on equal footing with her ex. In fact, if Norman Michaels was anywhere near as good as Drew claimed, she had a much stronger advantage than Ken did.

The office was just as nice, but not nearly as alienating as Gil Dubois' had been. The friendly secretary smiled at Cami as she introduced herself, then told her to go right in because the lawyer was already waiting on her.

"Mr. Michaels?" Cami asked as she stepped into the room.

The man in question smiled warmly at her and rose to lean over the desk and shake her hand. "Please," he said, motioning for her to take a seat across from him. "Call me Norm. Everyone does."

Despite his smile and friendly demeanor, however, Cami found him extremely intimidating. She couldn't help but be glad that he was on her side and not Ken's.

"So," Norm began once Cami was comfortable. "Drew Sloane told me a little of what was happening over the phone the other night, but I want to hear it all from you. Be as detailed as possible. Try not to leave anything out."

"Okay," Cami replied. "Where do you want me to start?"

"Start with the divorce," Norm told her. "Why you divorced, how the custody was decided then, anything else you feel is important. Do you mind if I record this?"

Cami nodded, composing her thoughts as Norm placed a recording device on the table before her.

"It's just so I don't miss anything later, and so my team can become aquatinted with your case," he assured her with a smile when she looked at it dubiously.

She nodded and began.

"Well, Ken and I divorced three years ago because his drinking had gotten out of hand. I guess that's not true. His drinking had been out of hand for a long time. But he started to get…not really violent, but as if he *could* get violent. Does that make any sense?" Norm nodded, so she continued. "He would scream and threaten me a lot. Every now and then he would push me, but nothing too forceful. And he was drunk almost every night. He was going out a lot. And I started to suspect that he was cheating on me. I brought it up, and he denied it—but that's what made me sure of it… He just *looked* guilty. Plus, I'd seen the way he was acting around his secretary, Natalie—the woman who is now his fiancée. Even then, I think, something was going on between them."

"So what was the final straw?"

"That conversation, where he denied cheating and I knew he was lying. He yelled and pushed me. It scared me. I didn't want Madison growing up around that."

"And so you left?"

"Yes. I left. And filed for divorce. My lawyer sucked, but he was all I could afford. And Ken's lawyers were amazing. He had a team. I didn't get any spousal support and barely any child support. It was fine though. All I really cared about was Madison. And I was awarded primary custody of Madison."

"How did you manage that, if your lawyer was so bad?"

"Ken wasn't concerned with custody at all at the time. He rarely even kept the weekends he was awarded with her. He saw her once a month, *maybe,* and then it was usually only for one night."

"What changed?"

"Natalie. They became serious, so Madison started going over there more, every other weekend. But then he called a few months ago and told me that he wanted primary custody. I refused, so he filed for full custody. He called me drunk the other night and let it slip that it's only because of Natalie. She wants kids and can't have any of her own. He couldn't care less about Madison himself."

"So he's still drinking?" Norm asked, leaning forward.

"Yeah," Cami replied. "He claimed he wasn't during our initial meeting—his lawyer talked about nearly two years of documented sobriety, but I had seen him drunk within the last year alone. And, of course, there was the other night."

"Tell me about the other night."

"Well, after our first meeting—the initial one with our lawyers—Ken called me. And I mean, *right* after. I was still in my car in the parking lot. And he tried to intimidate me into giving over primary custody. I don't know if he thought I had such a slim chance of winning or what, but he just assumed I'd hand Madison over. But, obviously, I laughed into the phone and I told him not to contact me again, except about his custody weekends with Madison. Anything else he could go through our lawyers."

"And since then?"

"I haven't really heard from him at all. Usually, he picks Madison up from my mother's so that I don't have to deal with him at all. I talked to him briefly on Sunday night of last week, when I picked Madison up from his house, but that was it—until the phone call Saturday night."

"Thank you, Ms. Hendricks," Norm replied, leaning over to turn off the recorder. "It sounds like a cut-and-dried case. If he's still drinking, I'll prove it. This should be over quickly. I have no doubt in my mind that we'll win. In fact, how would you feel about turning it around and petitioning for full custody yourself?"

"I think that would be ideal," Cami replied with a smile. "If you think I can win, I mean. I really don't want Madison around him at all. He's an abusive drunk."

"Of course not!" Norm said. "We can make that happen, I assure you. Now, if you'll just sign some papers, we can get the ball rolling.

The best part was, Cami didn't even have to fire her old lawyer. After the paperwork was signed, Norman's office would contact him themselves. Cami didn't have to worry about anything.

It really was the best Cami had felt in weeks. Her relationship with Drew was in a great place, she was still driving around in his BMW—though she had a sneaking suspicion that her car was fixed and Drew had just decided that it wasn't nice enough for her. Even that, which probably should have seemed creepy, made her smile. He really was trying to take care of her, just like he'd promised.

And now, not only was the custody battle looking up, but she and Madison appeared to have the opportunity to get rid of Ken completely. Maybe that way, Drew could adopt Madison as his own.

"Too soon!" Cami said aloud, trying once again to rein in her imagination. It was getting harder and harder to do so, however, as the days passed.

* * *

CAMI WAS IN SUCH A good mood that she decided to stop on the way in to work and get everyone coffee and donuts. It could be her apology for being late.

"Goodies!" Maggie squealed as Cami placed everything on the desk in the nurses' station.

"What did I miss? You haven't been slammed, have you?" she asked guiltily.

"I wish," Maggie griped before stuffing a donut in her mouth. "It's been absolutely dead. We've been out of our minds with boredom. Ashley and I have been playing hangman for the last half-hour." She motioned to the open notepad with half a stick figure drawn on it.

"I heard my name," Ashley chirped, walking up behind Cami. "Oh, what did you bring us?"

"An apology for being late," Cami replied. "Though I hear it's been dead."

"Ugh…miserable."

"So," Maggie began after swallowing her donut. "How did things go with the fancy new lawyer man?"

"Great!" Cami replied, wiping the smile off her face. "But how did you know about that? I haven't talked to you all weekend."

"Had dinner with Drew and Grant last night," Maggie replied. The mischief in her eyes made Cami nervous. Thankfully, Ashley spoke up before Maggie could continue.

"What new lawyer?" she asked.

"Drew hooked me up with a new lawyer," Cami said, trying to down play it a little. "I guess he's really good. He's helping Drew's sister through a divorce right now. He seemed really confident about my chances. He thinks that I could not only win, but could be awarded full custody."

"That would be amazing!" Ashley said. "Then you'd never have to deal with that slime ball again."

"I know. It would be so nice to have Ken out of our lives for good," Cami responded.

"And that would leave Madison available for adoption for any man you may marry," Maggie added. Cami shot her a look, so she added, "In the future. You know. If you met the right man."

"Shut up, Maggie," Cami said. "It is way too early to think about things like that." She'd been thinking about them almost constantly herself, but she wasn't about to admit that, even to her best friend.

"What?" Ashley asked. "Am I missing something? Why am I always out of the loop? Are we talking about Drew? Is he back in the picture? I thought you two were done."

"Yeah, Cami. What's going on with Drew?" Maggie gave Cami a look, raising her eyebrow questioningly.

Cami could tell that Maggie knew more than she was letting on.

"We've been seeing each other again," Cami answered.

"Since when?" Ashley asked with a frown.

"About a week," Cami admitted, feeling guilty for keeping it from the girls. But it had still been so new and she had spent most of the week waiting for something to go wrong again. "Since last Sunday. He showed up right as my car wouldn't start and gave me a ride to pick up Madison from Ken's."

“I bet Ken loved that,” Maggie said.

“Oh, it was awesome. I made Drew wait in the car but he spent the entire time glaring. Ken had the most constipated look on his face. I loved it!”

“So, then what? You guys made up?” Ashley asked, half a donut forgotten in her hand as she listened excitedly.

“Well, that night he took us to Chuck-E-Cheese. It was great. He spent hours playing with Madison. Then, the next night, he showed up and cooked us both dinner. And he’s been doing that pretty much every day since…except when we’ve gone over to his house. Oh, and he gave me his BMW to drive, which I’ve yet to give back.”

Both Ashley and Maggie were watching her with rapt attention. They looked almost as excited by the news as Cami’s mother had been.

“So, then what’s wrong?” Maggie asked.

“Nothing is wrong. What makes you think something is wrong?” Cami asked.

“You’ve just seemed rather anxious this week,” Ashley volunteered. “Not as happy as that news would suggest.”

“I…” Cami paused, collecting her thoughts. It would probably help to talk to these girls about her fears and insecurities. “I guess, I’m just waiting for the other shoe to drop, you know? Up until this week, my experience with Drew has been inconsistent. He’s super into me one minute, absent the next. And…and

I think I'm falling in love with him. And my daughter is half in love with him as well. That's a scary prospect when we're talking about someone I can't completely trust not to turn around and break my heart."

Ashley nodded in understanding, but Maggie just smiled.

"Trust me," Maggie said. "You have *nothing* to worry about."

"What do you mean?" Cami questioned.

"I shouldn't be telling you this," Maggie said, biting her lip and pretending to look torn though Cami knew that her mind had already been made up. Knowing Maggie, she'd probably come in that day planning on telling Cami whatever it was that she knew.

"Come on," Cami said. "Out with it."

"I told you that Grant and I had dinner with Drew last night, right?"

"Yeah," Cami replied.

"Well, Drew wouldn't shut up about you," Maggie continued. "He said that he's madly in love with you. He just doesn't want to tell you yet because he's worried it will scare you away. He says you're still acting a little skittish and he doesn't want to overwhelm you so he was going to wait to say it for a while. He even went on and on about how much he loved Madison. It would have been disgusting if it weren't so sweet. So trust me, the guy is in this for the long haul."

"Oh my God," Ashley gasped. "That's so awesome."

"Yeah," Maggie agreed. "You know Drew's parents were poor and spent all of their time working, so he and his sister were left alone to practically raise themselves. He was saying that, because of his childhood experience, he's always wanted a big family."

A new line of insecurity began working its way into Cami's mind at those words.

"You don't think that's the only reason why he likes me, do you?" she asked hesitantly. "I mean, does he just want to be with me and Madison because we're a ready-made family?"

"Don't be silly," Ashley replied. "Now it seems like you're just looking for problems where there are none."

"I have to agree with Ashley on this, Cam," Maggie said. "Plus, he didn't even know you were a mother when he met you on the beach. You said he didn't learn that until way later, when he picked you up for your first date. But he was gushing about you to Grant that first weekend, talking about how much he liked you and wanted to see you again. Remember?"

"I remember," Cami assured her.

Perhaps her insecurities really were all in her mind. Perhaps this time, things were finally going to work out. Maybe Drew really did feel the same way about her as she did about him.

That thought kept a smile on Cami's face for the rest of the day.

CHAPTER EIGHT
Cami

By the end of the second week that Cami and Drew had been together officially—since the car incident—Cami had grown accustomed to Drew being in her home, and in her life.

She was still driving the car he loaned her, having finally stopped asking about her crappy old car after the fiftieth time Drew had blown her off or changed the subject. It wasn't like she was excited to go back to driving the clunker after spending time in a luxury car. So, Cami just let it go.

She also couldn't remember the last time she'd actually cooked her own dinner. On the rare evenings when Drew didn't visit or they didn't go over to Drew's house, Cami and Madison ate leftovers from whatever meal Drew had prepared last. Cami reasoned that, since the man was just so much better of a cook than she was, spending her time preparing mediocre meals when Drew was happy to make amazing ones just seemed wrong.

And so, Cami had taken to relaxing with Madison after work while Drew prepared dinner. He was currently making hamburgers and French fries while Cami helped Madison color at the table. The two adults talked about their respective days while going about this all-too-domesticated business. It just felt so natural at this point that Cami barely questioned it anymore.

"So," Drew was saying, "because there isn't already a food bank in the area, I'm working with a couple of people at the homeless shelter to establish one. It's a little frustrating to realize that this town doesn't even have a system in place to help feed hungry families. Especially considering all of the wealth here."

"Yeah," Cami said, thinking about Ken and Drew's old business investor, James Cook. "But most wealthy people have no interest in helping the poor. They haven't been there themselves, so they don't have the ability to empathize."

"It makes me angry," Drew growled as he pulled the baked fries out of the oven. Cami couldn't help but think that he was adorable when he was being passionate about his foundation.

"Don't be angry," Madison said, looking up from her pictures.

"No, sweetheart," Drew said, coming over to the table so that he could kiss the top of Madison's head. "I'm not angry. Not really."

"Good," Madison replied. "Wanna color?"

"Not right now. I'm making dinner, remember?" Drew was still standing at the table, absentmindedly running his hand through Madison's hair as he smiled down at the picture she was coloring nowhere near in the lines.

Even though Drew was around almost every day, it still warmed Cami's heart to watch the way he interacted with her daughter.

"Burgers," Madison replied in answer to Drew's question.

"Yep," Drew confirmed. "Burgers." With that he moved over towards the stove where the burgers in question were grilling.

"Anyway," he continued, speaking to Cami again. "That's what I did all morning. I also spoke on the phone to the head of the local Habitat for Humanity chapter this afternoon. Thankfully, that's something I don't have to waste time trying to get up and running."

"You know," Cami said, watching Drew flip the burgers, "you really should look into hiring someone."

"Eventually, yeah," Drew replied. "But, honestly, right now there is actually isn't that much to do. Not really. And I'm so used to working twelve to fifteen hour days, I'm a little bored. I think I'm more frustrated at people's apathy than I am at the lack of help."

"Well," Cami said as she began to pick up the crayons and put them away. "If you do need help, and there's anything *I* can do, just let me know."

"Yeah?" Drew asked, turning to look at her.

"Yeah!" Cami assured him as she picked up all of the coloring supplies and put them away to make room for dinner. "I would love to help."

"Because there *is* something you could do, if you had time," Drew said, looking at her with some anxiety as he compiled the juicy burgers and plated them along with generous portions of fries.

"Sure, anything," Cami said.

"You could look into whether or not there are any low cost or no cost health clinics in town. My initial research shows none, but I haven't had time yet to look into what already existing hospitals or doctor's offices offer. I figured that, with your medical experience, you'd be more qualified to do that than I would."

"Of course," Cami responded, excited to have a task she felt confident in being able to perform. "I can start on that tomorrow, since I'm not working Fridays at the moment."

In fact, between Drew covering her legal bills and purchasing the bulk of the groceries he used to cook, Cami hadn't had to pick up any overtime in the last few weeks. Her days off were now just that—days off. It was nice. But she didn't mind spending a few hours of that precious free time helping Drew with his philanthropic foundation. In fact, she couldn't think of a worthier thing to do with her time—that didn't involve spending time with Madison, of course.

They were just settling down for dinner when there was a knock at the door. Knock was probably the wrong word, actually. It was like someone was banging on the door as hard as they possibly could. Cami could feel every nerve ending in her body tense up, and the hair at the back of her neck stood on end. Madison's eyes grew big and frightened, and Drew turned towards the door worriedly.

"Expecting anyone?" he asked, a frown on his face.

"No," Cami replied.

"Open up, you bitch. I know you're in there," came Ken's loud, angry voice from the front porch.

"Daddy?" Madison asked uncertainly.

"I know you're in there. Your boyfriend's shitty BMW is in the driveway. Open up or it's going to get keyed."

"Daddy?" Madison asked again, though there were tears in her eyes now. She looked truly frightened.

Cami couldn't help but wonder how many times her daughter witnessed Ken's outbursts while over at his house for the weekend. More than ever, she promised herself that she'd keep her daughter away from that maniac. She was also extremely embarrassed that Drew had to witness this. What must he think of Cami for choosing to marry such a man? Was he regretting loaning her his car? Was he regretting getting involved with her at all? Cami couldn't help but feel like her life was often way more drama than Drew could possibly put up with.

"Cami," Drew said in a deep, serious voice. "I think you should take Madison into your bedroom and let me handle this."

"No," Cami replied stubbornly. The last thing she wanted was to put more of her shit off on Drew. He'd already been so helpful—too helpful. She couldn't ask for more. This was her mess to clean up. "He is my ex and my problem. I've dealt with him in this state before. I can do it again now."

Drew's jaw clenched. She could tell he wanted to argue, but after a moment, he offered her a quick nod.

"Fine," he growled. "But Madison needs to be in your room with the door shut and the TV on."

"Agreed," Cami replied, picking up her daughter and heading towards the master bedroom.

"We're going to watch a movie in bed, okay?" Cami asked, turning on the television without waiting for a response from Madison.

In fact, Madison wasn't responding at all. Her eyes were still wide and she was shaking. Cami had half of a mind to give in to Drew and stay in here with her daughter. But she had to go deal with Ken—it was her responsibility. So she put a Disney movie on and kissed her daughter on the forehead before heading back out into the hall, shutting the door securely behind her.

Ken was still banging on the door, screaming obscenities. Cami knew that if her neighbors hadn't called the cops yet, they were sure to do so soon. Drew was standing in the middle of the living room, his jaw still clenched as he curled and uncurled his hands into fists, staring at the door.

"Calm down. Let me handle this. It's probably best if you stay out of sight."

Drew glared for a moment longer before nodding and heading into the kitchen. Cami took a deep breath and opened the door. Ken stood still for a moment, as if in shock, just glaring at her. His eyes were glassy and bloodshot, and Cami could tell that he was incredibly drunk. After a second, Ken pushed past her and marched into the house.

"Where the fuck is my daughter?" he growled. "Madison!"

"You will not be seeing Madison in this state," Cami said curtly. "What are you thinking, showing up like this?" she demanded. "Are you trying to traumatize your daughter?"

"Shut up, you stupid bitch," Ken snarled. "This is all your fault!"

"What is?" Cami replied, trying hard not to raise her voice enough to worry Madison. The little girl was already stressed enough without having to listen to her mother shout. "I have no idea what you're talking about."

"Your stupid fucking lawyer. He thinks he can just come and shove some stupid DUIs down my throat and expect me to back off? He doesn't get to do that. How dare he? And of course now, Natalie knows about them. And she's pissed. And it's all your fault. You and your fucking lawyer."

"No," Cami said, seething with rage. "This is all *your* fault, Ken. You brought this on yourself. It was your idea to sue for more custody—or at least you let Natalie push you into it. Things were fine as they were. Now I'm going to make sure you never see your daughter again, you drunken asshole."

"How dare you talk to me like that," he snarled, stalking towards her. Cami refused to step backwards. She refused to let him intimidate her. "And you have no say over what I can and can't do with my daughter. Madison is *mine,* and I can see her if I want to. Madison!" he screamed again.

"You need to leave right now, Ken. If you don't, I'm going to call the cops." Cami reached for her purse on the counter by the door and pulled out her phone. She held it up to him, as if to emphasize that she was serious.

"You can't scare me, bitch," he growled, lunging towards her.

This time Cami did step backwards, letting out a little shriek as she did so. As it turned out, that was completely unnecessary, because, as soon as Ken had started towards her, Drew stepped out of the shadows and held him back, pushing him until he was pinned against the wall.

"What the fuck?" Ken asked as he whirled around, attempting to swing at Drew but missing.

Cami had never seen Drew look so angry; his eyes were full of rage as he glared at Ken.

"Cami," Drew said without taking his eyes away her ex-husband. "I want you to go into the bedroom with Madison and call the police. I will deal with this."

Cami wanted to argue. She even opened her mouth to respond, but then Drew shot her a look over Ken's shoulder that implied that there would be no discussing this. Drew meant business. Cami just nodded, pulling her phone up to dial 911 as she hurried back into the bedroom.

"And lock the door behind you," she heard Drew call.

Cami did not need to be told twice.

CHAPTER NINE
Drew

Drew was having a really great day. He'd spent the morning making plans for a new food bank, then spent the afternoon coordinating with the local Habitat for Humanity chapter. He'd then gone to the store and prepared to cook for his little family. That's how Drew had been thinking about Cami and Madison—as *his* family. He made dinner while Madison and Cami spent time in the kitchen, just being close to him as he cooked.

It was so different than when he'd been with his ex. She'd never really wanted to spend time with him, unless it involved going out and squandering his money. Cami and her daughter seemed content just to be in the same room with him, talking about their days and coloring pictures.

As he was cooking, Drew couldn't help but think about the future, planning for the day that he would invite Cami and Madison to come live with him. He would put a nice-sized table in his kitchen, since no one really sat at the grand dining room table anyway. Instead, he would make an area where his girls could hang out with him while he cooked—where they could all eat as a family.

That's what he was thinking of when there was a loud bang across the door. Soon, the obviously drunken voice of Cami's ex rang out across the house. Madison was petrified, and for that reason alone, Drew could have knocked the man clear into next week. But when he started screaming obscenities at Cami through the door, Drew knew that he would make sure Ken got what was coming to him.

He tried to convince Cami to go wait in the bedroom with Madison, but—of course—Cami would have none of it. So, after Madison was safe and secure in the back of the house, Drew moved into the kitchen, still close enough to intervene if he felt like his girlfriend was being at all threatened, when Cami opened the door.

At first, Drew just smirked at Ken's words, recognizing them for what they were—petulant cries of a desperate man, a man who already knew he lost. When he mentioned that his fiancée didn't know about his stack of DUIs until the lawyers dug them up, it was all Drew could do not to laugh. He also couldn't help but admire the strength and tenacity with which Cami stood up to the man. She wasn't backing down. She wasn't showing even the slightest bit of intimidation. And Drew couldn't help but love her more for it, even as he wished that she was a little more careful with her own safety.

But then Ken lunged. Drew didn't even think, he just moved. He charged from the kitchen and towards the man, catching his arm before he could swing it towards Cami and pressing him back against the wall with both hands. Cami was far enough away to have missed the punch, proving once again that she was more than capable of taking care of herself. But it still sent a wave of fury through Drew's body, which was already pumping with anger and adrenaline. At the moment, he felt like he could rip Cami's ex-husband to pieces with his bare hands.

"What the fuck?" Ken asked, not having realized that Drew was in the room until he'd grabbed a hold of him.

It was all Drew could do not to pummel the man right then and there. But he didn't want to do that in front of Cami. Instead, he took a deep breath and tried to calm down, all the while still holding the thrashing Ken tightly in his grasp.

"Cami," he began when he was calm enough to speak. "I want you to go into the bedroom with Madison and call the police. I will deal with this." He could hear Ken cussing under his breath as Cami turned to leave. "And lock the door behind you," he called out to her as she went.

"I don't know who you think you are, dirt-bag,"

Ken began, twisting in Drew's grasp. "But that's *my* wife and child in there and—"

"Ex-wife," Drew interjected. "And Madison won't be your daughter for much longer. I'm going to make sure of it. Especially after the shit you've pulled tonight."

"Like you can control that, you asshole," Ken said, twisting to try and knee Drew in the crotch.

But Ken was drunk, and his movements were slow and obvious. Plus, Drew had the feeling that he was in a much better shape. But just the fact that he'd tried, pissed Drew off even more. Giving in to his baser nature, he let go of Ken with one hand, pulled back, and punched him hard in the face. Ken's head ricocheted back and hit the wall, blood pouring from his nose as he slowly sank towards the floor.

Drew shook his fist, though he pain pumping through it was entirely worth it to see the douche bag curled up in a pile. Drew turned away, smiling. He'd been wanting to do that for weeks.

He moved towards the hall, planning on checking on Cami and Madison, when he heard a shuffle behind him. He spun around quickly to find Ken staggering towards him, his expression contorted in rage as blood ran down his face. Now, with injury as well as inebriation, Ken's actions were even slower and easier to figure out. As he lunged at Drew, Drew moved, bringing his knee up to collide with Ken's stomach. Ken groaned in pain as he once again collapsed on the ground.

"You really want to stay down this time," Drew warned. "Trust me."

Ken just moaned in reply. He didn't seem like he was going to try and fight anymore, but Drew decided it was better to stay where he was until the police arrived. He was sure that Cami and Madison were safe in the bedroom, no matter how badly he wanted to go check on them.

Instead, he tried, as hard as he could, not to grind his foot into Ken's shoulder blades as he waited for the familiar wail of sirens.

CHAPTER TEN
Cami

Cami hung on the phone with the emergency operator until she heard sirens wail in the background. She was extremely embarrassed that her neighbors would be able to see her ex-husband being led from her house in handcuffs, but she tried her best to push that out of her mind. There was nothing she could do about it, after all. What she *could* do was ensure that Madison didn't have to witness her father being led from her home in handcuffs.

After hearing Drew open the door and the sound of new voices in the living room, Madison sat up and looked towards the door worriedly. She hadn't spoken a word since being led away from the kitchen table, and her obvious fear was tormenting Cami. She hated to see her daughter that way—hated to see her have to go through something as traumatic as what had just happened.

"Mommy has to go out and talk to the men, sweetie," Cami said, stroking her daughter's hair. "I need you to stay in here and watch your movie."

Madison nodded and stared at the screen. *The Little Mermaid* was playing—one of Madison's favorite movies—but she seemed to be looking through the television more than watching it. Giving her daughter one last look, she slipped from the bedroom, making sure to shut the door securely behind her.

In the living room, one police officer was handcuffing Ken while another read him his rights. Cami was surprised—thought not too surprised—to see blood on his clothes and dripping down his face. When he saw Cami, he tried, once again, to lunge at her.

"This is all your fault," he shouted, though his words were somewhat obscured by his drunken state.

The police officer was none too gentle with him as he yanked Ken back away from Cami.

"Why don't you go put him in the car while I get their statements?" the other officer suggested.

While Ken was being led from the house, Cami ushered the other officer into the kitchen, where she invited him to have a seat. She sat down next to him, though Drew chose to stand and pace across the floor.

"So," the officer said with a kind smile, "why don't you start from the beginning?"

"We were just sitting down to eat when Ken came banging at the door," Cami began.

"Ken is the man who was just arrested?" the officer asked.

"Yes," Cami clarified. "Ken Bellamy. My ex-husband."

"And who all was here eating dinner?"

"Myself, my boyfriend Drew..." Cami motioned towards Drew, trying not to cringe. This was the first time she'd used the term *boyfriend* and she hated that it was in such unfortunate circumstances. She hoped she hadn't overstepped her bounds, but Drew's reassuring smile put her at ease. "And my daughter Madison."

"And is Madison Mr. Bellamy's daughter, or Drew's?" the officer asked.

"Ken's," Cami replied. "Mr. Bellamy's. We're actually in the middle of a pretty bad custody battle right now. I guess my lawyers found some proof that he wasn't as sober as he claimed to be, and he was pissed."

"Well, if they didn't have proof before, they have it now," Drew said with a sigh.

Cami offered him a soft smile.

"Yeah," the officer agreed. "This will all go into his arrest record, so it will be available to the judge in the custody case."

"I guess, one good thing came from this," Cami replied.

"So, then what happened when he arrived?" the officer prompted.

"I tucked Madison into the back bedroom and turned on the TV really loud. I then opened the front door."

"And where were you?" the officer asked Drew.

"I was in the kitchen, watching everything but trying to remain out of sight. I wanted to handle it myself but Cami thought Ken wouldn't react well to me."

"So, what happened once you opened?" The officer turned back to Cami as he posed the question.

"He pushed inside and started raving about how it was my fault that my lawyer had uncovered some DUIs that he'd been trying to hide from his fiancée. I guess she found out and she was upset with him. And I think, he was starting to realize that he wasn't going to win the case. I asked him to leave and he wouldn't. Then he tried to take a swing at me. Drew stepped in and prevented Ken from attacking me, then told me to go to the bedroom with Madison while I called the police. And that's where I was until you arrived."

"And what happened out here?" The officer turned back towards Drew, waiting for an answer.

"When he lunged at Cami, I pinned him against the wall. I was holding him there after she went back to the bedroom, but he started to struggle and tried to attack me. So I punched him in the face. He fell to the ground, and I thought the struggle was over, so I turned to go check on Cami and Madison. But I then heard him getting up so I turned around in time to see him lunge at me again. But he was drunk and slow and easy to avoid, so I kneed him in the stomach."

The officer was making notes on a pad in front of him, and Cami felt herself grow worried.

"Drew won't be in trouble will he?" Cami asked. "He was only defending himself—and me."

"I highly doubt it," the officer assured her. "Your ex-husband may try to press assault charges—he seems like the type—but it would be hard to make it stick. I mean, he was in your home uninvited and he swung first, even if he failed to hit anyone. And I'm sure the tox screen will come back with a high level of alcohol in his blood. It would be very unlikely that he'd even find a judge willing to try a case like that."

"Good," Cami said, offering Drew a weak smile.

"Listen," the officer said as he stood. "I know this was a scary thing to happen, but I can guarantee you that it almost certainly won your custody battle for you. And if you need me or my partner to testify about his behavior here tonight, we'd be more than happy to. I grew up with a drunk for a father, you see. So I know all about women trying to stand up to their piss-poor excuses of husbands. My mom was one."

"Thank you," Cami said, shaking the officer's hand.

She let Drew see the man out as she went to check on Madison. Her daughter was still curled up where Cami had left her, staring vacantly at the screen.

"Hey, honey," Cami said, crawling across the bed towards her daughter. "How are you?"

"Daddy?" Madison asked, and it broke Cami's heart a little bit. "Is Daddy here?"

"No, honey," Cami answered. "Daddy is gone. Daddy is gone, and he isn't coming back."

"Oh. Okay," Madison replied, not actually looking very upset over that information. Perhaps she didn't really understand. Or, perhaps, she wouldn't actually miss her father.

Cami reached out and pulled her daughter into her lap, holding her tight until Drew came back into the room. He sat down on the bed next to Cami and stroked Madison's hair for a moment.

"I'm going to clean up the dinner mess," he told Cami, "then I'll head home. It's been a stressful night for you two, and you probably want to be alone."

"No!" the little girl cried.

Both Cami and Drew looked at Madison, who was trying to crawl out of Cami's lap and into Drew's. Cami, of course, was more than happy to let her.

"Don't go," Madison begged, fisting her hands in Drew's shirt. "Me scared."

"Oh, sweetheart," Drew uttered against her hair as he held her tight and kissed the top of her head. "There is nothing to be scared of. Not anymore. But I'll stay anyway, just to make sure you're safe."

"Okay," Madison said, not relaxing her grip on Drew's shirt.

Eventually, the three of them ended up in Cami's bed, watching the second half of *The Little Mermaid*. By the time the movie was over, Madison was fast asleep, snuggled securely between Cami and Drew.

As the credits rolled, Cami stood and moved to pick up her sleeping daughter.

"Let me," Drew said, easily lifting Madison and carrying her down the hall.

Cami padded after him, feeling her heart melt all over again at the sight of Drew putting Madison to bed. They tucked her in together and each kissed her on the forehead before heading back into the living room.

"I'm so sorry about tonight," Cami said, shifting from foot to foot.

On one hand, it had been amazing watching Drew stick up for her and her daughter, then the way Madison had clung to him and asked him to stay. He'd even helped put her to bed! But, at the same time, Cami was half expecting Drew to decide that her life was just too much drama for him. She really was humiliated by what happened.

"Don't be," Drew told her, pulling her into his arms. "I'm not. I mean, I'm sorry that Madison had to experience as much as she did today. But she seemed okay by the end of the night. And if it's what had to happen in order to ensure that Ken is out of our lives, it's a small price to pay. Think about what the officer said, Cami. He basically lost the trial tonight. We're free of him. Forever!"

There was the *we* again. Even after all that happened, Drew was still in this with her. They were in it together. They were a *we*.

"I love you so much," she whispered against his chest before she could register what she was saying. But, as soon as she did realize what she'd just admitted, she froze. Her heart began to race and she tried to figure out a way to take the words back. "I mean—"

To her surprise, Drew just laughed and hugged her closer.

"Nope," he said. "You're not allowed to back-pedal on that."

"I didn't mean to say it," Cami admitted, still not pulling her face away from the security of his strong chest.

"But did you mean it?" his deep voice asked in her ear.

She had half a mind to lie and deny it…tell him that she wasn't in love with him. But she couldn't bring herself to do it, so she nodded against him.

"Yes."

Drew eventually pulled away, and Cami began to panic. It *had* been too soon. She tried not to look at him, but Drew's strong hands came to each side of her face.

"Look at me Cami," he said. Hesitantly, Cami raised her eyes to his. They were full of warmth and passion. He smiled softly at her, stroking her cheeks with his thumbs. "I love you, too," he said.

For a moment, Cami forgot to breathe. Yes, Maggie had said as much the other day, but it had been second-hand information. And Maggie often liked to embellish things. But now it was coming from Drew's own mouth. He *loved* her. This was real.

When Drew's lips pressed against hers, it was with all of the tenderness and love she'd just seen in his eyes. It was sweet at first. An extension of the feelings they'd just confessed to each other.

But it quickly deepened, growing in passion and urgency. After the tense night and the love confession, they both just needed to lose themselves in each other. Or rather, Cami was sure that she needed to lose herself in Drew. And, by the way he was moaning and licking into her mouth, she assumed he felt the same.

Cami was surprised when Drew bent and effortlessly lifted her off the floor. He didn't break their kiss, even for a second, as he carried her bridal style to the bedroom.

Cami used the opportunity to push her hands into his thick dark hair, pulling his lips against hers even harder. She couldn't get enough of his strong, muscled arms and chest, carrying her so easily. Cami never would have guessed that she loved being manhandled, but it turned out that she did—a lot.

In the bedroom, Drew sat on the edge of the mattress, still holding Cami tight. He finally pulled out of the kiss to look down into her face. His dark amber eyes were full of all the words he'd already spoken.

"God, I love you," he said again, a small smile spreading across his lips.

Cami melted further into his arms, the combination of his words and touch sending bolts of heat crashing through her body. She opened her mouth to respond in kind, but Drew's mouth swallowed her words. Since he already knew how she felt, she let him devour her hungrily instead.

After a few more minutes of heated kissing, they both pulled away, panting. Drew then began to kiss and lick his way down her jaw and across her neck until he found the little spot behind her ear that drove her wild.

"Oh, Drew," she moaned against him.

"I love the way you moan my name," he responded breathlessly.

Drew then set about displaying yet another set of impressive skills by quickly and seamlessly removing Cami's shirt and bra, one handed. He let out a guttural moan as her breasts sprang free, bouncing the way only large, natural breasts do. Cami sometimes felt insecure about her chest, definitely not as perky as the fake boobs most women of the same bra-size had. But it was impossible to feel self-conscious with the way Drew was looking at her breasts now, all hunger and naked want.

"So beautiful," he murmured as his hand slid up to caress one mound, squeezing and pulling at the rapidly hardening nipple. “I wanted you from the first moment I laid eyes on you. With your round curves and fiery hair and wild personality. I think I loved you from the moment I saw you.”

Cami wanted to scoff at his cheesy words, but there was a part of her—a large part—that were eating those words up. Plus, once he lowered his hot, greedy mouth to her other breast, she was incapable of forming any comprehensible speech. Instead, she just moaned and arched against his tongue, which was lapping at the nipple held gently between his teeth.

Cami had never felt anything like this before. It was so amazing, the feel of the rough heat of his tongue laving at her sensitive flesh. She felt like she was going to explode. It was so intense that it was almost painful by the time he finally pulled away from her.

Cami was almost incoherent with need, helpless to do anything but cling to him, enjoying the sensation as he licked and sucked his way up her breasts. She knew that he was probably leaving marks, but she didn’t care. In fact, she liked the idea of Drew marking her as his. She *was* his and wanted the world to know it.

While Drew’s mouth was caressing Cami’s neck and chest, his hands were exploring lower, from the soft flesh of her stomach to the wide curve of her hips. Then his fingers were working on her fly, unfastening it before pulling her pants down her legs. Cami allowed Drew to lift her slightly as he removed her pants and underwear.

As she shifted, she could feel the press of his clothed erection against her bare bottom. There was something extremely erotic about sitting in Drew's lap, completely naked, while he was fully clothed. She couldn't help but grind down on the delicious hardness pressing against her through his jeans.

Suddenly, Drew lifted Cami off his lap and tossed her gently on the bed. Cami let her body relax against the soft comforter, spreading her legs invitingly and allowing Drew a fuller view of her body as she lay there before him. His gaze was hungry and wild as he devoured her with his eyes.

Cami could feel her own juices begin to drip on to her thighs and wondered if Drew could see that from where he stood. She hoped so. She wanted him to know that she was ready for him, as hungry and wild as he was.

"Cami," he whispered breathlessly. "You're so beautiful."

Cami preened at this, opening her legs even further and running her hands slowly along her body, stopping for a minute to play with her breasts before moving down between her legs. Cami played with herself leisurely, slowly circling her clit as she watched Drew undress. He made quick work of his clothes, tossing them on the floor as he went. Soon, he was naked, standing over her, stroking his full, throbbing erection.

Cami examined his body ravenously, licking her lips as her eyes fell on his huge, leaking manhood. There was a bead of pre-cum hanging from the tip, and Cami wanted more than anything to taste it.

Unable to help herself, she was on her hands and knees and crawling towards him. When she got to the edge of the bed, she reached out and grabbed his hips, pulling him towards her as she ran her tongue slowly up his cock until she was able to lick the pre-cum off the tip. They moaned as one as she savored the salty taste in her mouth.

Cami looked up into Drew's eyes. He was looking down at her pleadingly. Without him having to say a word, Cami knew exactly what he wanted. He elicited a raw, dirty sound as she gripped the base of his length and guided it between her wet lips.

Drew moaned again and brought his hands up into Cami's hair, bucking his hips slightly. He stilled, as if catching himself, but Cami hummed in encouragement and used her hands to direct his hips until he was thrusting into her face in earnest. Cami was dizzy with the taste of him. Like an aged port that was both bitter and sweet, it was driving her crazy with want and need.

The noises Drew was making, small whimpers of need, were also going straight to Cami's head—and her sex. She was pulsating with desire. As much as she loved the feel of him in her mouth, she needed more. She felt like she might spontaneously combust at any minute if she didn't find relief.

Drew whined loudly in protest as Cami finally pulled her mouth off his cock. But, as she spread herself out on the mattress, opening her legs in invitation, he got the message. Drew reached into the bedside table to grab a condom, then crawled onto the bed beside her.

First, he slowly ran his hands up and down her body before sliding between her thighs. When he slipped a finger between the lips of her pussy and circled her clit, Cami nearly screamed and arched off the bed. She was so tightly wound at that point that he felt like she was about to explode.

The sensation was amazing, sending shivers up and down Cami's spine. But it wasn't enough.

"Please," Cami begged, thrusting against Drew's hand.

"Please what, my dear?" Drew asked with a smirk, though Cami was sure he knew full well what she needed.

"Take me," she panted, her brain barely able to form words, much less sentences. "I'm ready. I just need you."

"You have me, baby," Drew said, moving to crawl between her legs.

He slowly rolled the condom onto his swollen length, squeezing the base of his cock before grabbing

Cami's hips and pulling her towards him. He quickly lined his swollen manhood up to Cami's tight little sex, then sank deep into her body, burying himself to the hilt. Cami cried out at the sensation of being filled and stretched and owned. She wanted nothing more than to feel this way for the rest of her life—like she completely belonged to Drew.

Cami could feel her nails digging into the flesh of Drew's arm so hard that they would leave marks. That thought send a possessive quiver through her body. She opened her thighs wider and thrust back against his hard length. Drew quickly lifted her legs until they were against his shoulders, then leaned down to press his lips to hers as he finally began to pound into Cami the way she needed.

"Yes!" she cried as he impaled her again and again on his girth.

Drew snapped his hips savagely, pounding into Cami hard and fast. Cami wanted to scream at the painful pleasure whipping through her body with each of Drew's thrusts. The only way she could keep herself from crying out loud enough to wake her daughter was to turn her head and bite down hard on Drew's shoulder as the most explosive orgasm she'd ever experienced burned through her body.

When the bolts of electricity finally subsided, Cami realized that her teeth were still sunk deep in Drew's flesh. The bite wasn't hard enough to break the skin, but Cami knew that Drew would have a mark on his shoulder for a long time.

Good, she thought. "I want everyone to know you're mine."

"Yes," Drew cried out against her neck, thrusting into her wildly as he chased his own release deep within her body. "I'm yours, just as you're mine. Completely. Forever."

Cami felt a second's worth of embarrassment at realizing that she'd said those possessive words out loud. But, given that they were enough to send Drew over the edge into his own body-shaking orgasm, she couldn't bring herself to care for very long.

Cami soon felt a bit awkward, still positioned beneath Drew with her legs up over her own head, and wiggled until she could stretch out beside him. Drew rose and disposed of the condom. Cami used the opportunity to crawl between the soft sheets.

"I'm just going to rest for a minute," Drew promised. "Then I'll get up and go."

"No," Cami replied. "Stay. I want you to stay the night."

"But what about Madison?" he asked uncertainly.

"What about Madison?" Cami asked, rolling over onto her side until they were facing each other. "She asked for you to stay. She'll be disappointed if you don't."

"Won't it confuse her?" he asked, but Cami knew that he was just working through his own insecurities as this point.

She could tell that he wanted to stay as much as she wanted him to.

"No," Cami replied with confidence. "This is real. This is serious. So she needs to get used to it—used to you. She already loves you though. She won't mind. We'll go to breakfast tomorrow—the three of us. It will be great. You'll see."

"If you're sure," Drew said, though he was now beaming.

"I'm sure," Cami promised him as she rolled over and pushed back up against him until he was spooning her just right. She then slowly drifted off to sleep.

As it turned out, Madison was absolutely delighted to find Drew still there in the morning. Drew told her later that it made him never want to spend a night away from them ever again. And Cami told him that she was okay with that.

CHAPTER ELEVEN
Epilogue

Cami shifted nervously, watching through a crack in the door as her daughter teetered in her brand-new shoes, the frilly white dress she was wearing swaying with each step. Cami knew that she shouldn't be peeking, but she couldn't help herself.

Madison clung to Robbie's hand as the two of them made their way up the aisle. Robbie took his place between Drew and Grant. Madison stepped up beside Maggie, in front of the empty pulpit where Cami was about to stand.

The music changed. Cami knew that was her cue. Her mother stepped up beside her, taking her arm. Her mom looked amazing in a crisp off-white tux, her long gray hair pinned up in a tasteful bun. Cami had told her mom that she didn't need to wear men's attire, even though she was walking her daughter down the aisle. Her mother, of course, would hear nothing of it, excitedly shopping for a tuxedo specifically tailored to a woman's body. She hadn't found the right one—becoming pickier than Cami had been about her dress—and they'd eventually had one tailored specifically for her.

Just because Drew had handed Cami a credit card with her name on it and told her to spare no expense hadn't meant that Cami wanted to go wild. She'd tried her best to plan the most frugal wedding possible—whenever she could. But there were just a few things Cami had splurged on, including her mother's suit and the Vera Wang gown that she herself was about to walk down the aisle in. It was custom-made and absolutely perfect, worth every penny, with a jewel-crowned corset and miles of silky tulle trailing after her.

When she stepped out into the aisle, on her mother's arm, Drew's expression took her breath away. She could see tears in his eyes as she slowly walked towards him and knew that she was shedding a few of her own as well.

The ceremony was short and sweet, as they said their vows in front of friends and family and Madison and Robbie served as 'honorary' Maid of Honor and Best Man, respectively. The reception that followed, however, was another matter.

They'd decided to host the wedding at their own house, since they'd finally gotten the place properly landscaped. An enormous white tent was set up in the lawn, on the other side of the house from the pasture that housed Madison's pony, Peanut. No one wanted to spend the evening eating and dancing with the smell of pony wafting through the air.

The wedding had been a little rushed. Though they'd been engaged for a while, Cami and Drew found themselves with the surprising—though not at all unwelcomed—news that they were expecting a few months back, and Cami wanted to rush the wedding before she was the size of a barn.

Also, since the custody battle was won quickly, awarding full custody rights to Cami and relinquishing all parental rights from Ken, Drew had been able to easily adopt Madison and she had taken on his last name a few months ago. She was now Madison Sloane, and Cami was anxious to hurry up and become a Sloane herself. Now they would both have a new name—a better name. A name that would be shared with Madison's new brother or sister incubating in Cami's belly as she and Drew danced and laughed—celebrating their love with all of their friends and family.

Cami's mother took Madison home with her that night, so that Cami and Drew could spend their first night together as husband and wife alone in their house. It wasn't as kinky and erotic has many of their times together had been before, but it was sweet and loving and reinforced exactly what it was that they felt for each other.

The next morning, the two of them rose early and started the long drive to their honeymoon, the location of which Drew still wasn't willing to divulge. It wasn't until they turned down a somewhat familiar street that Cami realized where they were.

"Wait," she said, sitting up excitedly. "Are we heading towards the Emersons' beach house?"

"Close," Drew said with a smile. "But no cigar."

As he spoke the words, Cami noticed that their car passed the turnoff for the driveway for the Emersons' house. So they were in the area. Cami remained quiet, patiently waiting for Drew's surprise to be revealed.

Eventually, Drew did pull down a drive. It was longer and more wooded than the Emersons' and seemed to go on forever. Finally, the trees broke, revealing a beautiful, white sandy beach and a large house—though nowhere near as large as the Emersons'—with a two-story deck. As they drove around to the side to park, Cami noticed that the entire side of the house that was facing the ocean was made of glass.

"That doesn't look too private," she said, though she really didn't mind.

"It's a private beach," Drew told her, grinning. "No one here but us."

"Wow… you rented an entire beach for our honeymoon?" Cami asked, imagining all of the naked sunbathing—and sexing—that would be going on.

"Actually," Drew said, a sly grin spreading across his face, "this is a kind of…honeymoon-slash-wedding present."

"I don't get it," Cami said with a frown.

Drew reached into his pocket and pulled something out. He then leaned over and placed it in Cami's hand. She opened it, looking down at a set of keys. She turned them over in her hand for a moment before what Drew was implying actually set in.

"You bought me a house?" Cami asked, her voice rising an octave…or three. "You bought me a beach house!?"

Drew's smile grew wider at her excitement.

"Yes," he replied. "I did. I figured, since we met on this beach—or a few miles north, I guess—it would be a great place to own a home here. It would be a way for us to commemorate."

"Also a great reason to have sex on the beach," Cami added knowingly—not that she was complaining.

"Yes," Drew replied, "and a great reason to have sex on the beach. It's a private beach, so it's not illegal. And no one will see us. I've been planning on doing this for a while. I've had my eye out for anything in this area for sale practically since we first got together. And then this house just went on the market last month. Since it was so close to our wedding, I thought it would make a great present."

"Oh my God," Cami practically yelled. "You bought me a beach house as a wedding present! I can't believe this is my life."

"You're welcome," Drew said, laughing a little at her reaction.

"I only got you a watch," Cami replied sheepishly.

"You got me so much more than a watch," Drew said, his voice deep and earnest. He brought a hand up to stroke her belly, reminding both of them of the new life growing there. "So much more." They sat in silence for a moment, just grinning at each other.

"Now," Drew began, clearing his throat, "let's go in and explore our new house—make sure you actually like it before you thank me properly."

Cami did like the house. Actually, she loved it. It was already tastefully furnished, though Drew assured her that they could change things to make it more their own. The master bedroom was on the side of the house with the glass walls, with an amazing view of the ocean. The sun was already setting over the water as Cami dropped her bags and flopped down on the king-sized bed.

"Shall we break it in?" Drew asked with a smirk as he followed her into the bedroom and sat at the end of the bed.

"Actually," Cami replied, rubbing her pregnant belly, "I'm starving. Plus, I have other plans for you tonight."

After a quick meal from the fully stocked kitchen, Cami grabbed Drew's hand and pulled him down onto the beach, where they strolled through the darkness for a while. Eventually, Cami collapsed down into the sand, pulling Drew with her. After pushing him back against the sand, Cami straddled him, leaning down to kiss him deeply.

"God, I love you," Cami whispered when she finally pulled back for air.

"I love you, too," Drew replied, bucking his hips a little to make sure that Cami was aware of the way in which his body was responding.

She was aware. "The first night we were together—when we fooled around on the beach—you got me off with your fingers, but when I wanted to stop, you stopped—even though you hadn't gotten off yet. You were such a gentleman. I think I fell in love with you a little right then."

"That was the first day we met," Drew reminded her.

"Yes," Cami replied. "I've loved you since the day we met."

"I said it first," Drew said teasingly.

"Shush," Cami whispered against his mouth as she leaned down to kiss him, "or you won't get your reward."

Drew obliged, proving his willingness to be quiet by pressing his lips against hers.

Cami smiled into the kiss. Then, crawling on top of her husband, she set about treating him in the same way he'd shown her all those months ago—and demonstrating her love for him, which had come to life that night, long ago.

The End

Have you read **The Reckless Secret***, another hot romance by Alexa Wilder? This is a story about Maggie and Declan, so if you haven't had a chance to grab it, here is your sneak peek:*

SNEAK PEEK: THE RECKLESS SECRET

Chapter One: Maggie

Maggie couldn't really call this one of her better mornings.

Hot travel mug scorching her one hand and the purse sliding off her opposite shoulder, she dodged a group of elderly tourists checking out the monument on the corner and almost rushed head first into the path of a UPS truck.

"Oh sh—" Her heart leapt into her throat as she stumbled back up the curb, UPS truck honking its horn as it raced past, yanking the attention of all passersby directly to her.

Her face burned hotter than the palm wrapped around her hastily brewed coffee.

She took another step back to avoid any more near-death experiences and await a safe crossing, and brought her heel down on something that made a man shout, "Ow!" into her ear, like stepping on the press of a pedal trash can.

"God, sorry," she said, moving off the man's toe and turning to face his livid death stare. "I'm so sorry."

Thick eyebrows hung low over his ice-cold eyes.

"Um," she said.

"*Go*," he snarled, looking behind her pointedly, and she turned back around to see everyone now crossing the street, traffic paused. She was very much blocking this angry man's way.

Which he rectified a split second later by barging past her and knocking the travel mug out of her hand. She watched, as if in slow motion, as the cup hit the ground on the edge of the street, burst open, and splattered all up the left leg of a passing nun.

After a full minute of flustered apologies and offers to dry-clean the nun's clothes, she finally made it across the street and halfway to work before her phone rang and had her fumbling in her overstuffed purse.

"Hey, can I call you back later?" she panted into the phone, contents of her purse threatening to spill out onto the filthy sidewalk as she attempted to close the zip. "I'm *so* late—"

"Just a quick thing," her brother said, and there was something odd in his voice. Something strained and cracked, not his usual rich tones. "I can't make Jen's wedding this weekend."

The words stopped her dead in her tracks, forcing several people to swerve around her, muttering their irritation. "Sorry," she mumbled vaguely to no one in particular, and then hurried over to an empty doorway, turning to face the wall to create some privacy. "What're you talking about?"

"I can't make it." Grant sounded entirely unapologetic, and that alone was enough to set her on edge. Her brother didn't let her down. Not him.

"But—you have to. You promised." Because he knew how difficult she found these things, attending events with her cousins and aunts and other relatives who didn't understand her, who judged her, who thought she needed to remember her place in the world—of country clubs and jewelry and brunch four times a week. Relatives who saw her chosen profession as an insult to the upbringing the family had given her. "We'll find you a medical charity to assist; I'm sure there's a board somewhere with a seat for you," they told her, back when she expressed her ambition of nursing. "At least become a *surgeon*."

Her father had been apoplectic. "I didn't pay to send you to all the best schools just so you could become a damn *nurse*!" he'd raged at her, for weeks on end, every time she saw him and watched that stain of disappointment blacken his eyes.

But her father's opinion didn't matter, not anymore—not since she was ten, and he turned her entire world upside down. Tore it apart with a savagery she would never forget.

Grant, her older brother, was the only man in her life who mattered to her from that point on, the only man she trusted. The one who promised to look after her, to protect her, to be everything her father couldn't.

And he spent the next fourteen years doing just that. Until recently, when hints of a different side of Grant started showing—a side of him she'd never seen before. A disheveled Grant, like the last time she'd seen him, showing up to her cousin Jen's rehearsal dinner with bloodshot eyes, messy hair, his T-shirt inside out, and a scruff on his face at least three days old. And he never came through with the money for his half of the wedding gift, always *next week, I promise,* and brief, cold texts about being busy.

"I don't have time to argue about it now, Mags," he told her abruptly, and while his tone wasn't unkind, he still sounded so very much like the opposite of her caring brother that it took her aback. "I gotta go. Sorry."

"Grant—wait—" But he'd already hung up.

Blinking stupidly at the grimy wall before her, Maggie took a moment to worry about her brother. A vague, abstract sort of worry, the kind without a defining cause she could focus on, think of ways to fix. But she had no time to analyze the change in him, not right now—she was already late for work, and there were a couple of people there who'd delight in her being reprimanded for tardiness. One person in particular.

And he didn't disappoint. Ronald Mitchell, Maggie's mistake of an ex-boyfriend, had a sneer the size of Texas on his face when she hurried in, breathless and apologetic.

"For someone so determined to have *independence,*" he said, spitting the same word back at her that she'd yelled at him months ago, "you'd think you might figure out how to set an alarm."

"Family crisis," she snapped at him, half lying, as she yanked off her coat and stuffed it in her locker. "Don't you have work to do?"

He was always here in the staff room with her whenever she needed to use it, almost like he was stalking her, but for the sole purpose of chipping away at her, berating her, reminding her—daily—of why she'd split up with him.

"Unlike you, I've been here since dawn."

"And unlike *you,*" she said, "I don't have my mom at home to wake me up every morning." The sass came out without any real bite, and she sighed as she slumped onto the bench, bending over to pull off her shoes. "I couldn't fall asleep."

He paused. And then, stiffly: "I told you to stop drinking coffee so late in the day."

"You also told me to quit my job and spend my life serving you." Work shoes slipped on, she smiled up at him as she stood. "So forgive me if I completely ignore you."

The icy smugness of his voice stopped her as she headed for the door. "Dr. Stevens is looking for you," he drawled, the unpleasantness of it creeping down her spine, "so I'd wipe that smirk off my face if I were you."

She swallowed and turned to face him, biting back her utter repulsion of his presence enough to ask, "Did he say what he wanted?"

He sniffed in a way that said he knew *exactly* what it was, but he wasn't going to tell her about it.

She huffed, rolled her eyes. "Fine, whatever," she said, leaving the room with what she hoped was a modicum of dignity, even as her heart hammered against her ribcage and her stomach churned with anxiety. Dr. Stevens hated her, and there was no way he wanted to see her for anything that would put a smile on her face.

But neither could she think of anything she might have done wrong, except her lateness this morning—and that wasn't enough for him to punish her in any way, was it? She was only late by a few minutes, and she still had twenty minutes before her first round.

She passed her friend Ashley at the nurses' station as she headed to Dr. Stevens' office, and they shared a troubled smile, making Maggie's stomach tense even more as she realized that Ashley knew, too. Whatever it was. Whatever had happened this morning that she'd missed, being a couple of damn minutes late. And Ashley wasn't the only one: three other people gave Maggie worried looks as she walked past, almost like she was heading down the green mile and at the end of it was her last meal…

There was a slight tremble to her hand as she knocked on Dr. Stevens' office door.

He called her in, and then didn't bother to look up at her as she entered the room, closed the door, and stood in front of his desk. He continued to write instead, scrawling on a large document, glasses perched on the edge of his bulbous nose and the silence in this room so thick and oppressive that the *scratch-scratch* of his messy writing was deafening to her, matching the amplification of her thunderous heartbeat in her ears.

"Ah, Ms. Emerson," he said eventually, his tone soft and sneering. He placed his pen back in its holder and folded his hands on the desktop. "Good of you to join us."

"I'm sorry, sir. I overslept, and traffic coming in this morning—"

"Traffic?" He raised a disdainful eyebrow. "I would've thought your driver might know how to avoid midtown rush hour…"

She blinked. "My driver?"

"Yes," he said, dragging the word out. "Your family makes use of an entire fleet of town cars, do they not?"

"I—yes?" This was new. Dr. Stevens wasn't exactly subtle about his dislike for her, but he'd never brought her family into it before. "I don't, though."

He tipped his head as if to say, "If you say so," his disbelief entirely evident, and she had half a mind to set him straight, if it wasn't for him catching her off guard with his next words.

"You know about the stealing, yes?"

It was like someone had very slowly, very delicately, dropped an ice cube into her gut. "No. I don't know anything about the stealing."

He observed her for a long moment. "Hmm," he said, and then, "Have a seat, Ms. Emerson."

When she sat, he rose from his chair, walked around the desk to perch on the end of it, and stared down at her. From this angle, he was relentlessly formidable.

"Where were you at four p.m. yesterday?"

She swallowed thickly. "I was here, sir. Working."

"Yes," he said conversationally, rubbing a thumb along his jawline. "And again on Monday afternoon, correct?"

"Yes…"

He let silence hang between them, staring at her while she tried not to squirm, not to panic, not to blurt out something wholly inappropriate and land herself in a world of trouble. She'd wait it out.

She didn't have to wait long, it turned out.

"Someone is stealing drugs from the nurses' store cupboard in your department, Ms. Emerson, and I'm sure it's no surprise for you to hear that right now it's all pointing to you."

The screech of her chair scraping back registered before she knew she was moving, and once on her feet, her pulse hammering in her ears, she found the voice she'd kept subdued since entering this office.

"Are you accusing me of *theft*, sir? What do you mean, it's no surprise to me? Are you suggesting—because let me tell you—"

"You'll tell me nothing," he said calmly, straightening a cuff. "The matter is under investigation, and for now you'll return to work until such a time as we have more substantial evidence."

"Evidence..." Her mouth ran dry, and she cast about wildly for the thread of her composure. "Evidence. What evidence?"

"That's confidential at the moment."

"I think I have a right to know!" she said, waving a hand in his general direction. "Considering I'm the one in the frame here."

"Are you?" he said, narrowing his eyes. "Would you put yourself in the frame?"

"Oh, for God's sake." She let out a billowing huff of a breath and shoved a hand into her hair. "This is insane. I've never stolen anything in my life!"

"Well, I'd hardly expect you to admit it, would I?" He sniffed again, then gave her a long, appraising look from her feet to her head. She felt naked all of a sudden, and she resisted the urge to hug her arms around herself. "Still, I wanted to give you the opportunity to come clean. Pity," he added delicately. "You can go now. We'll talk about this in due course."

She stared at him, entirely gobsmacked—watched him walk back around his desk and take a seat, pick up his pen and examine his document like he hadn't just tipped her on her ass.

"No."

He looked up at her, eyebrows raised. "No?"

"No." She folded her arms, making an attempt at hardening her expression. "I'm not leaving until you tell me why I—out of everyone in this hospital—am the one accused of stealing drugs."

"Like I said, Ms. Emerson, it's currently confidential infor—" The beeping of his pager cut him off and he looked at it, muttered under his breath, and then stood. "I don't have time for this now," he said to her, reminding her of her brother's abruptness not thirty minutes ago. As mornings went, this one wasn't her best.

She watched, entirely helplessly, as he swept past her, unable to stop him and demand more of his time when the pager was no doubt calling him out to perform some kind of life-saving procedure.

He paused in the doorway, framed by the hustle and bustle of the corridor behind him, his weathered face highlighted by unforgiving neon lighting. When he looked at her this time, he made no effort to mask quite how much the very existence of her displeased him.

"Call it a hunch," was all he said, the hint of a smirk on his face. And then he was gone, leaving her in a solitary panic.

Because it wasn't a hunch. He had evidence. And that meant everything she worked for, everything she'd put ahead of her family's wishes, all her years of hard work and dedication and her lifelong desire to help people—all of it, every last moment of it, was in danger.

And with Dr. Stevens refusing to tell her the evidence, to give her any information at all, the whole situation was completely out of her control.

Which was the most terrifying thing of all.

End of Preview

Also by Alexa Wilder

Don't Miss Out on New Releases, Free Stories and More!!

Join Alexa's Readers Group!

AlexaWilder.com/readers-group/

Visit Alexa on Facebook:

Facebook.com/AuthorAlexaWilder

The Wedding Rescue

The Courtship Maneuver

The Stubborn Suitor

The Reckless Secret

The Temptation Trap

The Surprising Catch

40333227R00213

Made in the USA
Middletown, DE
10 February 2017